Page One: Hit and Run

A Robin Hamilton Mystery

Page One: Hit and Run

A Robin Hamilton Mystery

Nancy Barr

A

Arbutus Press
Traverse City

Page One: Hit and Run
A Robin Hamilton Mystery
© 2006 Nancy Barr

ISBN 1-933926-15-5
ISBN 978-1-933926-15-5

Arbutus Press
Traverse City, Michigan
www.Arbutuspress.com

Printed in the United States of America

To my parents

Harry, for always believing in me

and

Patricia (1931-1981) for sharing her love of mystery

Author's Note

In the course of writing this novel, several people assisted me in numerous ways. Susan Bays and Pamela Grath were invaluable in editing the manuscript, sharing ideas and guiding me through the process of publishing my first book. A special thank you goes to my friend "George" for sharing my enthusiasm, reading the manuscript and encouraging me when I felt nothing but despair. Paul Cousineau, Escanaba Public Safety; John Bruno, Michigan State Police; and retired Delta County Sheriff Gary Carlson patiently answered my many questions about law enforcement procedures and deserve special thanks. Any errors in fact are mine. Lastly, I would like to thank the great people of Delta County, Michigan. I could not have asked for a better place in which to grow up.

Chapter One

IT ALWAYS STARTS WITH THE pounding at the door. The sound of fist meeting oak ricochets inside my head. I jump out of bed, pull on a robe and open the door. Two big burly Chicago cops are standing in the hall, their features grim. The older one, a sergeant with steel-colored hair, looks down at me with cold gray eyes, confirms that I'm Robin Hamilton and asks to come in. I know what they are going to say. I don't want to hear it. I want to slam the door in their serious faces, run back to bed and pull the covers over my head, never to awaken again. Instead, I open the door wider and they file into my tiny apartment. The younger one speaks. He is Hispanic, with a kind face and warm voice. His hands are even warmer as he draws mine—small, pale, shaking—into them. Mitch is dead. I scream and wake up.

It had been two months since that horrid night, but the nightmares kept it fresh in my mind. My bleary eyes found the digital clock atop my dresser on the other side of the room. Its red lights sneered at me. Three a.m. I had to get up for work in another two and a half hours. I uttered a curse. Now wide awake, I'd have a hell of a time trying to get any more sleep.

Belle, my faithful companion of a year and a half, had no such trouble. The basset hound grunted, heaved a deep sigh and rolled her thick body over on her side, her choke chain rattling softly as it settled on the hardwood floor next to my bed. Her white legs and chest were all I could see in the pale light cast by the street lamps outside my second-story apartment. The ease with which she slept made me jealous. I hadn't slept through the night since Mitch died.

I pounded my pillow and flopped back down, but sleep was elusive. Despite the slight breeze, the air felt warm and sticky. The last few nights

I had slept with just a sheet covering me, but now I kicked that off to the side as well. I let my mind wander and, for the thousandth time, asked myself if I'd made the right decision in coming back to Escanaba so soon after my fiancé's murder. An afternoon shift sergeant with a suburban police department, he was shot and killed late one night on a deserted road with no witnesses and suddenly Chicago, the beautiful city by the lake we had explored on so many weekends, seemed like a violent, cold, ugly prison from which I had to escape.

A few weeks after Mitch's funeral, my dad called to tell me that my initial training ground of three years, the Daily Press in Escanaba, Michigan, was looking for a police reporter/copy editor. I had the job after a ten-minute conversation with my crusty former boss. It meant a sharp decrease in pay and status from the big city daily news desk I had occupied for six years, but I saw it as a knotted rope of sheets leading out from my prison cell of pain and despair. At least, that was my hope.

My hometown is like many other small Midwestern enclaves—on the way down the ladder of economic prosperity along with too many of its thirteen thousand residents—but it is also close-knit and relatively crime-free. Situated on a bay along the northern shore of Lake Michigan, Escanaba is touted by the Chamber of Commerce as a great place to raise a family. It is—if you don't mind a little isolation and a lot of cold, snowy weather. Growing up, I couldn't wait to get the hell out. Now I had boomeranged back, a little older, a lot wiser but no richer, seeking peace and quiet.

I finally drifted off to a tortured sleep, reaching out for Mitch and finding only an emptiness I couldn't seem to escape even in my dreams.

⌐❦⌐

When the alarm clock blared at five-thirty I dragged myself out of bed and groaned as I crossed the room and fumbled for the off button. I'm not a morning person, and my friends never understand why I work in a profession that requires me to get up at such ungodly hours.

After trudging downstairs, putting Belle on her chain in the back yard and taking a quick cool shower, I wrapped a towel around myself and turned on the radio in the kitchen to hear what had happened overnight. The first newscast of the morning was just beginning, with a story about the Escanaba City Council meeting the night before. The big bone of contention seemed to be too many teenagers loitering along Ludington Street, driving away business for downtown retailers. That was followed

by news of the city's plans for the biggest Fourth of July fireworks display
in its history. No murders, robberies, assaults, or other nefarious deeds,
which meant I would probably have a nice, quiet Friday morning.

As I dug through my closet, already a mess after the one month I'd
lived in the apartment, I heard the snip-snip of my landlady's pruning
shears. With my towel still clutched around me with one hand and a
sleeveless cotton dress in the other hand, I walked to the living room
window overlooking the front yard and peeked around the blind. Mrs.
Easton was working on a cluster of leafy green bushes to my left. Wearing a hot pink golf shirt, baggy jeans, sneakers and gardening gloves, she
worked quickly with a smile on her pleasant face. Later, when the sun
was high, she would don one of those big, floppy straw hats favored by
older gentlewomen.

I admired the view beyond the front yard. The two-story, Queen
Anne style house that had been in Mrs. Easton's family since it was built
in 1892 was situated on the northern end of Lake Shore Drive along with
some of the largest, oldest homes in the city. Across the street was Ludington Park, which lined the lake for nearly a mile. Known as one of the
most beautiful parks in the state, it had a man-made island for swimming
built in the 1940s, a marina with about a hundred slips, four lighted tennis courts, two sand volleyball courts and a playground designed to look
like a castle from the Middle Ages.

A distant patch of clouds ranging in color from purple to a rosy peach
announced that the sun was about to peek above the horizon. Seagulls
dipped and swooped around several garbage cans bursting with trash
from gatherings the night before. The gulls' shrieks were the only sound
other than Mrs. Easton's pruning shears. Soon the park would be full of
walkers, joggers and bicyclists enjoying the cool breeze off the lake. A lone
man was now making his way into the park at the southern end, walking
with an easy, athletic gait. He was one of the park regulars, always beating the morning rush by about forty-five minutes. I didn't recall his name
but recognized him as an accountant who had taught a few courses when
I was in college. Unfortunately, I hadn't taken any of his classes, which
might explain why my checking account was overdrawn by a few dollars
several times a year.

To the north, an ore freighter was heading for the docks to pick
up a load of pellets from the iron mines up north and deliver them to
ports in Indiana, Detroit or Cleveland. The vessel, a newer red and
white one resembling a giant barge, stretched about a thousand feet

and made no sound as it slowly rounded the point of the park and headed into the bay.

I returned to my bedroom, got dressed and put on just enough make-up to give my green eyes a little definition while the radio announcer delivered the weather forecast with an exaggerated, heavy tone of voice. And why not, it was miserable—more extreme heat and humidity for at least another week. Thousands of "snowbirds," migratory humans who wintered in Florida or Arizona, fled north each summer to the comparatively cool Upper Peninsula, but they were receiving little relief this year. A high-pressure system out of the Gulf of Mexico was swirling around the nation's mid-section, making even the most avid outdoors-lover weary of venturing outside. For the past week, temperatures had been hovering in the lower to mid-nineties with a humidity level around eighty-five percent.

I strapped on my gold watch, a graduation present from my dad, and saw it was nearly six o'clock. Still plenty of time before I had to leave for work. I went to the kitchen and popped an English muffin in the toaster. The morning crew on the radio had slipped into their usual inane chatter, so I switched off the receiver.

Almost immediately a piercing scream and the squeal of tires shattered the quiet. I ran to the living room window and scanned for Mrs. Easton. She was standing at the edge of the yard, staring across the street at something in the park.

"Mrs. Easton!" I shouted, "What's wrong?"

She turned to me with a horror-stricken look, holding her gloved hands up to her cheeks, unable to speak. Then she looked back to the park. Following her gaze, my eyes found the crumpled body of the man I had just seen walking. Now he lay, unmoving, in a position even the scarecrow in the "Wizard of Oz" would have found uncomfortable. I could make out heavy tracks of rubber laid down by a vehicle speeding away from the scene. The vehicle itself was nowhere in sight.

Grabbing the phone, I punched in the emergency number and told the female dispatcher what little I knew—that a man had apparently been struck by a vehicle while walking in the park. As I talked, I pulled on my running shoes. As soon as I hung up, I bolted out the door and down the back steps. Dashing around to the front yard, I found Mrs. Easton in the same position, still staring at the man in the grass about fifty yards away.

"I called the police. They should be here any minute," I said, wrapping my hand around her upper left arm and giving it a gentle squeeze. She barely nodded. I sprinted across the park to where the man lay in the grass about two feet to the left of the roadway winding through the park. The faint wail of distant Sirens grew louder with each step I took, and the heavy dew of the night before soaked my shoes by the time I reached the limp body.

He was dead, all right. If it hadn't been obvious from the contorted position of his limbs, the blank stare of his deep blue eyes announced the fact. Just to be sure, I put two fingers to his right wrist. Nothing. Blood trickled from his mouth, and his once-white t-shirt was streaked with dirt, grass stains and blood. It appeared he had hit the windshield of the vehicle before being thrown into the air and landing on his head, breaking his neck. He had just missed striking one of the many towering oak trees that lined Jenkins Drive.

I finally remembered his name—Frank Thompson, a well-known popular accountant involved in many local charitable causes. He often had his picture in the newspaper for some honor or donation.

I looked back in the direction from which he had been walking, along the left side of the road, against traffic. Whoever hit him would have had to cross into the opposite lane. There were faint imprints of rubber tracks starting a few hundred yards back, indicating where the vehicle began to swerve into the other lane at a high rate of speed. The tracks ended in the left lane. I couldn't immediately tell where the point of impact was, but what looked like part of the headlight and turn signal assembly lay in the roadway about 80 feet from Thompson. A darker set of tracks, those I had noticed earlier, showed where the vehicle had sped away from the scene.

Mrs. Easton was still standing in the front yard and had been joined by Alan Clark, our neighbor to the north. He had his arm around her shoulders and appeared to be trying to get her to go inside. Meanwhile, the Sirens had grown to a fever pitch, then quit all at once as four police cars and an ambulance converged on the scene at the same time. The shift lieutenant, Dale Olsen, a man I remembered from my early reporting days, leaped out of his patrol car and jogged to where I knelt next to Thompson.

"That's Frank Thompson! What the hell happened?" he asked in disbelief. Not waiting for an answer, he surveyed the scene with a long, sweeping gaze and began barking orders to three officers standing close by.

"Jim, get the accident reconstructionist over here. Carl, find some witnesses. Start with the houses on this block. Alex, barricade both entrances to the park with you at one end, and put Gary at the other end when he gets here." The officers scattered like schoolchildren headed for the playground at recess, eager for action despite the fact that they were entering the last hour of a twelve-hour shift.

Olsen turned to me as if he suddenly remembered I was standing a few feet away. A tall, slim man in his early forties, with blond hair gradually turning to gray, he filled out his navy blue uniform nicely. When I last worked in Escanaba, he had just made midnight sergeant and was not particularly friendly with the media. I wondered if he remembered me. His eyes squinted against the sun rising behind me as he asked, "You're that new reporter with the paper, aren't you?"

"Yes, I'm Robin Hamilton," I said and held out my hand. He shook it with a quick, firm grip but eyed me with suspicion.

"It sure didn't take you long to get here. Where are the rest of the maggots?" Being called a maggot would probably offend most people, but I'm used to it. Most of the time it's even appropriate: news people are like maggots, swarming around a human carcass as soon as we catch wind of the stench of death.

I smiled and said my associates in television and radio were sure to follow soon. "I live in an upstairs apartment across the street," I said and pointed at my house. He followed my finger and nodded.

"Rose Easton's place, okay. Did you see what happened?" he asked.

"Not really. I looked out the front window on the left there this morning and saw Mr. Thompson walking down the hill into the park. A few minutes later I heard Mrs. Easton scream and then tires squealing."

Olsen pressed a button on the radio microphone attached to his chest and told Officer Carl Parker to interview Mrs. Easton in the big white house directly across from the accident scene.

As he gave out orders, the two-person ambulance crew worked frantically to get Thompson's heart started. They cut away his blood-spattered t-shirt and attached electrodes from an automatic defibrillator to his chest. After a few jolts through the limp body, it was apparent that their efforts were doing no good. Thompson was beyond human help. When the medical examiner arrived about ten minutes after the accident, he pronounced Thompson dead, and a yellow plastic sheet was drawn over the broken body.

I couldn't help feeling sick. I hardly knew the guy, but it was a pathetic way to leave this world—lying in a twisted heap like a discarded rag doll. The final insult was having an ugly tarp thrown over you as though you were a lawn mower being stored for the winter.

Officer Jim Banks had returned to his lieutenant's side. Olsen heaved a big sigh and said, "Jim, you're pretty good at this stuff, so I'm going to send you to tell Victoria Thompson her husband is dead. Call Dispatch on the cell phone and get her address."

As Jim walked towards his patrol car, I went numb. Suddenly it was two in the morning on April 20. The cops were pounding on my door.

"We're very sorry. Sergeant Montgomery was shot tonight. He didn't make it." The words were always in the back of my mind, sometimes echoing loudly as they were now but usually just lying in wait for the right time to come up and bite me like a pissed-off Rottweiler. The officers had stayed with me until a member of the local Police Aid Association arrived to console me, even though Mitch and I weren't to be married for another fifteen months. At the funeral, the chief of police, tears rolling down his care-worn face, handed me the flag that had draped Mitch's coffin. It was stored now in a trunk in my bedroom. Someday I would display it. Not now, though. Not yet.

My throat grew tight and my eyes stung. Then I became aware that Olsen was staring at me and saying something.

"I'm sorry, what did you say?" I asked.

"I said, are you all right?"

"Yeah, yeah. I'm fine," I lied.

"You look like you just saw a ghost," he said, eyes narrowed.

"In a way I did," I said, forcing a smile. Diverting his attention, I told Olsen I would be contacting the department in about an hour to see what official information they were releasing to the media.

I ran back to the yard, but Mrs. Easton was nowhere to be seen. As I walked around the north side of the house, past an open window in the dining room, I heard a male voice ask, "Were you able to see who was driving?" I paused to listen.

"Well, sort of, but, well…. No, I guess not. Oh, I don't know! I can't think," she moaned, her voice choked with tears. I could picture her slight figure trembling. "I saw a man with dark, short hair, but I couldn't see his face. He was too far away and frankly, I wasn't paying too much attention. I was so shocked when he hit that man." She broke into soft sobs.

Mrs. Easton, a retired high school home economics teacher, didn't have the kind of personality that dealt well with tragedy. But there was nothing I could do for her at this point, so I continued on to my apartment, resolving to check on her later. She was the kind of person who liked to talk out everything in her life, and I doubted this incident would be any different.

Belle was pacing around the back yard, upset with all the commotion in the park, which she could hear but not see. I let her off her chain, and she ran for the back door and bounded up the stairs. Once inside, she jumped up on a chair near the window and studied the scene outside.

While she watched the police at work, I called the newspaper. The office didn't open to the public until eight o'clock, but the news staff began arriving around six. It was now six twenty-five. I got Carol Dinby, the news editor, on the phone. A sweet-voiced woman of about fifty-five, Dinby was one of my mentors, a reporter who could make the most irate person walk away feeling blessed to have spoken to her. She had uncovered some of the ugliest scandals in the county in her thirty-year career and written features so touching, People magazine would be jealous.

"Carol, this is Robin. There's been a hit-and-run fatality in Ludington Park. The victim is Frank Thompson, the accountant. Get a photographer down here as soon as possible. I don't have a camera." After explaining the few other details I knew, I hung up the phone.

My workday usually began with visits to the city and county police agencies, but that would have to wait today. With just two and a half hours until deadline, I had a lot of work ahead of me. I still didn't know what had happened to Thompson. Was he trying to cross the street when someone hit him? Was it deliberate? Who had hit him, and what was the culprit driving? Was the driver drunk? Joyriding? Mrs. Easton had witnessed the accident, but had anyone else? The police were asking all these questions and more at this very minute, but I doubted they would share many of the answers with me, at least not this morning.

Returning to the accident scene, I thought about potential suspects and figured it wouldn't be more than a few days before the driver was caught. Hit-and-run cases are usually easy to solve when the police have witnesses, especially in a small town where someone is bound to recognize the offending vehicle. I had no idea how right and yet how wrong I would be about that.

Chapter Two

STILL HAD PLENTY OF TIME to find more information, get to my desk at the newspaper and start writing, so I hung around on the wide swath of grass between Lake Shore Drive and Jenkins Drive. Thompson's body still lay on the grass under that gaudy yellow tarp.

For a reporter, these kinds of stories bring out a mix of emotions including the thrill of trying to get the facts in a short period of time and put them all together in a story that is accurate and touches people. But I always feel like a ghoul, too, hovering around a death scene, waiting for something to happen or chasing down witnesses or family members who usually have no deSire to talk to the media. Few reporters enjoy sticking a microphone or notebook in the face of someone who's just lost a loved one and asking, "How do you feel?"

The Daily Press photographer, Kevin Watkins, came up from behind and tapped me on the shoulder.

"Hey, what's up?" he asked with a smile.

A young photographer looking to break into national magazines, Kevin was a rare treat at a small newspaper—loaded with talent but not an egomaniac.

After I filled him in on what I knew, he drifted over to where some officers were taking measurements. The humanitarian in me wished Thompson's body had been removed already. Gruesome pictures splashed across the front page, in my opinion, have the effect of cheapening human life.

A couple officers helped the accident reconstructionist from the state police post in the neighboring town of Gladstone take measurements and mark the location of tire marks and debris, presumably from the offending vehicle. Lieutenant Olsen was briefing another small group of cops

I recognized from the day shift, probably called in early to help with the search for the vehicle. I edged closer to listen in on Olsen's instructions.

"...I'm thinking we're looking for a younger guy, but keep your eyes peeled for anything that looks like it matches the description of that truck. Everyone understand? Any questions?" he asked as he scanned the group. All assembled shook their heads. "All right then, get to work."

The heat was getting heavier as the sun rose higher. Sweat glistened on the faces of the officers. Their dark blue uniforms and Kevlar vests absorbed the bright hot sunlight, making them shift uneasily as sweat trickled down their necks. Officer Carl Parker approached Lieutenant Olsen with a shirt soaked down the back and a deep rosy flush on his round face, the exertion of walking from house to house in search of witnesses in such heat a bit too much for him.

"Too hot for this kind of thing, Lieutenant," he said, mopping his brow with a fleshy hand.

"Carl, when the hell are you going to get serious about that diet? You're gonna drop dead of a heart attack before you're forty if you keep this up," Olsen admonished.

Parker smiled sheepishly. "I'm trying, Sir, but it's hard to lose weight. I can't help it, I love food," he said.

"Humph! Got anything more since you called me?" Olsen asked. Only then did I notice the compact black cellular phone strapped to his gun belt along with the traditional police paraphernalia. Escanaba had gone high-tech while I'd been away.

"No, Sir. Just that one lady saw what happened. Everyone else was either asleep or busy doing something else when the truck struck him," Parker said.

"All right. Go back to the station and write up what you have. I already put out a BOL for the pickup. I'll take care of the media," Olsen said, pointing at me. Then he sniffed the air and made a retching sound. It was a bad summer for alewives washing up on the beach, and the stench of the rotting fish was getting strong.

"Parker?" he called.

"Yes, Sir?" he stopped and turned back to his boss.

"Get Public Works over here to clean up the beach. It smells like a damned processing plant out here."

Parker laughed. "Yes, Sir," he said and loped back to his car.

Olsen walked over to me. He wiped a hand across his forehead, took a deep breath and shook his head.

"What a morning!" He paused, as if organizing his thoughts before he made the mistake of vocalizing too much information. He finally said, "We don't have much, just a vague vehicle description—an older, light blue, full-size pickup with a dark-haired male, possibly early twenties, at the wheel. We're not sure if there were any passengers. Asshole didn't even slow down after he hit him." He jerked a thumb in the direction of Frank's body, which the paramedics had placed on a stretcher and were loading into the ambulance now that the measurements were complete.

"Are you ready to release his name?" I asked.

"Yeah," he said, after some hesitation. "His wife Victoria was told about 15 minutes ago. Took it pretty hard, Jim said. Sure as hell wasn't expecting her husband to be run down in the street like a dog," he said, adding quickly, "Don't print that last part." I wouldn't have, even though it would have made a great quote and echoed what I was thinking.

"What do you think happened? Was it an accident or intentional?" I asked.

Olsen gave me a look as though I had kicked him, then laughed.

"Intentional? I remember you now. You're Hank Hamilton's daughter, the one who's won tons of awards and spent the last several years working down in Chicago. Well, sweetheart, this ain't Chicago. Hell, there are a lot less conspicuous ways to murder someone than to run them over in broad daylight in a public park," he scoffed.

"This couldn't have been too conspicuous, considering there's only one witness. There aren't too many people out at six in the morning," I countered. "And if I'm not mistaken, Thompson walks this route at the same time every day. It wouldn't be too hard to plan a little accident."

Olsen's eyes narrowed. "Don't go making too much of this. We average about one murder every five years in this town, and I don't think this here deal will fill the quota," he said, his voice rising. He wiped his forehead again

"The way I see it," he continued a little more calmly, "some drunk was trying to get home, got lost, and came through the park. He came around that curve too fast and hit Thompson walking along the edge of the road. Then he got scared and bolted. Either that, or it was one of those damn joyriding kids."

"You guys know most of the drunks and kids out and about at night. Do you have a suspect in mind?" I asked, while scribbling in my little notebook.

"No comment. Sorry, Robin, that's all I can tell you right now," he said and started to walk away. He headed towards the accident reconstructionist. I followed.

"How many people do you have working on finding the pickup?" I called after him.

He stopped and turned to look at me through squinted eyelids.

"The vehicle description has been put out over the radio, and every dayshift cop in the county is on the lookout. Now look, I've got to get back to my end of the investigation. When we have something new, we'll tell you," he said.

As Olsen walked away, the reporter for the local television station turned onto Jenkins Drive. You couldn't miss the white Chevy sedan with a large red Channel 3 emblazoned on each side. Olsen joined the reconstructionist, a short, solid-looking woman in her thirties with short dark hair and bright blue eyes. She held a clipboard and was making some sort of drawing on it with a pencil. She and Olsen spied the reporter's car and groaned together. From the other direction, I saw one of the radio news directors approaching the scene in another vehicle. The media onslaught was just beginning. I laughed and headed for home.

I had all I was going to get out of the cops that morning. It was time to get to the office and start putting together the story for that day's paper.

I could have tried to get a quote from Mrs. Easton, and if she hadn't been my landlady I probably would have, but I didn't feel comfortable pressing her in her agitated state. Must be going soft, I thought. Instead I retrieved my purse from the apartment and filled Belle's water and food dishes. After checking my hair and what little make-up I wore, both wilted from the heat and humidity, I locked the door behind me and headed to the garage to my decade-old Jeep. Half of the two-car garage was a rare perk for an apartment dweller in Escanaba, one I'd be especially grateful for come January with a foot of snow on the ground.

Just a three-minute drive from my apartment to the Daily Press, or about six blocks, the short commute was a benefit of small town life I appreciated after driving in a city where it took an hour to go ten miles most days. I parked the Jeep in the lot behind the building, a large two-story brick structure that stretched half a block in length and width.

The newsroom felt like a walk-in cooler compared to the sweltering conditions outside, and it was bustling with activity. The other four news reporters on staff were all clicking away at computers, each computer on an identical modern beige desk with fake wood top. A rookie out of college less than a month looked up when I walked by and said, "Hey, got some excitement this morning, I hear." Craig Myers' eyes were shining with envy. He was assigned to cover Escanaba school and city meetings, neither of which offered much in the way of excitement for an eager young cub reporter.

"Nothing like the double homicide I covered on Chicago's Gold Coast last year. This is just a little ol' hit-and-run," I said with a twisted smile.

Myers waved me off with a laugh.

Any kind of fatality in a small community— accident, fire or murder—is always big news. It's especially noteworthy when the deceased is well known. Frank Thompson fit the bill. It seemed nearly everyone in the newsroom had some tidbit about him and shared it with me as I passed their desks. Not just a prominent accountant, he was also active in several nonprofit groups, including Little League and the Red Cross. He was also on the board of directors of the Chamber of Commerce, something that carried a lot of weight in town. Childless, he still enjoyed attending high school sporting events, was an avid golfer, and he swung a pretty mean tennis racket.

"Hey, Robin, do the cops know what happened yet?" Greg Hale, the sports editor, shouted from his desk in the rear of the newsroom.

"It's a hit-and-run. They're looking for a kid driving a blue pickup. Have you talked to your son lately?" I yelled back. Hale had a 19-year-old son home from college and raising hell.

"Ha, ha, ha. That lump of coal is sound asleep in his room. He crawled home at two o'clock this morning. Oh, to be young again," Hale said before returning to his computer.

I sat at my own desk near the front of the newsroom and flipped on my screen. As the terminal came to life, I thought about what to write. There wasn't a lot to say and no time to do a lengthy obituary. I quickly typed out about four hundred words relating what Olsen had told me and what I had seen for myself. The police couldn't censor a reporter's eyes and ears. Despite the lack of solid information, adrenaline made the words flow like a river during spring thaw. As I filed my story on network server, the newspaper's long-time editor-in-chief shuffled up to my desk. As usual, I heard Bob Hunter before I saw him.

A lanky man in his mid-fifties, his pant legs rustled together as he moved slowly across the floor, but his slowness was not from age. It was simply a lack of deSire to move any faster. A lifelong resident of Escanaba, he was a walking archive of news stories from the last 40 years or more, full of vast amounts of information that could be processed and called up at any time with complete accuracy. Hunter had a way with the written word that could bring goose bumps to the reader. My first month on the job, I was summoned to his office to go over a story I had written about a 92-year-old man who maintained the most spectacular flower garden in the county with no help from anyone.

Hunter had leaned back in his favorite old wooden chair, which creaked and groaned no matter how much it was oiled, put his feet up on the desk and tossed a copy of my story at me.

"This is not worth the paper it's printed on," he had said. My fledgling ego crumbled as I gathered the two sheets of paper from my lap. "Do you know why?"

"No, Sir," I had muttered.

He took his feet down, leaned towards me with his elbows on the desk, his cat-like hazel eyes boring into mine until I shrank back in my chair from the intensity. "There's no heart in it. You gave me a bunch of facts. So what? A first-grader could have given me the facts," he said. "You're a writer, not just a fact-finder. Your job is to make me care about this man and get excited about his life. You can do a lot better than that."

After Hunter's lecture, I spent the rest of the day pouring my heart into that story. Six months later I collected my first statewide journalism award for it and gave Hunter a thank-you card and a bottle of 12-year-old Scotch.

"Well?" he drawled now, standing with his hands in the pockets of his baggy corduroy pants.

"The main story is in. Do we have someone working on a sidebar about his role in the community?" I asked.

"No. It's eight forty-five, and no one's available. The superintendent of Manistique schools quit without warning at last night's board meeting, so I've got two people working on that. You can spend the day following up on the accident. Do a good job, lots of details. This man was important to the community," he said and shuffled away.

As soon as Hunter was gone, I heard a woman's quick little footsteps trot to my desk.

"Isn't that awful about Frank Thompson?" she said in a stricken voice.

I looked up to see Molly Ashbrook, one of the accounting clerks, dabbing an eye with a tissue.

"Yeah, tragic. Did you know him?" I asked.

"I worked with him for several years. He was a very nice man. You know, there's quite a story there." Molly sighed and scurried away before I could ask what she meant.

Chapter Three

HAD DONE MORE THAN a few obituaries about prominent people. They all took the same course—friends, co-work-
ers, business associates, etc., all say something complimentary about
the deceased, even if they have to grit their teeth to do so (which a
few have). After two or three of these stories, a reporter grows to
hate them. Even if the dead person was a first-class pain the ass, you
can't write that. It's an unwritten rule. The obituary must show the
deceased in a good light. There is also too much of the old micro-
phone-in-the-face routine—"How do you feel now that so-and-so is
dead?" That's why I decided to talk to Thompson's partners at his
accounting firm first, so I could be done with it and move on to more
pleasant topics.

Figuring I'd have better luck getting someone to talk to me if I
showed up in person rather than phoning (reporters are harder to ignore
when they're standing in your lobby), I left the office on foot after the
paper was put to bed.

The office of Thompson, Klegle, Jordan and Company was located in
a light red brick, one-story building four blocks east of the Daily Press.
Along the way I passed the allegedly haunted House of Ludington, a
popular hotel and restaurant built in the 1860s. The large Victorian
brick and wood building, like so many places in Michigan, had supposedly been a hideout for Chicago gangsters on the lam during a bygone
era. Nearby were professional offices, a bait and tackle shop, and assorted
government buildings. Above the offices were apartments rented mostly
by college-age kids or low-wage workers from one of the many restau-
rants or hotels in Escanaba or the Native American casino about thirteen
miles west of town.

The accounting firm marked the end of the downtown and occupied a prime piece of real estate overlooking the bay. A small but well-used park and the municipal dock, where nothing ever moored except an occasional Coast Guard vessel, stretched to its east.

The large oak front door swung open easily when I pushed on the brass handle. Sunlight flooded the interior from two huge windows on either side of the door. The fluorescent lights overhead were a waste of electricity today, but the air conditioning felt good. A pretty receptionist approaching middle age, strawberry-blonde pageboy falling across one blue eye, greeted me with a weak attempt at a smile, her face red and streaked from tears. I swallowed hard and took a deep breath.

"Good morning, I'm Robin Hamilton," I said in what I hoped was my most sympathetic voice. "I'm a reporter with the Daily Press. I'm working on the story about Frank Thompson. I know this is a difficult time."

"I know why you're here. I'll get Mr. Klegle," she said quietly and disappeared down a hallway to my right. I took the opportunity to look around.

The walls were covered with a matte beige wallpaper with several outdoor prints spaced evenly at about eye level. The carpet was a plush, deep forest green and looked new. The hint of formaldehyde still lingered in the air. In fact, the whole building had the smell of recent serious redecorating. The office was quiet, almost eerie. I guessed there were at least six or seven people who worked in the building, but I didn't hear a sound—no talking on the phone, no fax machine or phone ringing, no clicking away at a keyboard. As if in response to my line of thinking, the phone rang on the desk in front of me. Next to the phone I noticed a photo of three plump orange tabbies snuggled together on what looked like a couch. The receptionist—the nameplate on her desk said Cindy—returned from around the corner and said to me, "Mr. Klegle will be right with you," then answered the phone. "Thompson, Klegle, Jordan and Company. This is Cindy. How may I help you?"

Her voice was pleasant, almost mechanical, her face arranged in that same weak smile with which she had greeted me. I've heard you should smile when you answer the phone because the person on the other end can sense the smile in your voice. I guess Cindy had heard the same thing. She still sounded sad to me.

"Thank you. Yes, we're all shocked. Mr. Jordan was too distraught to come in today, but Mr. Klegle is here. He's with someone right now, but I'll let him know you called," she said into the receiver.

I felt a presence behind me and turned to find the awkward Albert Klegle glaring down at me through horn-rimmed glasses with quarter-inch lenses. He looked like his name sounded—unpretentious and dull. His thinning mousy brown hair had receded to a semicircle at the middle of his crown. His brown eyes matched his brown suit. Made for a taller, heavier man, it hung on him like a wet dishtowel. His oxford shirt and tie were slightly different shades of tan. The overall effect was one of a dead tree that hadn't fallen over yet.

"Ms. Hamilton, I'm Albert Klegle. Thank you for coming," he said as he extended a hand and smiled wanly. I shook his hand, then followed as he led me to an office halfway down the hallway past a few closed doors.

"On account of what happened, the rest of the staff is off today. Cindy and I are here simply to answer calls, as I'm sure many of Frank's clients will be contacting us," Klegle explained.

His office was the only clue to his position as one of the partners in the firm. It was done in the same colors as the entry, with a large mahogany desk and deep reddish brown leather chair behind it, but the best feature was the view. The dark blue waters of Little Bay de Noc sparkled in the morning sun through a large square window stretching almost from floor to ceiling behind the desk, the glass shielded by fabric vertical blinds in beige. I could never work in an office like this, I thought to myself. I'd be looking out the window all the time.

We sat down, he in his big leather chair and I in a sturdy but comfortable straight mahogany chair with curved arms and a dark green vinyl cushion. Klegle leaned back as a solemn expression took over his countenance.

"I feel numb. I've lost one of my best friends. Frank established this firm and offered me a partnership twenty-some years ago." At that, his throat seemed to clench. He looked down at his hands clasped in his lap.

"I know this is difficult," I said again. My pen was poised over a steno pad as I waited for him to tell me what I needed for a moving portrait of Frank Thompson.

"You have a job to do, and I want everyone to know what a wonderful person Frank was," he said. Heaving a deep sign, he then plunged on without my having to utter another question. It was as if he had been through this before and knew exactly what I was going to ask.

"I met Frank when he went to work for the Lewis firm about twenty-three years ago. After about two years, Frank got bored. He had the talent and the guts, so he went out on his own and invited me to come with him. We invited Doug Jordan to join us a few years later because our list of clients had grown so large. We each had our areas of expertise. His was tax preparation for individuals. He knew the tax code like the Lord's Prayer and could take a $5,000 tax bill and turn it into $500 and keep it all legal. What a mind!" Klegle paused at some memory, then shook his head and went on. "He married Victoria about fifteen years ago. She was one of our secretaries—beautiful woman. They never had children, even though he loved kids. He spent his free time teaching at the college or volunteering. He was a great person, and he'll be missed."

He stopped talking and sat staring into space for some time. The interview was over. It wasn't much but enough to get started. I asked Klegle for a photograph of Frank Thompson, and he directed me back to Cindy. I found my way to her desk and asked for the photo. She opened a file drawer on the right-hand side of the desk and pulled out a thin manila file folder.

"We have photos of everyone—for media purposes, you know," she said. "Let's see, here's a black-and-white one of the entire firm, but it's several years old."

She held up an eight-by-ten of three women and five men. I recognized one of the women as Michelle Ashbrook. Thompson sat on a chair in between Klegle and Douglas Jordan. Klegle looked about as lively then as he did now. Jordan, on the other hand, looked quite the fashion plate, wearing a well-cut, expensive-looking dark suit, lighter-colored shirt and polka-dot tie. The photo showed Thompson as a thin fortyish man with dark hair and a mustache, light-colored eyes and a welcoming smile.

"That's a nice shot, but it would be hard to crop everyone else out and we'd rather have a color picture if you have one," I said.

Cindy leafed through a few more shots before pulling out another print.

"Oh, this is my favorite. It was taken last year," she said and handed me a five-by-seven professional portrait of Thompson. Here he had the same charming smile and bright eyes, although the hair looked a little grayer against his tanned skin. He was a handsome man, if a bit thin for my taste. His dark gray suit appeared to be tailored for his athletic frame.

"This is perfect. Thanks, I appreciate your time. I'll return it in a few days," I said and tucked the photograph in my notebook for safekeeping.

"Ms. Hamilton?" she called as I reached for the door handle to leave.

"Yes?" I said, turning back to face her.

"Frank was the most wonderful boss I ever had. I'll miss him terribly. Please put that in your article about him. My name's Cindy Carrigan. You can quote me," she said, her brown eyes shining with tears.

"Yes, Ma'am. I'm sorry," I said again and left.

I walked back to the Daily Press, sad for those who had lost a trusted friend and co-worker, yet enjoying the feel of the hot sun on my bare arms. Nothing like death to make you thankful to be alive. It was so humid I could feel the air move as I walked, but at least I was breathing. The House of Ludington was gearing up for the lunch trade, and the smell was heavenly. I thought about food all the way back to work.

By the time I entered the newspaper office, though, I was soaked with sweat, and the cold blast of air conditioning hit me like a slap. No wonder people got the worst colds in the summertime, I thought as I shivered to my desk. I made a call to the dean of instruction at the local college, but he was gone to a lunch meeting, so I left a message. I sat and stared at my computer screen, thinking about who Frank Thompson was. I knew I didn't have enough to write a meaningful tribute article yet. I decided to go home for lunch and then, in the afternoon, call the organizations for which he volunteered.

When I got home I put Belle on her leash and walked her around the block. She normally enjoyed a little exercise, but the heat left her listless and panting, so I took her back upstairs and sprayed some cold water on her droopy face. She settled on the rug next to the tub in the bathroom, the coolest room in the apartment. The dog days of summer had arrived ahead of schedule.

I went back downstairs and walked around to the wide front porch, where the front door to Mrs. Easton's apartment was open. I tapped on the screen door, then poked my head inside and called her name.

"Come in, dear. I'm in the kitchen," she called back from deep inside the house. I walked through the dark oak main hall past the living room, drawing room and a staircase leading upstairs but long since blocked off. Everything was on an elaborate scale in the house, characteristic of grand old Victorian homes. At the end of the hallway were a formal dining room to the right and a large bright kitchen to the left. Straight ahead was an odd little pantry created by the slant of the staircase leading from my apartment to the back door.

I found Mrs. Easton working at the counter, chopping romaine lettuce for a salad. Everything in the room seemed to produce light, from
the white cabinets with yellow trim to the stainless steel double sink.
Normally this was a peaceful scene, but today, after witnessing Thompson's death, Mrs. Easton was distraught. I was afraid she was going to
lop off a finger or two.

I sat down at the small breakfast table and asked her how she was
doing. Her back was to me, but I saw her shoulders shake as she started
to cry. I went over to her and put my arms around her frail body as she
rested her head on my shoulder.

"Oh, Robin, I just can't get the image out of my head! I see it over and
over in slow motion, like that awful video of President Kennedy's assas-
sination. You know the way they play that horrid thing every twenty-sec-
ond of November," she said through her tears.

"It must have been awful," I said quietly. "Do you want to tell me
about it?"

"Well. . .." She hesitated, then took a deep breath and let it out slowly.
"Why don't we sit down? I just put this salad together, and we'll have
some lunch first." She busied herself with the preparations while I got
plates and glasses from the cupboard and retrieved the pitcher of lemonade I knew she always had in the refrigerator.

We ate in silence, the crunching of the lettuce, cucumbers and tomatoes filling the air in a comforting, familiar way. After clearing the dishes,
she sat down again and took my hand.

"It started out such a beautiful morning. I woke up around five o'clock
and felt wonderful. The birds were chirping as if they were calling me to
come outside. So I got up, got dressed and set to work on the yard before
the heat got too bad. It's been just miserable, you know.

"Well, anyway, I was trimming back my rose bushes. You know how
scraggly those rugosa roses can get if you're not careful. This heat has
made everything grow tremendously. Anyway, I was completely absorbed,
thinking how beautiful they were and thanking God for the pleasure of
tending them, when I heard a vehicle speed up through the park." She
took a drink of lemonade and another deep breath.

"I saw that man walking, and then this truck hit the man, just hit him.
Bam!" She clapped her hands together to illustrate. "The man bounced
off the truck and flew through the air. It was horrible! The truck just kept
going. He never even slowed down." This last sentence was in a whisper,

each syllable accented. Mrs. Easton stared at the table, again clutching my left hand.

"I miss George so much right now," she whispered, referring to her late husband, who had died the previous summer. "He was such a comfort when I miscarried all those times. He was my rock."

I didn't say anything. What could I say? After a few minutes she asked me what the police would do to find the driver of the truck. I explained how they would use what they learned from her statement earlier that morning and evidence at the scene to identify the vehicle and go from there.

"Robin, who was he? The man who was killed, I mean," she asked with sorrowful eyes.

"Frank Thompson. He was an accountant with Thompson, Klegle, Jordan and Company."

"Oh, my. I know him. He married Victoria Holmes. She was a student of mine. She was a very pretty girl and a gifted student, but her home life was dreadful. Her father was an alcoholic. Poor thing, such pain in her life," she said.

She smiled for the first time since I'd arrived. "Listen to me go on. I'm sure that poor woman is going through a lot worse pain than I am. I shouldn't sit here and fuss so," she said. She sat up straight and shook her head. After giving her another hug, I thanked her for lunch and went back to work.

The afternoon went quickly as calls came back to me from Thompson's friends and associates, including the college dean, who made an odd observation.

"Frank was a good man, but he was changing. You might call it a mid-life crisis, I don't know. But he was changing, and it wasn't in a good way," he said.

I tried to get him to elaborate but to no avail. In the end I dismissed the remark, put together the positive comments and created a story I hoped reflected the life of a man I hardly knew.

Chapter Four

IT WAS ALMOST THREE-THIRTY by the time I finished the Thompson tribute. I stretched to loosen the muscles in my neck and shoulders, knotted after huddling over the computer with a phone receiver clutched to my ear for hours.

I decided to head over to the public safety department to see what new information I could squeeze from the men in blue. There were no women on the force of about thirty-five officers, who handled both police and firefighting duties for the city. Escanaba had combined the two departments about thirty years ago, and the transition brought some hard feelings to long-time veterans who had no interest in learning new jobs but supposedly the merger saved the city tens of thousands of dollars each year.

While the city, county and state office buildings were located within a block of each other on the eastern edge of downtown, the public safety department was built in what was pretty close to the center of town. It was located in a rather old, rundown section with several bars and a large supermarket. Typical of buildings designed and built in the 1960s and 70s, it was one story, brick and flat, with institutional green walls inside. I parked in the public lot to the east of the building and darted past a roving sprinkler showering the dry grass with water.

The lobby was more fortified than a bank, with both the dispatch center and records windows made of thick, wire-filled security glass. A little circle vent was placed in the center to allow people to speak to the protected class behind the glass. I approached the dispatch window and asked to speak to someone handling the Thompson case. I had to crane my neck to be heard because the folks that designed such contraptions assume everyone is at least five feet, eight inches tall. One of the two women seated at the radio consoles went off in search of some soul willing to talk to me. After a few minutes, I was pleasantly surprised to see Detective Sergeant Charlie Baker, whom I hadn't talked to since leaving Escanaba. He let me in through a locked door and swept me up in a bear hug. I followed him back to his office, a small but neat room with old metal office furniture and a new computer.

He settled his tall muscular frame, clad in a plain dark blue suit, behind the ancient gray metal desk that dominated the room. He motioned me to one of two matching old gray office chairs in front of the desk. Baker smiled crookedly at me for a moment then shook his head.

Charlie and I had first met when I was working behind the counter at McDonald's in college and he was a new patrolman on the midnight shift. His reddish-brown hair and mustache and his hazel eyes were captivating to my young heart, but we never found ourselves in a romance. We shared a love of 1940s-era mystery novels and old movies, and we developed a strong friendship. The bond had grown dusty with distance. It was evident from the warm expression on his face, though, that it hadn't been broken.

"I can't believe you came back. I thought the big city was the place for you. Danger, scandal, excitement and all that. How long have you been home?" he asked.

"About six weeks. The danger, scandal and excitement got old, especially after it hit home. Anyway, how have you been doing? I haven't seen you around at all. I would have called, but I didn't know your home number or if you were married," I said.

"I'm fine, not married, and no prospects. I'm too busy. In fact, I've been away for a few months for special investigations training. I just got back to work Monday," he said, resting his feet on the edge of the desk. His face grew solemn. "Listen, I'm sorry to hear about your fiancé. I saw your dad right after it happened, just before I left for California for that training. That's tough. Do they know what happened yet?"

My stomach lurched. I was fine as long as I didn't have to talk about it. My mind had been focused on Thompson's accident, leaving me unprepared for questions about Mitch. I muttered something like, "Thank you. No, they haven't found a suspect or anything. . . . At least they haven't told me anything," I added.

I changed the subject quickly. "What can you tell me about the Thompson hit-and-run?" I could tell he was aching to hear my personal story, but he studied me only for a moment then reached for a file on top of a pile of manila folders and various papers near his computer on the left side of his desk. He opened it and gazed at a page, then tossed it back on the pile.

"There's not much to go on so far. We know it was a light blue truck driven by a man with dark hair. The accident reconstruction crew did find a good-sized piece of the headlight and turn signal assembly at the point of impact. They're researching that end to see if we can get a make, model and year. Then we can try to run a check through the Secretary of State's office to see who has a truck like that in the area," he said.

"How long will that take?" I asked

"Hopefully not much longer. I haven't talked to the team yet, but I just heard they're making progress," he said, tossing the file back on his desk. "Off the record?"

I hated that phrase. Unfortunately, sometimes it was the only way to stay on top of a story. Even if you couldn't use them right away, "off the record" comments often led to great stories.

"Yeah, okay, off the record. What else have you got?" I finally said.

"The night shift guys are familiar with a kid in town who has a truck fitting that description. He has a couple drinking offenses on his record— you know, minor in possession, and a speeding ticket too. It could be that he got drunk last night, went for a joy ride, smacked Thompson, got scared and took off," Charlie said. He rubbed the back of his neck and added, "If that information comes back soon, it could be a long night."

I knew how he would answer my next question, but I asked it, anyway.

"Who is this suspect?"

"Can't tell ya," he said with a devilish smile, swiveling in his chair.

"If you know who it is, why not just bring him in for questioning and get a look at the truck?"

"That's where things are getting kind of sticky," he said, turning serious. "He's nowhere to be found, and neither is the truck. We went to his house, but no one answered the door when we knocked. He may have been at work. But if we start going around asking too many questions of too many people too early, we could scare him off—if he hasn't already left town. I don't think he has, though."

"I see what you mean," I said and dug out one of my business cards from my purse. I scrawled my home number on the back and handed it to him. "Keep me posted. Here's my home phone number," I said.

He took the card and studied it for a few seconds. "Staff writer/copy editor, huh? You came back for this? How come, really?" he said as he watched me quizzically.

"I had to get away from Chicago, Charlie. After Mitch was killed I needed a change of scenery. The buildings were closing in on me. Listen, I appreciate your concern. I'm just not ready to talk about this yet. I gotta go," I said.

"I'm sorry. I didn't mean to upset you, Robin. Look, I'll let you know when we hear something I can share," he said and stood up. "Despite the reason, I'm glad you're back."

With that, he walked me to the front door and wished me a good weekend. I walked slowly to the Jeep and got in but didn't start the engine right away. My mind went back to Frank Thompson instead. Something didn't feel right with what Charlie had told me about the suspect. Something about the scenario Charlie had laid out didn't make sense. Maybe it was the idea of a young man knowingly striking someone down and then fleeing without a trace. Most kids who commit a crime get scared and eventually go to the police or someone else and tell them what happened. They can't stand the pressure of their guilt, especially if they're local and know the victim. If Charlie were right and this kid was well known by the cops, vanishing in a small town or even within a hundred miles would be difficult. I was anxious to hear who Charlie's suspect was in this case.

Finally I started the ignition and went back to the Daily Press to write an update for the Saturday morning edition before going grocery shopping and heading home for the weekend.

⟶≍⟵

When I got home a little after six I found a note from Mrs. Easton taped to my door.

Robin,

Thank you so much for listening to an old woman prattle on about her problems over lunch. It helped. I'm feeling better and will spend the weekend with my sister at her cottage on Big Bay de Noc. Please water the flowers if it doesn't rain.

Love,
Rosie

She left a phone number where she could be reached. I was glad she had someone who could look after her.

Thinking about Mrs. Easton's family made me wonder how my father was doing. After putting Belle on her chain in the back yard, I called him.

A retired Escanaba firefighter, he was an attractive man with broad shoulders and only a hint of a paunch despite being sixty, toughened by thirty-three years of hard work and heartache, both on the job and off. My mother's death when I was ten had hit him hard, and I wasn't sure he had ever gotten over losing his infant son, Evan, to a heart ailment when I was three. He never mentioned Evan, but he did like to reminisce about my mother, and he never remarried, although he was pursued by more than a few widows and divorcees, some as much as twenty years younger. He lived alone in our old family house about a mile away on the far south side of town.

"Hey, Sweet Pea, how are you?" he said in his gruff voice as soon as I said hello. Not waiting for an answer, he plunged into the day's gossip. "Hey, what's the deal with Frank Thompson? The guys at the coffee shop said he was having some problems at home and work, and then this happens. Wow!"

"Hold on a minute. What do you mean by problems?" I asked, my curiosity heightened tenfold.

"His wife—what's her name?—uh, Victoria. Well, she was reportedly running around on him. No surprise there. She sure is a looker," he said.

"Dad!" I groaned. "Just because a woman is attractive doesn't mean she's running around."

"I know that. But she's got this way about her, like she's always looking for the next best thing. Hell, she even batted her eyelashes my way a few times at the country club. But I don't need none of that business," he said.

I laughed. Dad enjoyed a beer once in a while and a bit of gossip, but he could never be called a skirt-chaser. And his gossip was usually pretty accurate since it came from a group of retired cops, firefighters and court employees who gathered every morning at the coffee shop on Ludington Street for about an hour.

"Who was she supposedly running around with?" I asked.

"I think it was some guy she met through Frank's office, but I'm not sure," he answered.

Albert Klegle? I stifled a giggle at the thought. I remembered Victoria from a few of my forays on the golf course with my dad. Good ol' Albert, with his overbite and horn-rimmed glasses, wasn't her type. I couldn't imagine him attracting the likes of the fiery, auburn-haired Victoria Thompson. Maybe it was Doug Jordan, I thought, before deciding I didn't care.

"Anyway, Dad, the police are still trying to find the guy that hit Frank. They've got a few leads, so maybe in the next day or two they'll have something. Did you know Frank?"

"Yup. He was a pretty good golfer. We played a few scrambles together. Nice guy, loved kids, good at his job. I liked him," he said.

We talked for a few more minutes and then hung up. It was still hot and steamy, so I fixed myself a turkey sandwich and lettuce and tomato salad for dinner and turned on all three fans in the apartment. After dinner, I took Belle for a stroll through the park, retracing the route Frank had taken that morning. Ludington Park was packed with people trying to beat the unusual warmth. Groups of teens played basketball and volleyball or lounged around picnic tables listening to tuneless music with heavy bass. Over the music, sounds of children shouting at the beach carried on a light breeze that provided little relief.

Except for a few paint marks left by the police and the tire tracks burned into the asphalt, there was no hint that a fatal accident had occurred less than fifteen hours before. Belle, however, seemed morbidly drawn to the spot where the body had landed, her snout exploring the site. I yanked on her leash and walked home as fast as the heat and Belle's stubby little legs could handle.

⁕

I woke up the next morning around nine after yet another restless night and dusted and vacuumed before the heat grew stifling again. While I was vacuuming the living room, the phone rang. It was Charlie.

"We got him. Brett Lindstrom's his name. The lab reported the headlight piece at the scene matches his pickup, as we suspected. We arrested him this morning," he said, the excitement of the catch evident in his voice.

"Did he confess?" I asked.

"No. He says he doesn't know anything. He'll be arraigned Monday morning. I gotta go. Bye." He hung up before I could digest what he had told me.

Brett Lindstrom. The name seemed to echo in the deep reaches of my memory. I spent the rest of the weekend reading, trying to stay cool, and wracking my brain to remember who Brett Lindstrom was and why it mattered.

Chapter Five

HE TINY DISTRICT COURTROOM could hold about forty people and was filled to capacity when I arrived for the arraignment Monday morning at eight. I found a spot along the back wall in the left rear corner next to Kevin Watkins. He had his camera poised and ready. I nodded to him and scanned the room.

The majority of people already gathered appeared to be cops, alleged criminals, or families of those about to be formally charged. Families of victims rarely showed up at arraignments unless it was something serious like rape or murder. I saw no sign of Victoria Thompson or anyone from the accounting firm.

Three men and one scraggly-haired, overweight woman, all clad in orange jumpsuits with large black initials DCJ for Delta County Jail printed on the back, were seated on the first bench on the right. A sorry-looking kid sat at the defendant's table. From what I could see, he looked about twenty years old and sat slumped over, head down and face hidden. His hands, bound in handcuffs in front of him, were clenched tightly between his legs. He looked like he wanted to curl into a ball. An Escanaba cop sat beside him. From the looks of all five defendants gathered, I figured this one must be Brett Lindstrom. I couldn't picture the kid I saw joyriding through the park and striking a man dead, then running away.

Charlie Baker entered the courtroom through the door opening from the corridor that led to the jail. He nodded and stood next to me in the last available space on the wall.

"That him?" I whispered and nodded towards the young man up front.

"That's him, all right," Charlie whispered, his head bent close to my ear. "But we still haven't found the truck, and he's not saying a word. He spent the whole weekend telling everyone who would listen that he doesn't know what happened or why he was locked up."

The door to the judge's chamber opened, and the buzz in the room quieted. Prosecutor Esther Mattson appeared and let the door close behind her. Mattson placed a briefcase on the prosecution table on the left and motioned for Charlie to come talk to her. He sauntered up the aisle, and they whispered for a few minutes. Then he returned to his place on the wall.

Mattson began removing thin manila folders from her briefcase and methodically arranging them on the table. She had been an assistant when I was last in town, but Delta County citizens took a step forward when they elected their first female prosecutor five years ago, the first Republican in that position since before FDR was president. In her late forties and never married, Mattson was a no-nonsense woman who dressed in modestly cut suits in muted colors and wore her golden brown hair in a bun. But when she went in front of a judge and jury, she was like a ravenous tiger released from a cage, a side of beef waving in front of her nose. The number of cases that were pled out rather than brought to trial rose dramatically within months after her election because going to trial meant going to jail. Juries seemed to connect with Mattson. I was almost sorry for Lindstrom—if the cops had the evidence to convict him, he was going to prison.

The door to the judge's chambers opened again and the dull hum of voices ceased as the court reporter called, "All rise."

Judge Harvey Reed blew into the room, black robe billowing around him, and bounced up the two steps into his chair behind the massive oak bench. Although small in stature, his sharp gaze and purposeful demeanor made it clear he had control of the room without needing to utter a sound.

"Please be seated," he commanded, leafing through a stack of papers. The room's occupants obliged quickly.

"First order of business is the matter of the People versus Brett Lindstrom," he said, peering over his reading glasses at the young man still hunched and staring at his hands.

Mattson stood and recited the charges against Lindstrom—negligent homicide and leaving the scene of a personal injury accident, one felony and one misdemeanor.

"Your Honor, the defendant is accused of striking Mr. Frank Thompson on the morning of June twenty-sixth, killing him, and leaving the scene without so much as stopping to check on Mr. Thompson's condition," she stated in a clear staccato delivery.

Lindstrom kept his head down but was shaking it now, as if silently denying Mattson's diatribe against him. She continued, "Mr. Lindstrom has a history of reckless driving and underage drinking, as evidenced by his driving record. Because of the serious nature of the charges and his past disregard for the law, the State is asking that bond remain at $100,000 cash as set by the magistrate." At that, someone gasped, but I couldn't tell from whom the sound had come.

Judge Reed considered Mattson's request for a moment before asking Lindstrom if he had an attorney.

He mumbled something inaudible.

"I'm sorry, Mr. Lindstrom, but you'll have to speak louder so the recorder can pick up your voice," the judge said.

"No, Sir," Lindstrom repeated loudly.

"That's better, thank you. Do you have the finances to afford an attorney?" Judge Reed asked.

"I don't think so. I have a job at the sawmill, but it only pays six-fifty an hour, and it's only part-time," Lindstrom said, his head still down and his voice growing lower with each word.

"Would you like to have the court appoint an attorney for you, as is your right?"

"Yes, Sir."

With that, the judge set bond at the requested $100,000 and told Lindstrom a bond hearing to reduce it could be held after the young man had met with his attorney. A preliminary hearing to establish if there was indeed enough evidence to try the case was set for July thirteenth, two weeks away. Lindstrom was dismissed, and the judge moved on to the next defendant, a woman, charged with drunk driving.

The police officer at Lindstrom's side urged him to stand, and they walked together to the back of the courtroom. When they passed the last bench on the right, a woman dressed in a blue nurse's uniform reached out and grabbed Lindstrom's arm. Tears flowed from her blue eyes leaving trails through her make-up. She looked vaguely familiar.

"I love you," she choked.

Lindstrom looked at the woman—who, from her age and vague resemblance to the defendant, I guessed was his mother—and mirrored her weak smile. The officer gave a tug on his right arm, and they shuffled away.

I left the courtroom with Charlie in tow. After the door closed behind us, I stopped in the hallway and tugged on the sleeve of his sport coat.

"Who is that kid? Where does he work? What's his story? His name rings a bell with me, and his mother looks familiar," I said.

Charlie led me to a row of seats in the lobby and we sat down.

"You know, he's really not a bad kid. He's supposed to start his second year in the automotive technician program at the college this fall," Charlie said as he loosened his tie. "Like he said, he works part time at Stewart Lumber. He probably would be okay if he just had better taste in friends these days."

He stretched out his long legs, and we sat in silence for a minute or two. He seemed to be considering whether to tell me more. We had built a solid foundation of trust by the time I took over the police beat as a cub reporter just out of college, and he had been one of my best sources. When he told me to keep something under my hat, I did. But he also knew I had just come back from working for a newspaper where competition for scoops made reporters behave in ways that could leave behind a trail of pissed-off people sorry they had talked. Charlie decided to gamble.

"This has to be off the record," he said and leaned forward. "We went to his house Saturday morning. I knocked on the door, and one of the patrolmen walked around looking for any sign of the truck. Lindstrom's mother answered the door—that's who grabbed his arm in there. She said she was glad Brett finally called us. I thought, 'Great, we've got a confession.' But after she woke him up and brought him into the living room, he told me this story about how the truck turned up missing Friday afternoon when he went to leave for work but he didn't report it stolen because he figured his sister or his mother had borrowed it. So he walked the three miles to work. He said he found out that night that the truck must have been stolen, but he was waiting to report it until the next morning in case a friend had borrowed it. It was the most ridiculous thing I'd ever heard. But I'll tell you something, he sure made it sound convincing. He's going to be sorry he lied, though. It just makes my job harder."

"What did you mean about his friends?" I asked.

"He's not the sharpest tool in the shed, but I don't remember Brett ever getting into trouble in high school. It wasn't until he graduated that he started hanging around with Greg Connor and getting into all sorts of trouble. Connor runs with a bad crowd. We suspect he's involved in some minor drug dealing, mainly marijuana. I haven't seen him hanging around town much lately, though. I hear he got a real job at the same place this Lindstrom kid works," he said.

"Maybe this Connor guy was driving the truck and Lindstrom's just protecting him," I said.

Charlie laughed. He stood up to his full height of six feet, two inches, hooked his fingers in his waistband and adjusted his trousers.

"Your imagination's kicking into high gear already. You should have been a detective. We'll see what happens," he said and walked away.

As I walked back to the Daily Press offices, I pondered Charlie's tale. I had an easier time believing Lindstrom's story than accepting that he had senselessly struck a man dead and left him lying by the side of the road. Was I becoming a sucker for a sweet face in my old age? I couldn't shake the feeling that this case was more complicated than it looked on the surface.

Chapter Six

IT TOOK ME ABOUT twenty minutes to sum up the court hearing in a story for that day's paper. I spent the rest of the morning making calls on a few less sensational stories to which I was assigned and broke for lunch at eleven-thirty, feeling a sense of accomplishment at getting so much done.

At a quarter to four that afternoon, my neck was aching again, my eyes were watering, and the air conditioning had quit sometime around one o'clock. I considered heading home. The outside air temperature was ninety-two degrees, according to an announcer on a distant radio that was providing more static than music, but inside it felt like one hundred and two, with the dozens of computers throwing off heat and the florescent lights blazing overhead.

As I was lazily shuffling piles of files, various interoffice memos and other miscellaneous papers, a commotion started at the receptionist's desk.

"I told you I want to speak to Robin Hamilton," said the woman who had reached out for Brett Lindstrom at the hearing earlier, shaking a copy of that day's paper in poor Amy Winklebauer's face.

"Yes, Ma'am. Just a moment please," the receptionist said meekly.

Amy was not quite the professional gatekeeper that Albert Klegle's secretary was. A quiet natural redhead, small in stature and voice, she hid her best feature—big, blue-green eyes—behind a pair of wire-framed glasses. Just twenty years old and only two months on the job, she was still learning how to handle angry readers.

She scurried over to my desk and leaned close to me.

"Robin, there's a woman up front who wants to talk to you. She seems really angry," she whispered, wringing her hands. "Do you want me to send her away or have her talk to Bob?"

I laughed and patted her shoulder. "No, no. Bob's got enough to do. I'll talk to her. Send her back," I said.

What the hell, I figured. It certainly wouldn't be the first time someone was mad about something I had written. Talking to her might even result in more information about the case.

The woman stalked to my desk like a general on a mission. Her face, once attractive, I imagined, was contorted into a pained, tight-lipped grimace.

"I can't believe you, of all people, could write this kind of trash," she said in a shrill voice, throwing that day's paper on my desk. A picture of Brett Lindstrom being led from the courtroom was splashed across three columns under the headline "SUSPECT CHARGED IN HIT-AND-RUN DEATH."

I learned a long time ago that the best way to handle angry people is to remain calm and smile politely, which I did.

"I'm sorry you feel that way, Ma'am. Would you like to have a seat so we can discuss the article?" I said, gesturing to the straight-back chair beside my desk.

The tactic worked. She sighed deeply and sank into the chair, dropping her large leather purse to the floor with a thump. I took a moment to study her face.

She had obviously had a rough life. I guessed she was about forty, but the dark circles under her eyes and sallowness of her skin added at least five years to her appearance. Sleep was something she probably had not experienced in any reasonable quantity for several days. Her shoulder-length sandy blonde hair was natural, with the few strands of gray at the temples made more noticeable by the way her hair was pulled back in a low ponytail. Something about her jogged a memory. Something about a game of Monopoly at my dad's house when I was a kid.

"Why don't you start by telling me who you are and what it is about the article that upsets you," I said.

She looked at me, incredulous, as if I had pinched her bottom. "Don't you remember me, Robin? I took care of you after your mother died!" she exclaimed.

My mind went into rewind mode and stopped at a point just after my mother had died of cancer. Of course! Hannah Spencer was her name, or had been at least until she had run off with Jack Lindstrom when she was still quite young. The daughter of one of Dad's fellow firefighters, Hannah stayed with me at night when my dad had to work. For two years, we shared pizzas, laughs and many tears as I adjusted to life without my mother. Ten years older than I, she was a big sister to me. But what my dad didn't know when he hired her was that she was pregnant. The baby, a son, was born seven months after I turned ten, six months after my mother died. I remembered Dad being horrified but deciding to let her keep working for us because it was the only income she had except for an occasional check from Jack, who was in and out of her life like a recurring migraine. I learned how to feed, change and bathe the little boy. Then Jack finally decided to marry Hannah, and Dad figured I was old enough to take care of myself on the few nights I was alone. I lost touch with Hannah sometime in high school and had pretty much forgotten her.

Now, looking into her face, it was hard to connect this pathetic woman sitting before me with the bubbly teenager I had once known. And that little baby boy had grown into someone who might have recklessly taken the life of another man. I searched for something to say. The best I could do was an apology.

"I'm sorry. It's been so many years. I thought you looked familiar when I saw you in the courtroom, but I couldn't place you," I said.

Hannah sighed again, expelling her energy along with the air from her lungs. Her shoulders slumped, and she began to weep. I passed her a few tissues and let her cry.

When she got control of herself after a few minutes, she said through gritted teeth, "He didn't do it, Robin. He didn't kill that man. They're wrong. The police are wrong."

I was expecting that. After all, I would not want to believe someone I loved and shared a bloodline with was capable of carelessly killing someone, either.

"What do you think happened?" I asked.

Hannah stared at the tissue wadded up in her hands for a few seconds before answering. Beads of sweat drenched her upper lip and rolled down her temples.

"I'm really not sure. But," she stated emphatically, "I know there is a lot more to this than what Brett is saying."

"Like what? He told a rather weak story to the police when they arrested him," I said, shifting in my chair as a drop of sweat rolled lazily down the middle of my back.

"I know it's weak. That's why I'm here. There's some reason he told that story. It's not the truth. But I know the truth is not that he struck that man in the park, either. My God, Frank Thompson was Brett's Little

League coach for two years. He bought him a new glove and cleats, out of his own pocket, when my hours were cut back at the hospital," she choked. She blew her nose again and tossed the tissue in the small round metal trashcan behind me.

"I wasn't home that morning of the—the accident. I'm a registered nurse at St. Francis, and I mostly work the graveyard shift in the ER. In fact, I was working when the call came over the scanner at the nurses' station that a pedestrian had been hit by a vehicle in the park.

"I had no idea that call would put my family in the middle of a firestorm," she said, her voice dropping and head shaking slowly from side to side. She took a fresh tissue and wiped the perspiration from her face.

"It's awfully hot in here. Don't you have air conditioning?" she asked.

"We do, but wouldn't you know, it's broken, and on the hottest day of the year too," I chuckled bitterly.

She took another tissue, this time to wipe the moisture from her forehead and upper lip. "I came home at about eight-thirty Friday morning. My daughter, Sarah—she's seventeen—had spent the night at her best friend's house on Kemper Lake, so she wasn't home. Brett was asleep in his room. He had worked about ten hours the day before at the sawmill and come home exhausted about eleven Thursday night. He had parked his truck in the driveway. But when I got home Friday morning, it was gone. That's why I went to check on him, to see if he was home. I woke him up and asked him where his truck was. He said one of his friends had borrowed it and would bring it back later. But he had the strangest look on his face when he said that, like he was confused. When the truck hadn't shown up by seven that evening and I saw that Brett had walked the three miles to work and back, I begged him to call the police. He refused. He said his friend would bring it back. He even refused to tell me who borrowed the damn thing," Hannah said with her fists clenched.

"Something's wrong here. Brett's covering for someone, but he won't talk to me," she said, pausing to collect her thoughts. "Brett is—well, a little slow. He does great with mechanical things and is doing fine with his technical classes, but he doesn't communicate well. His IQ is around ninety-five. He's very impressionable and easy to take advantage of."

She grabbed my hand. "Robin, please help us. Your father says you're really smart and have experience investigating these sorts of things. I can't afford a private investigator, and I don't have much faith in the local cops. I don't think they'll dig deeper than Brett. I don't want him to go to prison for something he didn't do!"

I didn't answer right away. Instead, I pulled my hand away and propped my chin on it and considered her request. She was right about one thing. Something was wrong with Brett's story. For one thing, it didn't match what he had told police. For another, there was a hole in it big enough to pass an ore freighter through. If Brett was taking the fall for someone else, who and why? Few friendships are so strong that one person will go to prison for another. And if someone had borrowed the truck, was it with the intent of killing Thompson, or was that simply an accident? Or did Brett really kill Thompson by accident, ditch the truck, come home and concoct a story for his mother and the police?

I had to give some weight to Hannah's belief that her son was innocent. She sensed something. No one knows a person like a mother. There's a bond that can extend beyond the grave.

"Who does your son hang around with, Hannah? The police told me he has some bad friends," I asked.

She gave me a faint smile, understanding my question as acceptance of her request.

"Well, he doesn't have many friends, really. He's always been shy and small for his age and not very athletic. Like I said, he's a follower. He did have a couple nice friends in high school, but one went to college downstate and the other joined the army. Last year, he started hanging around with a new guy a few years older than him—a Greg something or other. Greg doesn't come around the house much. Brett's always going to meet him somewhere. Since they started hanging together, Brett's been staying out later and has gotten a few tickets. Nothing serious. Other than Greg, I don't know if Brett as any friends any more," she said.

"What about a girlfriend?"

"Oh no! Brett's so shy, he gets tongue-tied around girls. When Sarah's friends come over to the house, he hides," Hannah said, smirking.

"I'm not sure what I can do," I said. It was tough to be without friends, and if a kid didn't have many to begin with, he might guard the ones he did have to the point of lying for them. "The police don't have a very strong case without the truck, which means they're going to keep investigating until they find it, but they may come across something that will help in Brett's defense. In the meantime, I'll see what I can find out on my own. I'll warn you, despite what my dad may have told you, I'm not a detective."

Hannah's eyes brightened for the first time, and she smiled, revealing a simple beauty. "Thank you. Just try, that's all I ask," she said and clasped my hand in hers.

I walked her to the front door and gave her a pat on the shoulder, then went back to my desk and sat for a while, pondering the situation. I glanced at my watch. It was nearly five o'clock. I needed a cold shower, change of clothes, some food and an ear to bend.

I went home and took Belle for a short walk in the ninety-degree heat. After one trip around the block, she waddled eagerly back to the apartment, panting furiously. I took a quick ice-cold shower and changed into shorts and a t-shirt. I squirted Belle a few times with cold water as she continued to pant like an out-of-shape man in a marathon. Then we went back downstairs, where I lifted her into the Jeep and headed for the air-conditioned home of my most trusted confidant.

Chapter Seven

ESPITE MY DAD'S LOVE of gossip, if you told him to keep something to himself, he did. We were sitting in the space to the right of the kitchen, which served as a dining room and overlooked the patio. It was too hot to enjoy being outside, so we ate turkey club sandwiches, lightly salted cucumber slices, and cantaloupe at the dining room table while Belle watched from her makeshift bed on the mat in front of the sink. After dinner, we made our way to the living room with tall glasses of iced tea. My dad took a seat in his favorite blue corduroy easy chair, and I flopped down on the couch.

"I don't know, Dad. What do you think?" I asked, after relating what Hannah Lindstrom had told me earlier.

He took a slow drink, then said, "You know, Brett's old man was a low-life. He was never much of a father to those kids. He left Hannah and the two little ones about fifteen years ago. She struggled for a while but went back to school, got her nursing degree and did just fine. She was better off without him. He drank, ran around, even hit her a few times, if the rumors are true. I don't know where the hell he is now, but I hope he stays far away from here."

"That's interesting; but it doesn't answer my question," I said.

"Yes, it does," he said curtly. He put down his glass and leaned forward in his chair, resting his elbows on his bare knees. "Listen, I know your generation believes everyone ought to mind their own business, and generally that's not a bad thing. Sometimes, though, you have an obligation to help those in need, especially when they ask for help."

"So you think I should dive into this mess and do my own investigation," I said. While I had told Hannah I would look into Brett's story, I was not sure I had the time or energy to invest a lot of effort in a problem perhaps best handled by the police.

"Hannah helped us out at a time when I thought the world was coming to an end. We owe her a little bit in return," he said, settling back in his chair again.

My dad had a soft spot in his heart for people who had fallen on hard times. I, on the other hand, seemed to have developed such a cynical view of the world that I was content to let people stew in their own juices. I found myself wishing I could be more like him, that I could feel more warmth towards others, empathy or even sympathy. But since I'd lost Mitch I seemed incapable of feeling much of anything.

My gaze fell on the collection of framed photos artfully placed on the mantel over the small, white-painted brick fireplace. My mother smiled down at me from a large portrait framed in antique silver. The photograph was taken a few years before I was born and showed a woman full of grace, beauty and love of life. She was always the first person to lend a hand or a shoulder to cry on, to a friend, a neighbor, or the wife of one of my dad's fellow firefighters.

"All right, I'll do what I can to help the kid. In the event he's innocent, though, and I don't know that I believe he is, the police should be able to uncover the truth. Once they find the truck, there should be some evidence pinpointing who was at the wheel," I said.

"I know. But you have a God-given talent for uncovering the truth when people want it buried deep in the earth, and if there's anything to Brett's story, you'll find it," he said. Then he studied me for a long time with a concerned expression on his tanned face.

"You haven't been sleeping well. There are dark circles under your eyes. You've never had those before," he said.

I pulled my compact out of my purse and considered my reflection in the round dusty mirror. There were shadows under my green eyes that made me look older than I wanted to look.

"Heck, I'm thirty-one. Maybe they're a part of aging," I said. "I'll be all right. I'm just getting used to living in a new place. I'll sleep better when I get settled in. Besides, it's too hot to get a decent night's rest."

"Have you talked to anyone about Mitch?" he asked.

"What do you mean?"

"I mean, have you talked to a friend or a counselor or anyone? You certainly haven't talked to me. Believe me, Robin, bottling everything up inside does not make the pain go away," he said.

He was right, but I was afraid—afraid of the rage that burned inside me, of the despair that threatened to smother me whenever Mitch entered my mind, of the empty future that loomed ahead of me. Once I started to talk, I would start to cry, and then to scream. Once I started screaming, I was terrified I wouldn't be able to stop.

"I'm not ready yet," I finally said. "I'll be all right."

I could see he wasn't satisfied, but he didn't pursue further discussion. We parted with a hug, and I drove home in the still-sweltering heat with Belle, panting once again, perched proudly beside me. I scratched her soft floppy left ear as she gazed out the windshield.

When we arrived back home, Mrs. Easton's cream-colored Buick was parked on her side of the garage. After putting Belle upstairs, I found my landlady on the front porch, sipping a glass of ice water.

"Hi. How was the lake?" I asked.

She beamed and said, "It was wonderful, just what I needed. I feel so much better. My sister has the loveliest English garden you've ever seen. Makes my little bushes look sort of sad in comparison. How are you, dear?"

"Just fine. It's still pretty warm out, though. It's going to be another rough night for sleeping," I said. We said goodnight, and I went upstairs.

Once in bed, I tossed and turned until past midnight, then fell into a troubled sleep and dreamed I was being chased through the darkened halls of my old high school, hearing but not seeing the source of the roar of an engine revving furiously behind me.

The next morning, after the paper's deadline, I started my foray into private investigation. In my short time back in Escanaba, I hadn't had the opportunity to meet with the Public Safety director, Joe Nelson. When I left town, Nelson was a lieutenant in charge of the day shift. He had a reputation as a womanizer and heavy social drinker, and we never got on too well. He ignored me most of the time. I didn't really blame him. After all, then I was just a kid right out of college who didn't know a thing about police work other than what I had seen on TV. This time around I hoped to build a better working relationship.

"You've got five minutes, Ms. Hamilton," he said curtly after I was escorted to his large office, adorned with various plaques and shooting trophies to remind visitors of his greatness. I didn't like the way he sneered when he said my name, but I had enough experience now dealing with hard-ass cops not to let it rattle me. I flashed my best kill-'em-with-kindness smile.

"Thank you, Chief. I appreciate any time you can spare me," I said with all the charm I could muster.

"I'm back at the Daily Press, and I look forward to building a good working relationship with you and this department. Right now I'm looking into the Frank Thompson hit-and-run case," I said, still smiling.

Nelson sat behind a large oak desk with his elbows perched on the arms of his brown leather chair, his long tanned fingers pressed together forming a tent. The expression on his face was a mixture of boredom and contempt. He didn't utter a sound in response to my cheery introduction. I plunged forward, still not rattled.

"Brett Lindstrom was arrested, but I understand it's possible there may be others involved. Where does the investigation stand with regard to that?" I asked. I felt ridiculous. Nelson obviously had no intention of telling me squat about this case or any other. Yet I was unprepared for his vitriolic diatribe.

"Look, Ms. Hamilton," he growled. "I'm going to be straight with you. I don't like the media. You're a bunch of fleas feeding off the blood of human tragedy. But because this department is a public entity, I do what is required to keep the public informed. I do it through press releases issued by my lieutenants and captains. I don't have the time or deSire to sit here and answer a bunch of questions from some girl reporter."

Nelson stood up from his chair, strolled to the door, and opened it.

"Your five minutes are up."

I wasn't rattled even now. I was pissed. I got up and walked to the door, grabbed it from his grasp, shut it quietly, and looked directly into his dark brown eyes. He towered over me by nearly a foot and had at least a hundred pounds on me, but at the moment I felt like David taking on Goliath.

"Chief, you need me a hell of a lot more than I need you. If one of your boys out there—" I hooked a thumb in the direction of the squad room in back—"screws up, I can make your life miserable. Don't mess with me!"

I left the office before he could react, slamming the door so hard the glass inset rattled. So much for a good working relationship.

Chapter Eight

AFTER THE SCENE WITH Chief Nelson, I went home with the idea of eating lunch, but after staring into the refrigerator for about 10 seconds I slammed the door shut, hooked Belle to her leash and dragged her toward the park. It was still too hot for a walk, and Belle didn't make it half a mile before she let me know she wanted to go home. She stopped at every tree, shrub and weed along the way, forcing a tug-of-war match on her leash. That I was walking about twice as fast as her short legs could carry her barrel-shaped body may have had something to do with her reluctance to do the full two miles.

By the time we got back to the apartment, my sleeveless cotton shirt was soaked with sweat, but I felt calmer. I'm not the type of person to shoot her mouth off in general when challenged. The consequences usually aren't worth the bit of satisfaction received from letting someone have it with both barrels. I felt now embarrassed by my reaction to Nelson's idiotic behavior. Somehow I was going to have to find a way to work with the chief, since there were several years until his retirement party.

I went back to work and called Charlie Baker. The detective agreed to meet me for dinner at a popular downtown hangout, Hereford and Hops, a relatively new microbrewery and steakhouse. I figured Charlie might have some insights on Nelson and some new information on Lindstrom.

As soon as I walked into the restaurant, the heavenly aroma of greasy burgers and fries whetted my appetite. Charlie, still wearing a suit, was already seated at a small square table in the corner of the no-smoking section. He was sipping a glass of beer and watching the other patrons. The restaurant was about half-full, most of the customers business people. From the snippets of conversation I caught as I crossed the room, they were stopping in for a social drink with associates before either going to a meeting or to the country club for a late game of golf.

I sat down across from Charlie and plunked my purse on the floor. The waitress, a perky college-age brunette with a ponytail, was at my side within seconds. Not much of drinker, I decided to order a wine cooler, anyway, thinking it would quell what anger remained.

Charlie smiled slyly at me, observing my every move.

"I hear you and the chief, uh, had words," he chuckled.

I hid my face in my hands and groaned. It was probably all over the city that I had had a tiff with the chief. I finally looked up at Charlie with weary eyes and said, "We definitely did not hit it off. Did he say something to you?"

"No. Actually the dispatchers overheard your little tête-à-tête and passed it on," he said, still grinning.

I groaned again. This was the last thing I needed.

"I screwed up, Charlie. He pissed me off with his macho bullshit about not having to deal with women and not liking the media. I lost my temper," I said, shaking my head. "I'm going to have to work with that guy. Any suggestions?"

He took a swig of his beer and thought for a moment.

"I remember the day I met you. You were working the counter at that burger joint on the highway. It was Saturday night and you were dealing with an obnoxious guy in a thousand-dollar suit who was bitching about his hamburger having pickles. He wanted a new hamburger altogether, and you apologized, then suggested he simply pick them off because the place was packed, and the cooks were already running behind. He called you a few names. Then you called him a few names. The manager came over, the guy got his hamburger, and you got an ass-chewing," he said.

"Yeah, so? What does that have to do with this?" I asked, my face hot. I had forgotten all about that incident. I almost got fired over that hamburger.

"The point is, diplomacy has never been your strong suit when you're being attacked. You're very practical and strong-minded. I thought you were right about the hamburger ten years ago, and I think you're right about the chief. He's your typical male chauvinist pig. The only reason he got that job is that he and the city manager and half the city council have been buddies since high school." He took another slow drink of his beer. "That said, there are better ways to handle people like Nelson then playing hardball. You did some damage, kiddo, but I think it'll blow over. If anything, he may respect you a little more because you stood up to him."

I considered this and shrugged.

"I don't know. I hope you're right. I really don't want to apologize. And I still think he's a jackass," I muttered.

Charlie laughed. The ponytail returned with my wine cooler and took our orders, a steak sandwich for Charlie and a Caesar salad with grilled chicken for me.

"What started the argument, anyway?" Charlie asked after the ponytail left.

"I wanted to reacquaint myself with him and see what was new on the Thompson case. He went ballistic. His reaction was totally bizarre," I said.

"To his defense, Nelson has been going through a tough time. His wife finally left him this past winter after enduring about twenty-five years of his cattin' around. He took it hard. Go figure," he said and snorted.

"Men!" I huffed and rolled my eyes. Charlie laughed again. I liked hearing him laugh. It was a pleasant sound, comforting, like being wrapped in a favorite old quilt on a cold, rainy night.

"As far as the Thompson thing, there's really nothing new," Charlie said. "We still haven't found the damn truck. I'm thinking he may have ditched it in the woods on someone's back forty. If that's the case, we may not find it until deer season." He drained his glass with a gulp, motioned to the ponytail when she sailed by our table and ordered a diet soda. I cocked an eyebrow at him.

"One beer? What's this, you becoming a responsible citizen?" I teased. Charlie was known as a bit of party animal in his rookie days.

"Ha, ha. Actually, alcohol is full of empty calories. It's a pain in the ass to lose weight after you hit thirty," he said, patting his slightly protruding stomach. "The fun of a few beers isn't worth the extra two miles I have to do on the treadmill to get rid of them."

It was my turn to smile. I sort of envied him. I had never weighed more than a hundred and five pounds in my life and would have welcomed a little extra weight to add some curves to my frame.

"The reason I asked about Thompson is Brett Lindstrom's mother came to my office in tears yesterday. She said he's innocent, that he's covering for someone," I said. Charlie grimaced . "Yeah, I know," I went on. "They all say that. But we've already established that I'm no bleeding heart. I think she may be right. It's just a hunch, but things just aren't adding up."

The ponytail brought our food, and we postponed further conversation on the case until we had finished devouring our tasty meals. Then Charlie sat back in his chair and loosened his tie.

"I think you may be right about something not adding up. I've interviewed enough criminals to know when someone is just lying to try to avoid getting arrested and when someone is lying because they're scared. When I talked to Lindstrom on Saturday, he was scared out of his mind, and I don't think he was afraid of me. Something else had him spooked. He wasn't even that upset when I said I'd have to arrest him and lodge him in jail, although he kept denying he hit Thompson or knew where the truck was. But more than that, his story didn't make much sense. His mother said he never allowed her or his sister to drive that truck. What did she tell you?"

"She said Brett told her he'd let one of his friends borrow it and that he would bring it back. He wouldn't give a name, though," I said.

Charlie combed his reddish-brown mustache with his fingers.

"That's odd. I know for a fact he worked very hard to buy that truck and then put a lot of work into it. The guy he bought it from is a neighbor of mine. Why would he casually let someone borrow it and then not be supremely pissed off when something happened to it? The problem is, until he decides to tell the truth, there's not much we can do except go forward with our investigation against him. He's our only suspect," he said.

I mulled Brett's two stories over in my mind. Why did he tell his mother one thing and the police another? In his simple way of thinking maybe he thought he was protecting his friend by lying to the police but couldn't lie to his mother.

"Maybe this friend got rid of the truck for him. Maybe there were two people in the truck and the other guy was driving. Mrs. Easton was quite a distance away from the scene, and it happened so fast. Perhaps she just didn't see the passenger," I suggested.

"That's a definite possibility," Charlie said, his voice rising a little as the din in the restaurant grew. The place was full by now. "Yeah, I think that theory has some merit. If that is the case, though, he's only digging himself into a deeper hole by lying. If he just owned up to the whole thing, he'd probably get a year in jail, maybe two if he was the one driving and fleeing the scene. It just doesn't make sense," he said again.

The waitress brought our checks with a cheery smile. We paid our bill and walked outside. The blistering heat hit my skin as though a blanket soaked in boiling water had been wrapped around me.

"Man, I can't believe this heat. If I wanted to live in a climate like this, I'd move to Florida," Charlie moaned. He walked me to my Jeep. I got in and rolled down the window. Charlie propped his arms on the sill and leaned into the cab.

"Don't worry much about Nelson. I'll talk to him. He seems to like me. Let me know if you find out more on Lindstrom. You've got a knack for finding clues in odd places," he said.

"All right, but it's got to be a two-way street. I agreed to help Hannah Lindstrom find out the truth. I'm going to need your cooperation," I said.

"Don't get into this too deep. This is a police matter. If there's something to his story, we'll find it," Charlie said.

I said good-bye and drove home, where I cranked up the fans to the highest setting before collapsing on the couch. I lay in the path of a tall, floor-model fan, although it offered little relief. To take my mind off the heat, I focused on Lindstrom and contemplated my next move. Maybe, considering my personal history with his mother, I could get him to come clean out of concern for her. I fell asleep until eight-thirty when Belle's big wet cold nose nudged my leg telling me it was time for her walk.

Chapter Nine

CRACK OF THUNDER BLASTED me awake. Heavy rain pelted the house as a stiff wind blew the filmy white curtains in my bedroom out at a forty-five degree angle and made the blinds flap. I jumped out of bed and dashed from room to room to close the windows before the apartment was flooded. The sills were already soaked, so I went around again with a towel to mop up the water. Belle whimpered and panted heavily as she followed me. The wind and rain were so loud I could hardly hear my own voice telling Belle to calm down.

In the kitchen, I threw the wet towel in the sink and poured myself the remains of a week-old one-and-a-half liter bottle of cheap merlot, then settled into an easy chair in the corner of the living room, away from the windows. Belle climbed into my lap, her heavy breath in my face. I looked at the clock on the wall and cringed. Three forty-five. I would get no more sleep tonight. I stroked Belle's head and got lost in the storm.

Thunderstorms had thrilled me as a child. The louder the better— no cowering under the bed for me. When I began to understand their destructive power, I grew to respect a good storm. As a reporter, I had spent many hours working on stories about downed power lines, damaged homes and the occasional death. Finally, sitting in my old chair with Belle quivering in my lap, I realized why many people are afraid of thunder, lightning and wind.

A raging storm has a cruel way of making you feel isolated and vulnerable. For the first time in my life, I was almost afraid of the commotion outside.

The night Mitch died, a violent early spring storm had settled over northeastern Illinois. He had just been assigned to the afternoon shift in a small, remote suburb of Chicago and was patrolling the perimeter of the relatively rural community, searching for signs of damage. It was almost the end of the shift when he radioed in to dispatch that he was stopping to check a car parked along the side of a deserted road. The car had no license plate and appeared to be empty from his view in the patrol car. When he failed to check in again within ten minutes, the dispatcher tried calling him on the radio. No one answered. Another officer was sent to check on him, but it was too late. When the second officer arrived, he found the driver side window of Mitch's Ford Crown Victoria shattered and Mitch slumped over the steering wheel, dead of a shotgun blast to the head.

The parked car Mitch had reported was nowhere to be found, the heavy rain washing away any tire tracks or footprints his killer would have left behind. All the police had to go on was the general description Mitch had given over the radio of a dark-colored, late-model Cadillac. No motive. Nothing.

I was startled back to the present when Belle sat up and licked my face. A few hot, bitter tears had streamed down my cheeks. Hugging my dog, I felt a little less lonely. She seemed to understand. Mitch had given her to me for Christmas a year and a half before. Just eight weeks old, she made us laugh hysterically over her clumsy puppy antics, tripping over her humongous ears, slobbering all over anyone who treated her to a good tummy rub. I took her to visit Mitch's grave just before we moved. Sensing my sadness, she lay down next to his headstone, her head between her front paws, and whined softly. The memory now made my tears flow like a river.

There we sat until the alarm went off at five-thirty, wind howling, rain pounding, me crying and Belle in my arms, drawing out my sorrow. I wondered if the tears would ever stop.

⁓₩₦⁓

It was still raining when I left for work, but the monsoon had slowed to a heavy sprinkle. Branches were scattered in several front yards, and one small maple tree had toppled over a few blocks from my house, just missing a pickup parked in the driveway. I didn't see a lot of activity, so I figured the storm must not have done too much damage, my guess confirmed when I made my rounds to the city and county police stations. Except for a few downed trees and power lines, the area had survived unscathed.

As soon as I arrived at the Daily Press office, I was summoned to Bob Hunter's office. The editor was going over a list of major stories from the wire services and nursing what I guessed was his third cup of coffee of the day. He often joked about how he should walk around with an IV dripping coffee straight into his veins. It would be more efficient than running back to the break room to pour the dozen cups he drank every day. He still looked half-asleep most afternoons.

"Mornin', Robin," he drawled without looking up from his papers.

"Mornin' Bob. What's up?" I asked. My head hurt, and my eyes felt puffy.

He laid the papers and his coffee cup down and laced his fingers together on top of the pile. When he saw my face, he frowned.

"You all right?" he asked.

"I'm fine, Bob. The storm kept me up last night. So, what's up?" I said again.

He dropped the subject, either out of kindness or because he actually believed me, and I was grateful.

"Today is Frank Thompson's funeral. I'm going, and I think you should, too. This is worth a story. The church will be packed," he said.

Journalists usually love a good funeral. Coverage of presidential funerals has always been spectacular. And the round-the-clock, blow-by-blow reports of the funerals of Jackie Onassis and Diana, Princess of Wales, found a ready audience. Death and mourning attract curiosity, especially when well-known people die. And while Frank Thompson was a far cry from royalty, he was a popular man in town.

But I wasn't in the mood for a funeral, after crying my eyes out over Mitch just hours before, and I wasn't sure I could handle it. Mitch's funeral had been beautiful, with more than five hundred police officers from around the Midwest attending. A bagpiper had played a heart-wrenching version of "Amazing Grace." Mitch's mother held her husband's right hand and my left while my dad held my right hand throughout the service, a human chain of grief. It was beautiful, but I had no desire to relive the occasion.

Despite my private reluctance, at about ten-thirty Hunter and I piled into his Ford Taurus and drove to the Presbyterian church six blocks away. Hunter was right. Although the service wasn't scheduled to begin for another half hour, the parking lot was already nearly full.

The church was one of the largest in the city and could hold several hundred worshippers—or mourners. The gray stone structure loomed in front of us, almost sinister on this gloomy gray morning. The rain had stopped, but puddles dotted the street and sidewalk. The air smelled musty, while the trees lining the street were shrouded in fog. We made our way up the steps to the front doors along with several other people, most of them dressed in dark suits or dresses. I looked down at my khaki pants and white shirt and felt underdressed.

The vestibule was filled with massive bouquets of flowers. Their fragrance was heavy, almost suffocating in the damp air. Someone to my left sneezed. Between two sets of doors leading into the sanctuary stood three easels covered with pictures depicting Frank Thompson's life odyssey from tow-headed little boy to successful community leader. Hunter and I made our way through the crowd to view them. They were arranged chronologically, starting with a baby sitting on a blanket on the grass with a ball clutched in his chubby little hands and a big smile on his cherubic face. There were photos from Halloween parties long forgotten, sports team photos, high school and college graduation, and many snapshots with his wife Victoria taken at various social functions. There was even one showing him dressed in checked flannel and hunter orange, showing off an eight-point buck he had shot one recent November. I wouldn't have pictured him as the mighty hunter type, but considering firearm deer season is the U.P. version of Mardi Gras for a lot of men and a few women, I guess I shouldn't have been surprised.

All in all, the collection showed a popular, happy man who had loved life. My eyes were mostly drawn to the photos with Victoria, though. She was beautiful, indeed. Her straight white teeth glowed in each and every picture. Her glossy auburn hair always looked perfect, even when tousled by the wind. She and Frank appeared to be the epitome of the happily married couple, heading into middle age with few worries.

I didn't see any photos of children, not even nieces or nephews and pointed out the absence to Hunter in a whisper.

"Nope. She never wanted any children. Didn't like them. From what I hear, that was kind of a sore spot for them. Frank loved kids," he whispered.

We left the photo display and walked through the doors to the right and into the church, which was now almost full. We found seats about halfway towards the front. Victoria was standing by her husband's polished black casket, which was closed and draped with a massive blanket of white flowers. Dressed in a simple, shape-flattering black suit with a skirt that ended several inches above her knees, she looked like a model or an actress in a TV commercial. Her hair, done up in a French twist, gleamed under the soft candlelight. She dutifully shook hands with well-wishers and occasionally flashed that brilliant smile. I saw no tears.

Scanning the room for familiar faces, I saw many local dignitaries, including Grant Stewart, owner of Stewart Lumber Company, where Brett Lindstrom worked. Stewart was seated in the second row on the right, behind where I guessed Victoria and the rest of the family would be seated. Thompson's partners were sitting in the front pew on the left. Albert Klegle appeared relaxed but tired as he chatted with his drab little wife. Douglas Jordan, on the other hand, a normally attractive man in his mid-forties, sat stone-faced and stared straight ahead. His wife, the circuit court judge, was nowhere to be seen.

I turned to look behind me and saw Joe Nelson entering the sanctuary. Dressed in a tailored dark blue suit, he took a seat towards the back with the mayor. I had to admit Nelson wore his clothes well.

I wondered how many of those present had been Frank's friends and how many were there simply to be seen. Then I admonished myself for being so cynical again and settled into the hard wooden pew and to wait for the service to begin.

It was short, sweet and not too sappy—just a few songs, a brief sermon, and simple eulogy delivered by Doug Jordan. The partner talked about what a kind man Thompson was and how "his generosity of spirit, time and money will be missed in this fair community of ours, which was made a better place because of Frank."

When the service was over, Victoria Thompson made her way to the back of the church first and stood near the outside doors, thanking each person for coming. When it was my turn, I expressed my condolences and took a moment to study her.

She was a good four inches taller than I, taking away the black leather pumps. I was struck by her composure. Her hands felt soft and warm when she grasped mine, her manicured nails painted a soft peach. I realized her tan must be from a bottle because, although she had to be around forty, there was hardly a line on her face, a sure sign that she rarely went outside exposed to the elements. She smiled sweetly, thanked me for coming, then waved to someone further back in the line. She was hiding her grief well.

Outside, I lost myself in the crowd of people milling around, stopping to ask a few of them for a quote or two for one last tribute to Thompson. Suddenly I found myself face to face with Chief Nelson. He smiled, said "Good morning" and walked away before I could respond. Was it an act, or was Charlie right? Had I come up a notch or two in Nelson's mind by standing up to him?

I felt someone at my elbow and found Hunter motioning that it was time to leave. In the car, he turned to me and asked, "Is it just me, or does Victoria Thompson seem a bit too. . . . Oh, I don't know. . . . Social? She reminded me of a hostess at a dinner party, all smiles and pleasantries. It seemed out of place."

"I don't know. Everyone grieves in their own way. Maybe she's just not the crying type," I said. "Although I have to admit, in my experience, sudden deaths usually bring on more of a shell-shocked appearance. Maybe she's not sorry he's gone."

As soon as it was out of my mouth, Hunter turned and looked at me with one eyebrow raised.

"I'm sorry. That was a terrible thing to say. That was unfair," I said reproachfully.

"Why?" Hunter asked as he started the car. "I bet that's what nearly everyone in the place was thinking."

We drove back to work in silence, while I wondered whether Victoria really was sorry to see Frank dead. Did she have other plans? Had they been as happy as those photos seemed to show? Was there something more to the epitome of the happily married couple captured on Kodak paper? Or was my imagination running away with me?

Chapter Ten

WHEN WE GOT BACK to the office, I wrote a short article about the funeral and the little new information I had on the case. Actually, there was no new information, but I tried to make it sound new by rephrasing it. I debated whether to tell Hunter about the visit from Brett Lindstrom's mother but decided against it. Editors sometimes have a way of taking over stories and forcing them in directions reporters aren't yet ready to go. I wanted to talk to Lindstrom, but I had no intention of writing an article from the interview right now. I just wanted to hear his story first-hand. Maybe then I could plug the gaping holes in the tales he'd told to his mother and the police.

That's exactly what I told the young man's attorney over the phone just before lunch, but William Watson wasn't convinced. Considered one of the best criminal defense attorneys in the northern half of the state, Watson knew how to work the media to his advantage and had done so frequently. Working with him often felt like making a deal with the devil. But in this case, Watson was being unusually cautious, even for him.

"Perhaps I could understand your wanting an interview if there were some question of premeditation, but this is a simple case of a hit-and-run accident. What makes this case so compelling to you?" Watson asked.

"I'm not doing this for the newspaper, Bill. I'm doing this for his mother," I said.

"Hannah? Why? I don't understand," he said, the mistrust in his voice telling me I had an uphill battle.

"His mother was my babysitter for a few years after my mother died. She came to me Monday afternoon hoping I would help her get to the bottom of this. She believes Brett is innocent and may be covering for someone else," I explained.

"Yes, she mentioned something like that to me," he said. He paused, then surprised me with a statement I found strangely candid for an attorney. "Let me tell you why I'm hesitant. Brett is a very nice young man. Quiet and polite. He answers my questions to the best of his ability. But —and this is a big but—he is not the brightest client I've ever had. I know there's more to his story than what he's telling everyone. My concern is that it would further implicate him in this mess if he talked now. I'm working on him slowly. I don't really want interference, and I'm disappointed that Hannah didn't trust me enough to let me handle this on my own."

"I understand your concerns, Bill. Hannah said Brett's IQ was a little below normal and that he's a follower. She thinks he's frightened of something, and so do the police. But maybe he would be willing to talk about it because of my past history with his mother," I said.

"Well. . ." he said, voice wavering, "all right. I haven't been able to get anything out of him. Maybe he will talk to you. I guess it won't hurt. But I don't want to see anything in print, or you'll never get another word out of me. Got it?"

"That's fine, Bill. I told you I don't want a story, not right now, anyway. When can I see him?" I tried to keep the excitement building in me from creeping into my voice, surprised at how my adrenaline kicked in at Watson's acquiescence.

"I'll call the jail and set something up for 2 p.m. That's a good time for them. Listen now, if you learn anything that could help in his defense I want to hear about it, okay?"

"Sure, if Brett's comfortable with that, and only if I get something concrete. I'm not going to start spreading misinformation," I said.

I was relieved. I hadn't been sure Watson would go along with my plan, but I'd hoped his ego wouldn't be able to resist the thought of planning a brilliant defense based on information the police hadn't uncovered.

At about ten minutes to two, I walked to the jail, located behind the courthouse a few blocks from the newspaper. The courthouse/jail complex was sixties-style squat architecture and built in an area that had become the mecca for government offices. City Hall was on the next block and the state building across the street. The old courthouse and jail a few blocks from the lake had been torn down after a century of use, leaving a vacant lot. The new jail provided inmates with a recreation yard overlooking the bay.

The sun was now baking the blacktop, sending up waves of heat as I made my way across the parking lot to the jail. The jail administrator was expecting me and led me through several security doors to the interview room, a small, pale green cubicle with thick glass separating prisoner from visitor. I was immediately aware of the smell, reminiscent of old, dirty sweatsocks and perspiration, that seemed to fill every jail I had ever visited. It doesn't matter how clean the place is. Jails always stink.

Lindstrom was led in without handcuffs, wearing the ubiquitous orange jumpsuit. He sat in the chair across from me without looking me in the eye. His sandy brown hair was getting a bit long, big curls falling in his eyes. He looked the way he had in the courtroom—slumped shoulders, staring at his hands in his lap. This was not going to be easy. I decided to go for the direct approach.

"Hi, Brett. I'm Robin Hamilton, a friend of your mother's. She asked me to come talk to you. How are you doing?" I asked.

He finally looked up at me with sad, deep blue eyes and mumbled something that sounded like "I'm all right. How's my mom?"

"She's very worried about you. She believes you didn't hit that man who died, but she's afraid you're not being entirely honest about some things." I paused. He didn't respond except to turn his eyes back toward his hands. That alone told me more than a book full of words. He was hiding something.

I softened my voice a bit and said, "You could be facing a lengthy prison term here. The police think they've got enough to convict you." It was a bit of a lie. I didn't think they could get a conviction without the truck, but Brett didn't need to know that right now. "I don't think I need to tell you that prison is a horrible place, much worse than jail. Your mother would not handle it well if you were sent away to a place where human dignity has no meaning."

The broken-hearted mother bit was all I had, and I was worried that it wasn't going to fly. Then he looked up at me again, this time with more life than I had seen in his face yet.

"You don't understand!" he whispered fiercely. "I'm trying to protect her and Sarah!"

"What do you mean?" I asked.

He shook his head in frustration and looked at the guard standing a few feet away by the door.

"Hey, you're not doing your family any favors by sitting here in the clink, Brett. Your mother is aging a year for every day you're in here. Now what the hell's going on?" I whispered, matching his tone.

He sighed, then shot a quick glance at the guard again before he spoke. He looked long and hard into my eyes, as if trying to read my soul, then leaned as close as he could to the hole in the glass between us.

"You gotta believe me, I don't know what happened to my truck. All I know is that a friend of mine called me late Thursday night last week. It was like around midnight 'cause my mom was already gone to work. He said he wanted to borrow my truck and would bring it back the next morning. I didn't really want to 'cause that truck's all I've got, you know. But he's my friend, and I don't got many of them, so I said 'Yeah, sure, you can borrow the truck.' He showed up a half-hour later, took the keys, and told me to go back to bed. Then he said not to tell no one he took the truck 'cause it could get him in trouble. I said okay and went to bed. I woke up the next morning, and my truck was still gone. I waited and waited, and finally my mom started bugging me about calling the police, but I didn't want to get him in trouble. I started to get worried, though. I walked to work that day and walked home, 'cause I didn't want to tell no one who had my truck. By the time my mom went to work Friday night, my truck was still gone, but I didn't know nothin' about that accident." He paused to look over at the guard again. She was leaning against the door talking to someone outside the room. She periodically looked our way but otherwise seemed uninterested in our conversation.

"Go on," I prodded.

"Well, the next morning—it was like six o'clock 'cause I looked at the clock—the phone rang. I answered it—half-asleep, you know. This guy I don't know tells me to keep my mouth shut about who took my truck or else my mom and sister would end up just like Thompson. Then he hung up. I didn't know what he meant, but I was scared. I went downstairs to the kitchen to get some coffee and saw the newspaper on the kitchen table and read the story about Frank Thompson being run over in the park by a blue truck. I got even more scared because I knew that it was my truck they were talking about, and it was my friend who did it, and I can't tell anyone because Mom and Sarah will get hurt. You won't tell anyone, will you?" he pleaded, his eyes filled with fear.

I believed him, and my heart ached for this simple boy caught in someone else's clever trap.

"Brett, I'm trying to help you. What you've told me is very important. But it won't help if I can't tell the police what you've said. Brett, they can protect your mom and sister, but you have to trust them," I said.

"No, no, I can't," he said, shaking his head. His soft curls flopped back and forth across his forehead.

"All right, I'll go it alone. You have to tell me more, though. Do you know who threatened you on the phone? Was it your friend?" I asked.

He shook his head. "No. He sounded real mean, though, like he would really do what he said. No, if I have to go to prison, then I have to go. I don't want my mom and Sarah to get hurt."

He went back to staring at his hands, and we sat in silence for several minutes. It was a wild story, but it rang true. Brett Lindstrom was not the kind of person who could easily get away with a lie. The desperation and determination in his eyes told me he really was ready to go to prison.

"Brett, who took your truck?" I asked.

"I can't tell you," he said.

Okay, I thought, it shouldn't be too hard to find out on my own if he didn't have many friends.

I asked if he needed anything, to which he muttered "No," and he motioned to the guard and shuffled out of the room, head still down. As I walked back to my office, questions tumbled around in my mind like clothes in a dryer. Who took the truck? Was it the same person who hit Frank Thompson? Was Thompson's death an accident or planned? Who had called Brett and threatened his family? There were at least two unknown people involved. Brett would have recognized the friend's voice. Why was it so important that Brett took the fall?

I needed time to digest those questions and develop a plan of action. I changed my mind about returning to the office.

Chapter Eleven

RETRIEVED THE JEEP from the parking lot at work, then headed home. I put Belle in the back yard, changed into running clothes, and hit the pavement. Physical activity always clears the cobwebs and focuses my thinking. I headed for the park, running in the grass along the lake just before it turned into a hard sandy beach, which had mercifully been cleared of rotting, dead fish. Several days without exercise had set me back, but once I got into a rhythm of consistent breathing and speed, I began to turn Lindstrom's revelation over in my mind.

The first step would be to find out who borrowed the truck. I figured that would be easy—a few phone calls and maybe a visit or two, and I'd find the culprit. The hard part would be finding out who made the threatening phone call. I wasn't too concerned about the call yet because there didn't seem to be a strong enough reason for anyone to harm Brett Lindstrom's mother and sister. A few years in prison for a hit-and-run versus a decade or more for extortion and assault (or worse) made it unlikely anyone would carry out such a threat. The stakes would have to be much higher before a threat like that would be backed up by action.

The next question was how to locate the mysterious friend once I had him identified. My guess was that he had left town and that the truck would probably show up abandoned on some deserted road a few hundred miles away in the next few days. Or, as Charlie had suggested, on a back forty by some hunter this fall. I was hoping for the former because it would be easier for Brett.

After about four miles of easy jogging through the park and the east side of town, I felt ready for a shower and a fresh start on the investigation.

My first stop after a quick, pre-packaged salad supper was Hannah Lindstrom's home. From the smell of cooked sausage emanating from the kitchen, it appeared Brett's mother had just finished her equivalent of breakfast when I rang the doorbell shortly after six-thirty p.m. The Lindstroms lived in an older, pale yellow, two-story frame house about two miles from me on the north side of town in a working-class neighborhood with a large number of families of Croatian and Slavic descent. The house was in need of a coat of paint but looked neat. The yard was well kept with a colorful bed of annuals running along the front of the house, broken only by the wide concrete steps leading to the porch. The front door was open, so I knocked on the old wooden screen door. I was still getting used to living back in a small town where it was relatively safe to leave doors open when you were home. Many locals never even locked their doors when they were gone.

"Hello?" I called through the wire mesh.

Hannah appeared from somewhere towards the rear of the house and beamed when she saw me through the screen. When I stepped inside, despite the temperature in the mid-eighties outside, I could feel a cool breeze dance across my skin

"It's nice and cool in here, but I don't hear an air conditioner," I said as she led me through the living room. I noted that it was furnished with a faded but clean blue floral sofa and matching loveseat and recliner.

"I leave the front and back doors open when I'm up and around," she said. "This old house has great cross ventilation."

She motioned me to sit down at a breakfast table. The kitchen was decorated country-style, with quaint blue and white checks running through the wallpaper, towels, curtains, and tablecloth.

She brought two tall glasses of lemonade and sat down across from me. She still looked weary but not as forlorn as when she had visited my office Monday. Her thick, wavy hair was long and loose now, and the shadows under her eyes had faded a bit, making her look less tense. She tucked some flyaway strands of hair behind her ears and cocked her head to the side.

"Have you talked to Brett or found out anything?" she asked.

"Yes, I have. I need some help from you now," I said and took a big gulp of lemonade.

She threw up her hands and nodded emphatically.

"Anything. This is my only son. I'll do anything I can to get him through this," she said.

On the drive over, I had considered not telling her about the threat-ening phone call but decided finally that she should know the whole story. I'd promised Brett I wouldn't tell the police what he said, but his mother needed to know there might be someone ready to harm her and her other child as well.

"Is your daughter around?" I asked.

"No, she has a part-time job at as a checker at Elmer's grocery store. She'll be working until ten tonight," she said.

"Good. What I'm going to tell you came from Brett. I spent about an hour with him this afternoon. But this has to be just between you and me. You'll understand why when I'm through." I went on to relate Brett's story about his friend and the telephone call that had frightened him into silence. She sat quietly with her elbows on the table and hands propping up her face, her eyes fixed on me.

When I finished, she sat staring in disbelief for a minute before wail-ing, "Good God, what has he gotten himself into?"

"I don't know, Hannah. Can you give me the names of all of Brett's friends, everyone he's hung around with for the last five years or so?" I asked.

"Okay," she said, then got up and left the kitchen for a minute and returned with a notepad and pen. She began rattling off names and writ-ing them down.

"Let's see. There's Alex Smith. He's in the army, stationed in Japan. He was home on leave just a few months ago, so I don't think it could be him, unless he came back home. You never know with the military," she said, furrowing her brow as though trying to remember details. "Then there's Mike Callahan. He's a student at that technical university up north. He's home for the summer doing an internship at the paper mill. He lives over on South 18th Street, over near the football field. It's a real nice house. His dad runs one of the banks. Alex, Mike and Brett have been buddies since kindergarten, and my son's been lonely since they've left town. Now he's hanging around with that new guy from the sawmill. I think his name is Greg, but I've never met him so I can't tell you what he's like. I don't even know his last name. I think that's about it. Like I told you before, Brett's shy and has a tough time making friends. I've been trying to encourage him to step outside the bubble of this family, if you know what I mean."

"Actually, I'm impressed by how much you know about his friends," I said. With her work schedule and a teenage daughter to worry about as well, I wouldn't have been surprised if she'd had little information about Brett's activities away from home. I took the list and thanked her. She walked me to the front door and smiled warmly, grabbing my arm as I turned to leave. Her touch was firm but gentle.

"Thanks for your help, Robin. I knew I could count on you," she said. She gave me a gentle hug, then pulled away from me and seemed to want to say something else.

"What's wrong?" I asked encouragingly.

"Well. . . I have to admit I'm a little worried about that phone call you mentioned. I want you to get Brett out of jail and find the person responsible for him being there. But," she stressed, "I don't want Sarah dragged into this. She's having a tough time as it is with her brother being in the news damn near every night. She's seventeen, you know. That's a tough age. She feels the whole world is pointing an accusing finger at her. The thought of someone coming after her, trying to hurt her, is more than I can bear. What should I do?"

"Look, Hannah, right now I don't know how serious that threat is, or why it was made in the first place. I don't want you to live in fear, but I don't want you to disregard it, either. I'll leave it up to you whether to tell the police. I guess I would if I were in your shoes," I said.

"But that could put us in more danger, couldn't it? I mean Brett did say we would be hurt if he talked to anyone," Hannah said.

I didn't voice my opinion that there wasn't much the police could do, anyway. They weren't about to provide round-the-clock protection without a legitimate attempt made first to carry out the threat.

⚬⟜⟊⟊⟜⟝⚬

By the time I left the Lindstrom house it was past seven-thirty. I figured I had just enough time to check on at least one person from the list of Brett's friends. I concocted a story to found out if any of them were home at the time of the crime so I didn't sound like I was accusing them of anything.

I started with the first name, Alex Smith. Hannah had written down addresses for Smith and the college boy. Alex's family lived in a neat, older, large brick home a few blocks from downtown. I pulled up in front and waved to a man mowing the front yard. He looked about forty-five with a bit of a paunch, coarse, wavy black hair, and muscular shoulders and arms gleaming deep tan under his white, tank-style t-shirt.

He shut off the lawn mower engine and said hello. I walked over, stuck out my hand, and introduced myself as a friend of Hannah Lindstrom. A look of sincere concern came over his face at the mention of her name, and his dark brows knitted together.

"Marco Smith. Nice to meet you. How's she holding up? That's really sad about her boy. Brett and my son have been best friends since grade school, you know. I just can't see him doing something like that," he said with a shake of his head.

"Hannah's doing okay. She's very concerned about Brett, though. That's why I'm here. Brett's spirits are quite low, and he could really use the support of his friends right now," I said.

"Oh, I can imagine. It's too bad Alex is back in Okinawa. He was home just a few months ago. Hey, but maybe he could call Brett at the jail. Do you think they'd let him take the call?" he asked.

"Yes, I think so. Why don't you call the jail and find out when inmates can receive phone calls? I think that would be wonderful," I said, mentally scratching Alex Smith off the list of possible suspects.

I thanked Marco and left him to his mowing.

Deciding to push my luck a bit, I headed over to the address for Mike Callahan. The Callahan name was pretty well known in town with Mike Callahan, Sr., president of the largest bank in Escanaba. The family lived in a large, two-story home with cut stone and light gray vinyl siding in one of the newer subdivisions on the far south side. The neighborhood looked like something out of Better Homes and Gardens, with professionally tended lawns and precise landscaping. The Callahan house occupied a corner lot. There were two large sugar maples in the front yard and an in-ground pool in back—a rarity in the Upper Peninsula with its two-month-long summers and six-month-long winters.

I parked in the driveway in front of a two-car garage over which the second floor of the home extended, wondering just how many people lived there. The house had room for at least ten, from the looks of it. I rang the doorbell.

The day seemed to be getting hotter as the sun set. Another heat wave was rolling into the area. I couldn't remember a U.P. summer in my life this hot and miserable. If I'd wanted to go around dripping sweat all day and feeling lethargic, I would have moved to Mississippi. As I wiped my brow for about the tenth time that day, one of the oak double doors opened about six inches to reveal a petite, neatly dressed woman with short, stylish blond hair. She was wearing a pale yellow short set that enhanced her tan, and I realized that everyone involved in this case seemed to have a tan but me. This woman looked like she had just come from a day of golf and drinks with the ladies at the country club. Her eyes were bleary and bloodshot.

"Yes? May I help you?" she asked timidly.

"Mrs. Callahan?" I asked.

"Yes."

"Good evening. I'm Robin Hamilton, a friend of Hannah Lindstrom, Brett's mother. I understand your son is a friend of Brett's, am I right?" I asked in a chirpy voice. Good God, I thought, I sound like the Welcome Wagon calling.

"Yes, that's right," she said and opened the door wide. "Please come in."

The central air conditioning felt good on my sticky skin. Mrs. Callahan led me down a long hallway that divided the house in half. We ended up in the den, a large dark room with chunky pieces of black leather upholstered furniture arranged around a wide stone fireplace. It was masculine in design yet comfortable. She motioned to a chair to the left of the fireplace and took a seat near me on the edge of the couch where she must have been sitting alone before my arrival. A half-empty glass of amber liquid sat on a coaster on the low table in front of her.

"I was so sorry to hear about Brett. Hannah must be devastated. But then Brett always did have that streak in him. You know, with his father and everything," she said, pausing to take a drink of what smelled like whiskey. "That sort of thing is genetic, you can't get away from it. It finally caught up with him, I guess. You know, my husband never really approved of our son hanging around with Brett, but they got along so well. It can be hard for a boy like Brett to make friends. I sort of encouraged Mikey to stay involved with him. I thought he could be a good influence, show Brett what a real family looks like. I mean, certainly his mother is never around, always working at the hospital."

My blood hit an instant boil. I wanted to tell her what a snob she was and how Hannah was twice the woman she was, but I reminded myself that I was dealing with a different class of people. Not better, as they assumed, just different. To the Callahans, the Lindstroms were poor white trash who couldn't manage their piddly little lives without help from "good influences." I decided to use her sanctimonious attitude to my advantage and play along.

"That's very generous of you, Mrs. Callahan, and it's sort of why I came to speak with you. You see, Brett could really use some moral support from his friends. If Mike is around —."

"Oh, no! I know what you're going to say," she interrupted, eyes popping wide in alarm. "My husband would never allow Mike to visit Brett in jail."

She said the word jail as though she were saying leper colony.

"The Thompsons are—well, were—close friends of ours. Anyway, poor Victoria is devastated at Frank's death. Oh, it's all just so sad! No, no. I'm afraid the friendship between the boys is over now. You do understand, don't you?" she asked, smiling at me as though she were a kindergarten teacher explaining to one of her pupils why one has to wear boots when it's raining.

"No, Ma'am, frankly I don't understand. Is Mike around?" I asked with a slight edge in my voice. The Welcome Wagon had lost an axle.

Mrs. Callahan straightened and put her hands on her bare knees.

"No, Miss Hamilton, he's not. He is working as an intern at the mill during the afternoon shift. He won't be home until after midnight. But why does it matter? That Lindstrom boy got himself into this mess. We won't let him drag our son down with him." Her tone now was reasonable but firm.

I could see that any further attempts at discussion would only lead to a pointless argument. I thanked her for her time and left.

As I drove home, I considered the possibility that Mike Callahan, Jr., might not be the golden child his parents thought. If he got off work at midnight, he would have had time to get Brett's truck, do whatever damage he was going to do, and get home before his parents even knew he was late. There was no way of getting to him past his parents. I'd have to go right to the source.

It wouldn't be tonight, though. I was tired and cranky and not in the mood to talk to another Callahan.

Chapter Twelve

ON THURSDAY, I BREEZED through an uneventful day at work, then went home at four-thirty and took Belle for a brisk walk through the park. It gave me a chance to think and gave Belle some much-needed exercise. Mitch and I had alwa ys made it a point to take her on a two- to three-mile walking tour of the city every day, rain or shine. Since moving back to Escanaba, I'd had a lot less time and energy, which meant Belle had put on a few extra pounds—though I still couldn't seem to gain weight if I went a whole week eating nothing but steak, pizza and Ben & Jerry's ice cream. Also, I could tell Belle was feeling a bit neglected by the way she had been constantly following me around when I was home the last few days. Too much time without human companionship seemed to make Belle react like an insecure mate—clingy.

After our walk, I took a long nap, getting up at last for a late supper of soup, crackers and an apple. Then I loaded Belle into the Jeep and headed for the paper mill at about ten-thirty. Located about four miles outside of town on a county highway, the mill was the area's largest employer, with more than twelve hundred people on the payroll. The jobs paid well but were often dull and tedious for those not on salary. It also stank, liter-ally. The mill made an honest effort to be environmentally responsible, but there were always a few days a year, especially when it was clear and cold, when a big invisible cloud smelling like rotten eggs settled over the town. "The smell of money being made" was how old-timers referred to it because it was likely that, should the mill fold, so would the town. Most days, however, the smell just clung to the immediate vicinity of the mill. That was the case as Belle and I pulled into the enormous parking lot. The mill's lights glimmered like a small city in the dark night, illuminat-ing plumes of white smoke puffing from several tall stacks.

The night air was still uncomfortably warm, the air inside the Jeep stuffy. I sniffed. Belle needed a bath. I got out and leaned against the driver's side door. Belle crawled over and stuck her head out the window. I scratched her behind one long ear and surveyed the lot filled with pickup trucks, most of them American-made and not more than a few years old.

I heard a distant click and saw the door open to the gatehouse through which employees had to pass. A security guard stepped out and began to walk towards me. He approached casually, his eyes alert as he took in my size and demeanor.

He was a clean-cut blond in his early twenties. I guessed this was either his summer job as he worked on a degree in law enforcement or his stepping-stone to a police department. The mill often employed the children of long-time employees in summer positions, and many an Escanaba Public Safety officer had started out working security there.

"Good evening, Ma'am," he said with a smile when he got within about fifteen feet of me. He had a large flashlight in his left hand and shined it at me for a few seconds, then into the windows of the Jeep. Belle still had her head poked out the window. I could hear her tail thump against the seat as she got excited about the possibility of a new person to play with her. I patted her head and said to the guard, "Hi there, how's it going?"

"Just fine. How are you?" he said, still smiling. The inscription on his silver nameplate said L. Grenville.

"Great. Lovely evening, isn't it?" I said, returning his smile with what I hoped was a charming one of my own.

"Not really. It's too hot, and the heat makes the smell of this place even worse. It's also an odd time for an attractive lady like yourself to be here," he said. I liked the flattery. This kid had a future as a hostage negotiator.

"Well, the bars just aren't my scene, and I hear there are plenty of bachelors out here," I said.

L. Grenville laughed. He had nice teeth and a nice laugh, broad shoulders and sparkling bluish-green eyes.

"Are you looking for anyone in particular?" he asked, cocking one finely arched eyebrow.

"As a matter of fact, there is one young man who has captured my imagination. Do you happen to know an engineering intern by the name of Mike Callahan?" I asked.

"Yeah, I know him. He's a little young for you, though," he said, keeping the flashlight pointed over my right shoulder. He lost a few points with that crack, but I let it pass.

"Would you be so kind as to point him out when he leaves? I understand he's working tonight."

"May I ask why?"

"I'd like to speak with him about a mutual friend," I said.

"And who might that be?" he asked, still smiling but eyeing me intently.

"Is that important?" I asked.

"You shouldn't answer a question with a question. It makes me think you have something to hide," he said and shifted the flashlight as he walked closer to me and then to the front and back of the Jeep.

"Did you learn that in the police academy?" I asked.

"Yeah, Lesson Number Five, 'How to Determine When You're Being Lied To,'" he said with a grin and stopped near the driver's side door and scratched Belle behind an ear. She groaned in ecstasy. "Are you going to answer my question, Miss. . .?"

"Hamilton, Robin Hamilton," I said and offered my hand. He took it in a firm but relaxed handshake.

"Lee Grenville. Listen, Miss Hamilton, it's my job to make sure no one from this mill walks off with anything that doesn't belong to them. It's also my job to see that they leave the parking lot safely. Now, you look innocent enough. I'm sure Lizzy Borden did, too, before she gave her mother forty whacks with an ax. So, what's the deal?" he asked, cocking his eyebrow again.

I liked this guy. He had a lot of confidence and smarts for a college-age kid. I decided to quit playing coy and be straight with him.

"I'd like to ask Callahan a few questions about one of his high school buddies who's in a lot of trouble right now," I said.

Grenville's eyes narrowed, then flew open with recognition.

"You're a reporter aren't you? You work for the Daily Press. I've seen your name in the paper," he said and leaned against the Jeep. Belle licked the side of his face, and he stepped back, but chuckled good-naturedly and swiped the slobber away.

"Yes, I'm a reporter. Will you point Callahan out to me?" I asked again.

The midnight shift was beginning to trickle into the parking lot, which meant Grenville would have to get back to the gatehouse soon.

"I guess it would be all right. This is about Brett Lindstrom, isn't it? My sister went to high school with him. That's awful—what happened, I mean. Frank Thompson was my Little League coach. He was a good guy," he said.

"I'm sorry."

"Yeah, well, whatever," he said, shifting his feet. Grenville cleared his throat. "Callahan should be out in a few minutes. Why don't you come to the gatehouse and wait?"

I rolled the window up a bit so Belle couldn't jump out of the Jeep, then followed Grenville.

The gatehouse was a small structure with a control panel for various automatic doors and a bank of black and white TV screens showing views of the hallway leading to the exit and a few other locations I couldn't identify. I looked at my watch—five minutes to midnight. By now the parking lot was full of people carrying lunchboxes and thermoses, calling hellos to Grenville as they trudged by, ready to log in another eight hours.

Within minutes, the screens showed workers from within the mill making their way through the hallways and towards the gatehouse and exit. They looked quite a bit happier than the ones heading in. Suddenly Grenville gave me a light tap on the arm. He pointed to a screen showing the far end of one gray passageway. A young man with short wavy dark hair and wearing a white golf shirt, light-colored cotton pants and loafers was walking by himself in the direction of the gatehouse.

"That's him, Mike Callahan. What a wimp. His old man runs the bank," Grenville said with a snort. He seemed unimpressed by Mr. and Mrs. Callahan's "good influence" on the world.

I thanked him and left the gatehouse. When Callahan came out, I stepped in alongside him and introduced myself. He looked surprised, then stopped walking and turned a curious gaze on me.

"What's up?" he asked, his dark eyes squinting a bit as though he were nearsighted.

"I wanted to ask you a question or two about one of your friends, Brett Lindstrom. Have you seen him lately?"

He hesitated longer than necessary before answering.

"Wh-why do you want to know?" he stuttered.

"Look, there's nothing wrong. I was just asking. You may have heard Brett's in a tough spot right now and could use a little moral support from his friends. I understand from his mother you guys were buddies through high school," I said.

The scared look on his face raised a little alarm in the back of my mind. Something was saying all was not well with this kid.

He bit his lower lip, then said, "Listen, I don't know what you're all about, but you've got to understand something. I really care about Brett, he's like a brother, you know. But my parents think he's a low-life because he's a little slow and because his dad was in and out of trouble a lot. Brett's not like that, but my mom and dad told me to stay away from him. I still see him once in a while, but only where I know it won't get back to my parents. They're putting me through college, you see, and—well, you know how it is," he said, hanging his head.

I almost felt sorry for the kid. It was going to take a lot of years and a thousand miles before he got out of the shadow of Mr. and Mrs. Perfect.

"I'm not going to tell your parents you've been hanging around Brett. I just want to know the last time you saw him?" I was getting impatient.

"It was last week, Tuesday, maybe. I saw him at the Dairy Flo in Gladstone. He was there with this other guy he met at work, a Greg, um, Connor. We only talked for a few minutes," he said, then started digging a loafer-clad toe into the blacktop and scanning the parking lot as if he expected Mommy or Daddy to jump out from behind a pickup. "Look, I gotta get going."

"Okay, just one more question. What else do you know about this Greg Connor?" Callahan started backing away from me, but I stuck to him.

"I don't know. Connor's a tough guy, not the kind of person I'd want as a friend, you know. Is there anything else?" Callahan asked. He looked ready to make a run for it.

"No." I'd tortured him enough. "Thanks for your help, Mike, and good luck with your parents." He gave me a confused look and darted away. I watched him get into a late-model Buick LeSabre and drive slowly out of the parking lot.

I waved good-bye to Grenville, who was getting ready to change shifts himself.

"Miss Hamilton?" he called after me. I stopped and turned towards the gatehouse. He jogged towards me with a small black and white cooler in one hand and a jacket in the other. When he caught up to me, he said, "I'll walk you to your car."

We walked in silence. The parking lot was again empty of people by the time we reached the Jeep.

"What's up?" I asked. "You're not going to ask to do a strip search, are you?"

He laughed. "No, Miss Hamilton—."

"Ugh! Call me Robin, please. I can't be that much older than you," I said and unlocked the driver's side door.

"Okay, Robin. I heard you talking with Callahan about Greg Connor. I know him. Went to high school with him, actually. He was two years younger than me, which would make him about 22. That guy was bad news in school. If Lindstrom's hanging around with him now, it doesn't surprise me he's found himself in hot water. That guy's got a temper. Watch yourself," Grenville said.

"Thanks, I appreciate the warning," I said. So he was 24. I filed away his name and information for future use. "What are you doing here at the mill? You're too sharp for this place."

"I'm waiting for something to open at Public Safety," he said, flashing that dazzling smile again. I could have spent the whole night gazing at him. Unfortunately, I also had to go to work the next morning, and it was already going on midnight.

I wished him luck and got in the Jeep. Belle was asleep on the driver's seat. I gave her a nudge and, with a low grumble, she moved to the other side. I sat and thought about Mike Callahan and Greg Connor for a minute. I could see how Brett and Mike had become friends despite their different backgrounds. Both were misfits in their own way—one a prisoner of Mother Nature's cruel, genetically-dealt hand, the other a hostage to his parents. But where did Greg Connor fit into the picture?

I drove home satisfied with the results of the night's work. I could eliminate Alex Smith and Mike Callahan from the list of suspects. One was out of the country, and the other was unable to blow his nose without parental permission. Next on the list was the mysterious Greg Connor.

Chapter Thirteen

WHEN THE ALARM WENT off at five-thirty the next morning, I reset it for six-fifteen and went back to sleep. I still felt bone-tired when I finally slid out of bed and slunk to the shower. I let icy cold water splash on my body for about thirty seconds before I was fully conscious. Thank God it was Friday and I would be able to sleep in for the next two days.

It was a week since Frank Thompson had been run down less than a few hundred yards from where I called home. That was a disquieting thought. Although a suspect (possibly innocent) was in jail, I knew the police were frustrated by the lack of physical evidence that would put Brett Lindstrom behind the wheel of the infamous blue pickup at the scene of the crime. A strong feeling was building in my gut that said this was much more than a simple case of reckless driving. All I had were the suspicions of an anxious mother and a bizarre tale from Brett of threats and shadowy friendship. My hope was that Greg Connor would be able to shed some light on the case. But first I had to earn my lunch money.

Bob Hunter was waiting for me as soon as I walked into the newsroom. Leaning against the wall in the entryway, wearing his usual uniform of rumpled shirt, pants and tie, his shaggy gray hair in its usual disarray, he smiled, the devilish twinkle in his eye saying he was as pleased as a terrier with a mouse in its jaws.

"Good morning, Robin," he drawled. "I hear you're rattling some cages."

"Mornin', Bob. What do you mean?" I asked, a bit startled. "Whose cage am I rattling?" I stepped past him and headed towards my desk with Hunter on my heels.

"Mike Callahan called Burns last night and raised holy hell about you and that Lindstrom kid," he said, still smiling. He sat down in the same chair Hannah had occupied at the beginning of the week and looked at me with obvious pride. Nothing satisfied him more than making the high and mighty squirm. He especially loved it when those same people called upon the publisher, Sam Burns, to rein in one of his reporters. People didn't realize that while Burns was a successful businessman, he had a nose for news that made Bob Woodward look tame. It was a rare quality among publishers and one reason I had chosen to return to the Press.

"What's Callahan's beef?" I asked as I stuffed my purse in a drawer and plopped down in front of my computer. I wondered how Callahan could have known about my conversation with his son, unless he had waited up for the poor kid to come home from work.

"He told Burns you're trying to drum up support for Lindstrom, that you wanted his family to lend its 'good name' to help a, quote, 'murderer,'" Hunter said, holding up the middle and index finger of each hand when he said 'good name' and 'murderer.'

"Murderer? That's the first time I've heard this case referred to as a murder," I protested, rubbing my chin thoughtfully. Something wasn't right about Callahan's reactions to my questions. "That's pretty harsh since all I did was ask his wife if her son, supposedly one of Brett's best friends, could go visit the poor schmuck in jail. What's the big deal?"

"Are you sure that's all you did?" Hunter asked with a raised eyebrow. "It sounds to me like you pumped his kid for information last night. How come? Are you onto something?"

So Callahan did know about my parking lot meeting with his progeny. He had an even tighter hold on the boy than I thought. Maybe I shouldn't have scratched Mike Junior from the list of possible suspects so quickly. After all, what was the senior Callahan so worried about?

I still didn't want to reveal a lot of information until I had a better handle on what was going on behind the scenes, though. If the threatening phone call that had frightened Brett so much was for real, I didn't want word getting out that Brett was talking. So I hesitated before I answered Hunter.

"Yeah, Bob, I may be onto something. I don't know what, though, and I don't want to talk about it just yet. You'll have to trust me on this one." I looked him straight in the eye and waited.

He cocked his fuzzy head to one side and grinned slyly.

"Okay, it's a deal. Just don't hold out too long, and don't get yourself in trouble. Good luck!" He got up, gave me a pat on the back and strolled into his office.

"Thanks," I called after him. After making a mental note to ask Burns what exactly Callahan had said, I made the usual morning round of phone calls to police agencies in the paper's coverage area. All was quiet, fortunately. At ten o'clock, I headed off to interview a man who was retiring as fire chief of a local volunteer department after 40 years. A happy story for a change.

Following a pleasant couple hours spent collecting the reminiscences of the fire chief, I took five minutes to grab lunch at a fast food drive-thru and brought it back to my desk. As I absent-mindedly inhaled lunch, I called Mrs. Easton, asking her to let Belle out in the back yard, and returned a few other calls. Then it was time for a drive out to the Stewart Lumber Company.

The sawmill where Brett worked was nestled among a large stand of towering white pines and occupied about five acres of land a few miles from Escanaba along the federal highway heading west out of town. I parked in the small paved lot in front of a large two-story building with beige corrugated metal siding and huge double doors on the side. The doors were opened to reveal some sort of storage area for heavy equipment, and a sign on the front of the building said "OFFICE." I entered and found myself in a small reception area with a pretty young blonde girl seated behind a cheap tan metal desk. The walls were decorated with outdoor art, common in this part of the state, including one oil painting of a log cabin at the base of a mountain and another of a larger cabin near the bank of a calm river in twilight with a campfire burning. A few posters touted the advantages of different types of lumber.

"Hi! May I help you?" the blonde asked in a high-pitched voice. She flashed a thousand-watt smile and some serious cleavage as she leaned forward on her elbows.

I returned the smile, minus the cleavage, and said, "Yes, I'm looking for Greg Connor. I understand he works here. I just need a minute of his time."

The smile disappeared from the receptionist's face, although the friendly tone remained. "Let me see if I can find the manager. Hang on just a minute." She bounced up from behind the desk and out of the room, disappearing into a hallway veering to the left. I followed her to the door and looked down the hallway. One of her long, tan legs was sticking out into the hall as she leaned in to talk to some unseen person in another office. A door on the right led to the garage, I surmised from the sounds of activity behind it, and the hall turned left at the end where a flight of stairs ascended. The blonde returned with her smile back in place.

"Mr. Kirksen can help you. He's in the garage. I'll take you to him," she said brightly, her crystalline blue eyes sparkling.

"Great," I said enthusiastically, mimicking her perkiness. What was she so happy about, anyway?

Ms. Perky led me through the door to the garage, where we went down a few steps to a cement floor filling a space larger than it appeared from the outside. It was nearly empty now, with most of the equipment, mainly forklifts from the looks of the lumberyard, in use. It was amazingly clean considering its purpose. There were few grease or oil stains marring the floor. An elaborate ventilation system located near the roof drew out the polluted air from the machines and brought fresh air inside. Massive open double doors let in the bright noonday sun. I put my sunglasses back on and followed the receptionist over to a group of men who were discussing some type of schedule.

"Jack?"

A tall, attractive man turned to us. He looked about thirty-five, with light brown hair and hazel eyes with bright gold flecks that sparkled in his lean, tan face. Ms. Perky introduced him to me as Jack Kirksen and flitted away like a butterfly.

"I didn't get your name, Ma'am," Kirksen said, stepping away from the other workers. He talked in the clipped, crisp diction of a downstater. Maybe Lansing or Ann Arbor, I guessed. He smiled, revealing perfect teeth, and I nearly swooned. This guy could have been looking down from a billboard along the highway, touting some rugged-sounding cigarette brand.

I introduced myself and extended my hand. He took hold of it and gave it a quick shake. I was sorry when he let go. Then something about the way he smiled down at me reminded me of Mitch. The flood of another memory washed over me, and my face was suddenly hot, tears prickling. I swallowed hard and blinked several times behind my sunglasses to regain control.

"I'm trying to find a man named Greg Connor. Someone told me he works here," I said, somewhat abruptly.

Kirksen raised his thick but neat eyebrows and said, "Well, he did work here, but not any more. May I ask why you're looking for him?"

"A friend of his is in trouble. I was wondering if he could help," I said.

Kirksen threw back his head and let out a loud guffaw.

"Greg Connor help anybody? Lady, you obviously don't know him," he said, shaking his head. "That guy could work hard, but he was in it for himself only. I'll tell you something, I'm not sorry he's gone. Although it would have been nice if he had given a little warning, considering this is our busiest season. I'm already running three people short."

"So he just quit without notice?"

"Yeah, last week. In fact, it was Friday. He was scheduled to work Friday afternoon, but he never showed up, and he hasn't been back since," Kirksen said.

Bells went off in my head like a slot machine hitting the jackpot. "Do you know where he went or what happened?" I asked, trying to sound calm. Every nerve ending in my body was buzzing like a neon sign. This had to be the guy who "borrowed" Brett's truck.

Kirksen looked at me for a few seconds before answering, then motioned me to follow him outside the garage.

"I don't know where Greg is. I'm mighty curious to know that myself. It seems kind of funny that as soon as he disappears, one of my best employees lands in jail," he said once we were out of earshot of anyone else.

"That's why I'm here. What do you know about Greg?" I asked.

"He's worked here since he got out of high school about four or five years ago. He could work hard when he wanted to, but I thought he had an attitude. At one point last year, I wanted to fire him. He was just getting too damn cocky. But Stewart, the owner, he told me to give him a chance to grow up, said Greg was 'testing his limits.' Bull!" Kirksen growled and shook his head.

"Do you know why he quit?" I asked.

"Nope, don't have a clue. What makes it even more strange is that Stewart really took a liking to the kid, saw some kind of spark and took him under his wing, tried to show him the ropes of running the business. Then the kid goes and takes off without a thank-you, good-bye—nothing," he said.

"Do you know where he lives?" I asked, squinting into the afternoon sun despite my despite my dark lenses. My pale skin was starting to burn.

Kirksen hesitated. "I'm not supposed to give out that sort of information... Oh, what the hell! He lived in a duplex over on North Thirteenth Street, just off Ludington. I helped him move in a couple years ago, before he started getting on my nerves. I don't remember the address. It's an old white house with a broken-down porch. He lives upstairs."

"Thanks a lot, you've been a big help," I said, shaking his hand again. I started to walk away, then turned back.

"By the way, someone told me Connor had a wild streak. Did you ever see that side of him?" I asked.

"Oh, yeah! That guy doesn't like to be challenged on anything. He even tried to take a swing at me one day. I was a little too quick for him, though," he said with a chuckle, adding, "Like I said, I don't miss him."

"What's your impression of Brett Lindstrom?" I asked.

"Brett's a real nice kid. Not too bright and way too timid, but he did more than his fair share of work around here and never gave any lip. He kind of latched onto Connor as soon as he came here. I guess he needed a friend—oh, I see, that's the friend you were talking about, huh?" Kirksen asked, then snorted. "I'm afraid Greg's not going to be much help to Brett."

"Okay, thanks again. If you hear from Greg, would you let me know?" I handed him my business card.

He looked at it with concern.

"You're not going to quote anything I said, are you?" he asked.

"No, don't worry. This is for information purposes only. I would have told you if this was for an article," I assured him.

He looked relieved. As I began to walk away again he called after me again.

"Hey, I just remembered something. A couple of days before he left, I overheard Greg bragging about, and I quote, 'getting out of this hellhole town.' I didn't think anything of it at the time. Kids always seem to say stuff like that," he added, tapping my card on his left thumbnail.

"Interesting, thanks," I said and walked back to the Jeep. A forklift passed me, and the driver let out a wolf whistle, to which I answered with a smile and wave. As I was unlocking the door, a late model navy blue Lincoln Navigator pulled up next to me. Grant Stewart got out from behind the wheel and said, "Good afternoon." I nodded a greeting and watched him stroll into the office. A widower, it was rumored he was one of the richest, most eligible middle-aged bachelors in the northern part of the state. As I pulled onto the highway, I wondered what it would be like to be rich. Must be nice, I thought, and headed back to work.

Chapter Fourteen

{I}SPENT THE AFTERNOON trying to concentrate on copy editing the work of the other four reporters and writing my fire chief
feature, but my mind kept drifting over what the sawmill manager had
said about Connor. I knew he was the man I was looking for, and I could
barely wait to leave the Daily Press at four and check out his apartment.
I didn't expect him to be there—by now he would be long gone, possibly
across the country or maybe even out of it—but he might have left a
clue as to where he was going, something that could help get Brett out
of jail.

Before I left work, I tapped on the publisher's open door. Sam Burns'
office was simple, filled with four-drawer file cabinets, a few awards and
heaps of newspapers, spreadsheets and files. Like the rest of the building, it had that "old library" smell, evoking memories of pleasant hours
whiled away engrossed in a great story. Sam looked up from a pile of
spreadsheets on his mammoth, wrap-around desk and peered over the
top of his gold-rimmed spectacles.

"Hey, Sam, am I interrupting something?" I asked.

"Well, Robin, come in, come in. Have a seat. It's time for the semi-
annual reports to the big bosses," he said, waving his arms over the array
of papers. "I could use a break. Actually, I've been waiting for the opportunity to tell you how glad I am that you decided to return to small town
journalism. I'm sure you don't need me to tell you your work is excellent,
but I'll do it anyway."

He set the spreadsheets aside, took off his glasses and smiled at me.

"Thanks for the compliment. I appreciate it. Hunter told me this
morning that Mike Callahan had some unpleasant things to say about
my investigation of Frank Thompson's death. I was curious about what

exactly he told you," I said, settling into a burgundy tweed chair across from him and crossing my legs.

Burns laced his fingers together and chuckled.

"Yes, he called me early this morning at home, just after six, I think. He rattled on about one of my reporters harassing his son and dragging him into a murder investigation. He was very upset that you ambushed his son after work last night, after his wife told you not to talk to Mikey Junior," he said.

"Hmm," I said. "What did you say?"

"He didn't use your name, but I knew right away it was you. That's your style—aggressive—something we've needed here for a long time." Burns punched his fist in the air for emphasis. "I told him when my reporters are assigned to a story this big they're expected to dig in every nook and cranny for information. I said I was sorry he felt his son was harassed but I would not rein in a reporter unless I felt he or she was violating the law. Then he spouted something about a lawsuit and so on and so forth. Don't worry about it.

"But may I ask what your interest is in Mikey Callahan? The kid's a Casper Milquetoast if I ever saw one. He worked as a caddy at the country club last summer. He always looked to me like one unkind word would send him to the showers crying," Burns said with a scowl.

"My interest in Junior is really very minor at this point. He was once a close friend of Brett Lindstrom, the young man charged with Thompson's death. Lindstrom told me an interesting story that I'm investigating, and, no, I don't want to share the details," I said.

Burns chuckled again and shook his head.

"A regular Diane Sawyer, you are," he said.

"Why is Callahan Senior so jumpy about this, anyway? All I did was ask his kid a few questions about Brett."

"You must understand that Callahan and Thompson were best friends since—well, childhood, I guess. I know they were very close. My guess is, he's so angry about his friend's death that he resents the idea his son was friends with the person possibly responsible," Burns explained.

"I can see that. But why is he referring to this as a murder? Even the police aren't investigating this case as a homicide. They think it's an accident. Frankly, there is not one iota of evidence to indicate otherwise, right now," I said.

His eyes widened. "You know, you're right. I didn't think of it that way. Raises some interesting questions, doesn't it?"

"It makes me wonder if I was 'ambushing' the wrong Callahan," I said, then thanked Burns for his time and left.

It was a quarter after four, several hours since I had checked on Belle. I made a quick stop at the apartment to take her for a short walk. The heat seemed to have abated a bit, however, and Belle stretched the walk from around the block to around the park, more than a mile. She panted happily, stopping to sniff a fast food wrapper and other litter along the way. The park was again full of teens and twenty-somethings playing volleyball, tennis and basketball and hanging around laughing and listening to loud music. It made me think of the contrast with Brett Lindstrom's situation, stuck on a thin, smelly cot with not much to do all day but think and watch television. With that in mind, we returned to the apartment, Belle ready for a nap and fresh water and me all set to do more digging. I set off in search of the elusive Greg Connor.

The house Jack Kirksen had described was in a rough but clannish part of town, a ten-block stretch extending a few blocks north and south of Ludington Street, a neighborhood consisting of mostly older duplexes, apartments over storefronts and small homes. Escanaba has a Northtown and Southtown, each distinct in ethnicity and character, but this area smack in the middle is a no man's land, occupied primarily by the very elderly, low-wage workers or people on government assistance, some with criminal histories, mostly minor drug or theft offenses.

Connor's place was the second from the last house on the west end of the block. The white paint was peeling, and the cement front steps were cracked and crumbling in places. Dirty-faced children raced by on bikes and scooters. An elderly man wearing dingy, blue-gray overalls emerged from the front door as I walked carefully up the dilapidated steps to the porch. He stopped when he saw me and eyed me with suspicion.

"What do you want? You don't live here," he growled.

"No, Sir, I don't. Are you the owner of this house?" I asked.

"Yeah, what of it? You ain't with the city, are you? This place was inspected two months ago," he stated, jutting out his lower jaw with its two remaining front teeth showing. In addition to several hours with a good dentist, he needed a shave and a bath.

"No, I'm not with the city. My name is Robin Hamilton. I'm looking for Greg Connor. I understand he lives upstairs," I said.

"He ain't here no more. Son-of-a-bitch left a huge mess and stiffed me a month's rent, even left his piece-of-shit car here," he said and gestured to an early eighties model red Chevy Camaro with rust around the wheel wells.

"Did he say where he was going?" I asked.

The man removed his stained cap and scratched his balding head.

"Nah, he just took some clothes and stuff and left a note on the door saying he wasn't comin' back and to sell everything he left. Hah! There ain't nothin' in there worth more than two bucks at a rummage sale," he grumbled. Then he took a sudden step forward. "Hey, you one of his slimeball friends? I want my money!"

"No, I'm from the newspaper. I wanted to talk to Mr. Connor about an article I'm working on. When did he leave?" I backed up a step, not so much out of fear as to get clear of his rotten stench. A strong wave of body odor mixed with the smell of cheap liquor wafted between us.

"I don't know, Friday or Saturday of last week, I guess. What the hell does the newspaper want with him?" he asked. Suddenly perking up a bit, he didn't wait for an answer. "I've got a story for you. This whole city is corrupt. They're trying to put the small businessman out of business!"

To humor him, I played along and wrote a few words in my notebook.

"Why do you say that, Sir? By the way, what's your name?"

"Harold Adaminski. I own five houses in this town, take good care of each and every one," he said, drawing up to his full height of just over five feet. "But the city don't see it that way. No, they come in here, make up some damn complaint about some wire frayin' and make me pay a bunch of money to fund their coffers. They want to put me out of business, and I've been here all my life. An honest businessman, and they're trying to get rid of me!"

"Uh-huh. Well, Mr. Adaminski, I'll see what I can find out. Can I call you and use you as a source?" I asked.

"Oh no, no, no! That'll make 'em come down on me even worse! No, you'll have to find someone else. I gotta go. Got lots of work to do," he said and went quickly back into the house, slamming the door behind him.

I closed my notebook, got in the Jeep and drove home, dodging a little girl on a beat-up, sixteen-inch bike and two other children on in-line skates along the way.

⁓✠⁓

Mrs. Easton was working in her postage stamp vegetable garden in the back yard when I pulled up to the garage door and pressed the automatic opener. She spotted me from under her standard floppy straw hat and smiled and waved as I drove inside the garage.

I joined her and eyed the growing pile of weeds at the edge of the dirt patch.

"Isn't that something?" she said when she saw me staring at the pile. "The hot weather and that one night of rain made the weeds pop up all over."

"Everything looks good, though," I said. I know nothing about gardening. If it's green and not wilted, it looks good to me.

"Well, we'll have a bumper crop of tomatoes this year, but those little cottontail rabbits have done a number on the carrots," she said. She stood and brushed the dirt off the knees of her jeans. "Let's go in and have some dinner. I made a chicken Caesar salad from a new recipe I found in one of my gardening magazines," she said, picking up the weeds and dumping them on the compost heap next to the garden.

We went into her kitchen and washed our hands before sitting down to an appetizing salad and tall glasses of iced tea. After dinner, we sat in the swing on the wide front porch with Belle lying near my feet. It was a classic American summer evening. The park was still full of people, and cars and pickups zipped by on Lakeshore Drive, stereos blaring. A couple of large sailboats could be seen offshore, catching a brisk westerly breeze. After about half an hour of companionable silence, each of us lost in her own thoughts, Mrs. Easton spoke.

"You know something, Robin? I've been thinking about. . . well, that accident last week," she began timidly, pausing as her eyes drifted to the point in the park where it had happened. She sighed.

"I saw the picture in the newspaper of the young man the police arrested, the one they say was driving the truck. In fact, I've stared at it so many times this week I swear my eyes will cross," she said, chuckling sadly. She turned to meet my gaze. "I don't think that's the man I saw behind the wheel."

"You need to tell the police that, Mrs. Easton," I said, feeling a gleam of hope for Brett Lindstrom. "If they have the wrong guy, they need to know as soon as possible so they can find the right one."

"Yes, I know you're right. But I feel like such an old fool. I'm just not sure about it. The one in the paper doesn't look right, but I can't really explain it." She shook her fluffy gray curls. "Who do I talk to at the police station?"

"Ask for Detective Charlie Baker. He'll help you," I said.

"Okay, I remember him. He came over later the same day as the accident. A nice man, handsome too," she stated with a slight smile. I had to laugh at her expression.

"Well, I'm too old to attract them, but I can still look," she purred.

We spent the rest of the evening watching the cars go by and daylight dim as the sun set behind the house. It was a pleasant way to spend a summer evening, chatting about the past, present and future as we drank a pitcher of tea. I went to bed with a cool breeze blowing across me and fell asleep almost immediately, feeling a satisfaction that comes after good food and good company.

Chapter Fifteen

⁓ⵍⵍ⁓

THE NEXT DAY WAS Saturday, the Fourth of July. In my push to find Greg Connor, I had forgotten about the holiday, but my father called bright and early at seven to remind me and to urge me, since it was my first Fourth of July back home, to go with him to the festivities in Gladstone. I agreed reluctantly. Never big on holidays and still feeling tired, I could have happily spent the day loafing.

Trying to get in the spirit, I dressed in a pair of red denim shorts and a white and blue striped tank top. It was only nine o'clock and already 75 degrees, with not a hint of a cloud in the sky. I packed a bottle of sunblock, two one-liter bottles of ice water and some dog food into a tote bag. When I went to grab a pair of sneakers from my room, I spied a new Stephen King paperback sitting on the nightstand next to my bed and threw that in, too.

My dad had a three-by-five foot flag on a pole bolted to the left of his front door, not only for the holiday but just about every day spring through fall. I left Belle in the Jeep with the windows rolled down and walked to the door, knocking twice before opening the screen door and poking my head inside.

"Hello, it's me. Where are you?" I called.

"In the kitchen," came the reply from a distance.

I entered and shut the front door behind me, locking it. Chicago had taught me a few things. I found Dad in the kitchen making turkey and Swiss cheese sandwiches on wheat with Dijon mustard and lettuce. My favorite—he'd remembered. A small red and white cooler sat on the counter.

"What's this, a picnic lunch?" I asked, grabbing a slice of cheese and stuffing it in my mouth.

"Yup. I thought we'd go to the cemetery for the service, then to the parade. Is that all right with you?" he asked. He carefully secured the four sandwiches in zipped plastic baggies and placed them in the cooler a long with two oranges.

"Sounds great," I said, grabbing a slice of turkey.

"Didn't you eat breakfast?" he asked with a grimace as he watched my unorthodox meal.

"Nope," I said and picked up the cooler and a bunch of green grapes from the counter. Dad took a bag of pretzels from the cupboard and a large thermos of what I guessed to be iced tea from the refrigerator, and we headed for the Jeep. We loaded everything into the back except for the grapes, which I kept with me to munch on while driving.

Belle was secured with her seatbelt in the back seat, not only for her safety but to safeguard the picnic as well. She didn't particularly like the seatbelt and tried to gnaw at the strap for a few seconds until she caught a whiff of lunch. When she realized what was nearby, she pointed her big nose in the air, took a few hearty sniffs and gave a little whine.

"Quiet down," I said and reached back and patted her on the head. "There's food for you, too, later on,"

Once everyone was situated, I backed out of the driveway and drove north towards Lakeview Cemetery.

"I read in the paper that this year's parade is supposed to be the biggest ever. Fireworks, too," Dad said, glowing like a kid on his way to his first professional baseball game.

Like me, he was dressed for the day, wearing blue walking shorts, his white polo shirt with the Vietnam Veterans of American logo embroidered on the left front, and a white cap with the same design. The white showed off his deep tan and bright green eyes, eye color one of the few traits I had inherited from him. No doubt he'd be approached by a few of his lady friends later in the day.

It took about five minutes to get to Lakeview Cemetery, which was actually more than a mile from the lake. When the town was founded the town in the early 1860s, back before it was built up, visitors to the cemetery must have had a distant view of the bay. Today narrow roads winding through the six-acre site were jammed with vehicles when we arrived shortly before ten. We left Belle in the Jeep, parked under a big shade tree with the windows open. She stuck her head out the passenger side and watched us walk over to a group of Dad's friends.

"Hey, Hank, nice to see you again!" a gray-bearded man with a pot-belly called to him. "I see you've got your beautiful daughter with you. Looks just like her mother."

"Thank God for that," another man said, to which many, including my dad, laughed.

"She got her mother's brains, too," he said as he smiled proudly and put an arm around me.

I felt like I was five years old.

I was happy when the service began, drawn into the emotion of the speeches. I watched a few men wipe tears away as a trumpeter from the Escanaba High School band played taps at the end of a long line of uniformed Legionnaires holding American flags billowing lazily in the breeze. The soloist, a lovely teenager with shoulder-length dark hair and dressed in a long cream-colored summer frock, played each note beautifully. Then I spied the Callahan family standing off to her right, Mom and Dad looking on with pride.

Though I tried to concentrate on the speeches, my mind now drifted to Callahan's statement about murder. I watched Mike Callahan, Sr., intently from behind my dark sunglasses. He was a tall, good-looking man. Both of his older children had his dark hair and eyes. Two smaller children, about middle-school age and standing a few feet behind Mrs. Callahan looking bored, shared her blond coloring.

As soon as the service was completed, I whispered to my dad that I had to speak with someone and to wait for me by the Jeep. He looked at me with curiosity but nodded his head. I darted over to the Callahans, waited until they had congratulated the girl they called Lindsey on her performance, then caught Mike Senior's eye and motioned to him. I could tell he didn't recognize me, but he walked over to where I was standing. Only a mammoth headstone was close enough to overhear our conversation.

"Yes?" he inquired.

"Mr. Callahan, I'm Robin Hamilton, from the Daily Press," I said by way of introduction.

He smiled wryly and shook the hand I held out to him.

"Burns must have spoken to you. I understand you have a job to do, Miss Hamilton, but you must understand I'm simply trying to protect my family," he said. His wife called to him. He turned to her and motioned that he would only be a minute.

"Yes, I do understand, and I have no problem with you speaking to the publisher. That's your prerogative. What I'm curious about is why you referred to Mr. Thompson's death as murder. That's not how the police view it. At least, not yet," I added.

He cleared his throat, rocked back on his heels and said bluntly, "I'm not particularly fond of the media in general, but you have a point. The police aren't viewing Frank's death as a murder. I think they should be."

"Why?" I asked.

"Frank and I were very close friends. The last few months he was not himself at all. There were serious problems at the office. I know some of it but not everything. I can't be specific because I don't have anything concrete. He stopped confiding in me the last month or so, which was odd in itself. All I know is that something was terribly wrong. And he was afraid." Callahan spoke in a low voice, his head bent towards me.

"Of what? What was he afraid of, Mr. Callahan?" I prodded.

"I don't know, but he was watching his back. I mean literally watching his back. We would go out to lunch at least once a week. The last few times he spent most of the meal looking over his shoulder and paying more attention to who else was in the restaurant than to what little conversation we could carry on. That wasn't like him at all. He was normally a very open, very personable individual," he said.

"I think you should tell the police that, Mr. Callahan," I said. "This bit of news could turn the investigation in a new direction and expose a motive behind the 'accident.'"

"I don't want to get involved," he said, gritting his teeth. "If Frank was murdered, I don't want to endanger my family by blathering to the police about something I can't even confirm. No, I'm sorry, Miss Hamilton, but I will maintain my silence. I've already said too much."

With that, he turned on his heel and escorted his picture-perfect family away. Mrs. Callahan glanced back at me with concern on her face. Junior ignored me, intent on watching his feet as he shuffled along after his parents.

⚜

"What was that all about?" my dad asked when I got in the Jeep.

"That's Mike Callahan. He was a good friend of Frank Thompson," I said. Then, to change the subject, I added, "I imagine this weather will bring out a record crowd for the parade."

In thoughtful silence, I drove the six miles to Gladstone, where the parade and Fourth of July festivities were to be held. Also situated along Little Bay de Noc, a finger of water that reaches out from Lake Michigan, Gladstone is about a third the size of Escanaba, almost a suburb. Often referred to as "quaint" with an old downtown and many large Victorian homes built back in the lumber boom of the late 1800s, it was now home to many up-and-coming manufacturing firms and popular with walleye anglers.

I parked a few blocks from the parade route, and we hiked to Delta Avenue, the main street in town. We set up two folding chairs in the shade of an old two-story brick building housing the hardware store, and Belle sat obediently on the pavement between us. My dad chatted with an elderly couple seated next to him while I sat in silence studying the crowd of several thousand Delta County residents, young and old, turned out for the spectacle. I spotted a few people I knew and a few others who were vaguely familiar.

At exactly eleven o'clock, the Sirens wailed above the din of the crowd. A Gladstone Public Safety patrol car led the parade, followed by a sheriff's department car and then a contingent of local American Legion and VFW members carrying the colors. We all stood. My dad removed his cap as the flag-bearers passed us, and the Gladstone High School band played a Sousa march. Then came a menagerie of scout troops, different ages decked out in their blue, tan or green uniforms, followed by volunteers and local politicians passing out candy to the small children screaming and laughing on each side of the street. A few log trucks passed by, spit-polished for the occasion, one carrying a full load of fragrant, fresh-cut pine adorned with a signed proclaiming "Johnson Trucking Does It Best" and another sporting a float featuring a local 4-H group impersonating the signers of the Declaration of Independence.

It was no Macy's Thanksgiving Day parade, but it was a good representation of life in Upper Michigan. Belle looked bored lying on the sidewalk, raising her nose occasionally and letting out a low growl when other dogs dared enter her line of sight.

After the parade, we walked back to the Jeep and exchanged the lawn chairs for the cooler, then strolled the six blocks to the park that framed the southern edge of the city. Though not as large as Ludington Park in Escanaba, Van Cleve Park was still better than what most people had in their towns. As we strolled casually through the crowds, I saw several high school classmates. We stopped to exchange a few words, then moved on our way. I had been close to few people in school, being too skinny and brainy, and had little to say to them now beyond polite conversation. Michelle, my one true friend from Escanaba High School, was now a book editor in New York and never failed to tell me vehemently that I was nuts to return to Escanaba.

"You can do so much better," she had wailed when I told her I moved back to our hometown. "You could easily be working here for the Times or in Washington at the Post. Come crash at my place for a few months. Don't hide out in the boonies! You'll be bored out of your gourd by Halloween."

I wasn't bored out of my gourd yet, but Halloween was still four months off.

At about two o'clock, with the sun continuing to beat down relentlessly and the smell of grilling bratwurst whetting our appetite, we found a picnic table under a large oak tree about a hundred feet from the beach and ate our lunch. It was a relaxing way to spend an afternoon despite the crowd and the loud country and western band playing at the other end of the park. Across the bay, Escanaba's only skyscraper, a round, 18-story retirement community called Harbor Towers, stretched above the rooftops. Along the near shore, four preschoolers were trying to build a sand castle with a little help from two young women. Their laughter was as refreshing as the clean lake breeze. I was daydreaming when I realized my dad was speaking to me.

"I'm sorry, Dad, what did you say?" I asked.

"I said, you never told me what happened with Hannah Lindstrom after she visited you at the paper. Is she okay?" he asked, finishing the last bite of his sandwich.

"She's handling things pretty well, but she's worried about Brett and Sarah," I said, then explained what Brett had told me about the threatening phone call.

"I can see why she's worried," my dad said with concern. "Do you think the threat is serious?"

"There's no way to know until someone tries to carry it out. I just wish I knew who made the call. If it wasn't the person who took the truck, and Brett swears it wasn't, who was it and why would they do it?"

"Maybe it was one of that person's friends," my dad suggested.

"That's possible," I said. But not probable, I thought to myself. It didn't sound like Greg Connor had too many friends other than Brett.

"Sounds to me like you think Brett's innocent," my dad said with a slight smile, his eyebrows raised.

"I don't think he was the one behind the wheel. But I'm not ready to say he's completely innocent—not yet, anyway," I answered carefully.

Belle, lying in the shade under the table, rolled over onto my feet and groaned. I reached down and scratched her white belly.

"I've managed to track down a lead on who took Brett's truck. I haven't figured out why, though, and I probably won't until I find him. I think he skipped town and ditched the truck somewhere after he realized what he'd done. Who knows? He may even be the one who called Brett and simply disguised his voice," I said.

"Don't you think that's a pretty wild coincidence? That the morning after this person 'borrows' Brett's truck, a prominent man is run over during his daily walk?"

"Yes, I've thought of that. It opens up a whole new can of worms if it was deliberate." I said and heaved a sigh. "That's what that conversation with Mike Callahan was all about."

Before I could explain, I heard a female voice coo, "Oh, Hank!" from behind me. My dad looked up and over my shoulder and gave a hesitant smile.

"Hi, Clarice. How are you today?" he said to a plump woman whose curly hair was a muted shade of carrot orange. She wore a bright pink floral short set and large white straw hat with matching pink band.

"I'm fine, I'm fine. I'm so happy to see you! You don't come to the Y as much in the summer. We miss you," she fawned. I despised her on sight.

To battle a case of mild arthritis acquired after thirty years of climbing ladders and dragging hoses, Dad took water exercise classes at the YMCA during the winter. The classes were about ninety percent female, many of the women widowed or divorced, and they all adored him.

"Clarice, this is my daughter. Robin, this is Clarice Witherspoon. Her late husband was the mayor of Escanaba when you were just a toddler." The expression on his face said, "she's a pain, but be nice."

"It's nice to meet you, Mrs. Witherspoon," I said, shaking her soft, pale hand.

"Yes, we've heard so much about you from your father. He's so proud of you. You're so lovely. Are you married, dear?" she asked.

"No, Ma'am" was all I said. I turned to my dad and said, "Shouldn't we be going now?"

Clarice Witherspoon ignored my question to him and asked me, "Are you the one writing about that horrible accident that killed Frank Thompson?"

"Yes, that's me," I said, still wanting her to leave.

"Such a tragedy! My son is a junior accountant with the firm—just started in January, you know. He said Frank was having some problems with one of the partners before he died." She nodded her head knowingly.

Suddenly I didn't want her to leave. The old busybody might prove useful.

"What sort of problems?" I asked, trying to sound casual.

"Oh, not getting along, I guess. Sometimes those things happen. Oh, well, I must be going. My grandson is playing baseball soon. He's just eight years old and in Little League, but it might as well be the World Series for me. Toodle-oo," she said, waggling her fingers as she waddled away.

"Humph," I grunted after she was out of earshot. "How can you stand people like that?"

"Oh, she's all right. She means well. You're just a bit sensitive right now. That was interesting what she said about Thompson and his partners," he added as we packed up the remains of the picnic.

"Yeah, one more piece of the puzzle," I mumbled, trying to imagine where it fit. I wondered which one of Frank's partners he was having problems with—the dull, quiet Albert Klegle or the eloquent Doug Jordan.

It was four o'clock by the time we got back to the Jeep. Belle was hot and none too happy to be put in the stuffy back seat, where she grumbled until we got moving and air blew over her face. She seemed to smile with joy at the breeze, tongue hanging out the side of her mouth, ears flapping. Then she uttered one last grunt before lying down for her late afternoon nap.

I dropped my dad off at his house and made a beeline back to my apartment to call Michelle. She wasn't home, so I left a message on her answering machine and took a nap on the couch with a fan blowing over me.

About nine-thirty I woke up refreshed, splashed some cold water on my face and combed my hair, then hooked Belle to her leash so we could go to the park to watch the fireworks display put on by the City of Escanaba. Rose Easton was entertaining her sister and a few friends on the front porch and called out a greeting as we passed. I headed for the south end of the park where the city band was playing methodical versions of familiar patriotic tunes. Darkness comes late to this part of the country in summer, and there was still plenty of daylight until about ten o'clock. I spotted fellow reporter Craig Myers and his family on a large red plaid blanket to the right of the benches in front of the bandshell. They invited me to join them, and I did, keeping a tight hold on Belle's leash every time another dog scampered by.

Shortly after ten, the band cleared the stage, and the first charge rocketed into the air, exploding into a thousand brilliant shards of red, white and blue. The crowd cheered and whistled. The show continued for about half an hour and drew a long round of applause at its conclusion. After saying goodbye to the Myers family, I started back towards the apartment, but Belle had something else in mind and pulled me in the opposite direction. When a few tugs on her leash proved fruitless, I gave in and followed her.

She plodded along the beach behind the homes lining the west side of Lake Shore Drive south of the park. It was dark, the only light coming from the small bonfires and patio lights in the back yards we passed. I had no idea how far we had gone when I heard a familiar male voice, then a woman's laughter. The sounds caught Belle's attention, and she pulled me toward the voices. I resisted. We were trespassing as it was. Then I caught a glimpse of the couple and ducked behind a line of shrubs that separated one yard from what I recognized as the Thompson home. Standing in the amber glow of Chinese lanterns around the deck were Victoria Thompson and Joe Nelson, the public safety director, entwined in a passionate embrace, lips locked together in conflict, each trying to devour the other! I froze. This was not the sort of behavior I expected from a grieving widow of one week. Afraid that one of us would make a sound and reveal our eavesdropping, I yanked on Belle's leash and walked quickly home. I didn't know what to make of it all.

Chapter Sixteen

T HE RINGING OF THE bedside telephone shattered a sleep filled with twisted dreams, and it took a few more jarring rings before my head cleared. I reached into the darkness and felt for the annoying contraption.

"Hullo," I muttered into the receiver.

"Robin? Is that you?" The frantic tone at the other end made me sit up straight in bed, wide awake. My eyes fell on the clock across the room. Two-ten, too early for anything but very bad news.

"Yes, who is this?" I asked.

"Someone tried to kill my baby!" the woman's voice shrieked. It was Hannah. My blood went cold.

"What happened?"

"It's Sarah," she choked between sobs. "Someone ran her car off the road. It rolled over several times." She broke down, making anything else she tried to say unintelligible.

"Are you at the hospital?" I asked.

"Yes," she choked. "The police are here, too. I don't know what to tell them, Robin."

"It's all right. I'm on my way," I said and hung up.

I dressed in a pair of jeans and pullover sweater and raced to St. Francis Hospital. A mixture of fear and anger clutched at my throat like a vise grip. It was just too much of a coincidence for this not to be related to Brett Lindstrom and Frank Thompson. My mind churned over the events of the past several days, trying to determine who knew that Brett had talked with me. It was no use. I kept coming back to the main problem at hand: was Sarah going to be all right?

I parked in the visitor lot and sprinted into the building to the nurses' station in the emergency room. A plump, middle-aged brunette nurse indicated that Hannah was in the surgical waiting room. I half-walked, half-ran down several halls before I found her pacing in front of the double doors leading to the operating room. Leaning against a wall opposite the doors was a sheriff's deputy.

I hugged Hannah. She held onto me as if she were a tree drawing strength from me through her arms.

"How is she?" I asked.

"She's in surgery now," Hannah said, her voiced muffled by my hair. She drew back and removed a tissue from the pocket of her nurse's uniform and blew her red nose for what I guessed was probably the twentieth time that night. Her hair was in disarray, strands falling out of the loose twist that held it off her face. Her makeup was streaked, and mascara had pooled under her eyes.

"She was wearing her seatbelt, but she still has a head injury," she said, sniffling and starting to hyperventilate.

"Okay, take some deep breaths," I said. When she was breathing more normally, I led her to the waiting room and we sat down together.

"What happened?" I asked, taking her hand in mine.

"One of her friends was with her, Lacy Clark. She was in the front passenger seat and suffered a broken arm. Lacy said a truck of some sort drove up behind them without headlights. When it got right on their back bumper, the headlights came on—the brights—and blinded them. Then it pulled alongside and tapped the driver side corner of the front bumper. Sarah lost control, and the car hit the ditch and rolled over," she said, sniffling again.

"Where were they when this happened?" I asked.

"They had just dropped off another friend in Cornell and were coming back to town on the county road," she said. She took another deep breath and exhaled slowly. I rubbed my free hand across her back and tried to picture my local geography

Cornell is a farming community about ten miles northwest of Escanaba. The roads between are narrow, two-lane jobs that hold all sorts of dangers—deer darting out from the woods and fields, black ice in winter, potholes from lack of money for maintenance—you name it.

I turned to the young deputy who had come into the waiting room to listen to Hannah.

"Do you know about the threat made to Brett Lindstrom, her son?" I asked.

"I told him everything Brett said to you," Hannah answered for him.

"Yes, Ma'am," the deputy responded. "Detective Charlie Baker from the Escanaba Public Safety Department has been called as well. I understand he's the person assigned to oversee the Thompson accident investigation."

"Thank you, Deputy. . .?"

"Bradfield, Ma'am, Tom Bradfield," he said and tipped his brown saucer cap to me. I walked outside the room and motioned for him to follow.

"Is there a description of the vehicle?" I asked once we were out of Hannah's earshot.

"No, Ma'am, just a large, dark vehicle. We're guessing it's a truck of some sort, from what the girl said. That car's pretty banged up, it may be tough to get any evidence from it, like paint transfers. From what we saw in the dark, there wasn't any transfer. The girl thinks the truck's rear bumper is what hit them and forced them off the road."

I went back into the waiting room and sat in a hard plastic molded chair across from Hannah. The seat felt cold through my jeans. The whole place felt cold, harsh, unwelcoming. My head hurt, and my stomach roiled. The threat was for real, all right—but who was behind the wheel of the threatening vehicle? Greg Connor? It would have been bold of him to use Brett's own truck to try to kill Brett's sister after using it to kill Thompson, but from what his foreman, Jack Kirksen, had said, it wouldn't have been out of character. If Connor was the driver, it meant the man had no scruples and no fear of getting caught.

Whoever the driver had been, I wondered how he found out Brett had talked about someone taking his truck the night before Thompson's death. I mentally retraced my steps over the last week. Anyone I talked to could have made the connection between my questions and Brett's confession, but the best bet seemed to be someone at the sawmill. Brett's two other friends wouldn't have known Connor well, if at all. Was it the perky blonde receptionist who led me to Kirksen? Was she a Connor groupie? It was possible. I couldn't picture Kirksen tipping him off. He disliked Greg Connor too much.

I felt something akin to guilt well up in my gut. Perhaps I hadn't taken Brett's claim of a threat to his family seriously enough. Now his sister was possibly fighting for her life.

Hannah and I sat in silence for about ten minutes until I heard Charlie's voice in the hallway. He spent several minutes being briefed by the deputy, then came in and re-introduced himself to Hannah. She nodded a greeting and tried to speak, but no sound came out when she moved her lips. She sighed heavily and sat back in the chair with her eyes closed.

Here was the man who was trying to gather enough evidence to send her son to prison, and now he had the job of helping to find out who had tried to kill her daughter. It was awkward, to say the least. Charlie seemed to understand and nodded to me to join him in the hall. I squeezed her hand and gave her an encouraging smile before following him.

"I assume the deputy told you about the threat?" I said as we walked.

"Yeah. What exactly did Lindstrom say to you?" he asked, his mouth set in a grimace, his voice hard.

"Not much—something about a phone call from a man who told him to keep his mouth shut about whoever borrowed his pickup or else his family would be hurt. I'm not sure what that meant—injured or killed. You'll have to ask Brett. Maybe he'll be more willing to talk now," I said.

Charlie stopped and leaned against the cream-colored brick wall near the X-ray room. He rubbed his eyes and groaned, Wearing faded jeans and a dark blue t-shirt with the department's logo on the front and the word POLICE emblazoned on the back, he too looked recently jerked from dreams.

"Robin, why the hell didn't you tell me you talked to Brett?"

"Look, I told you before. I've got a job to do. Not only that, but I'm trying to help an old friend. I'm not trying to interfere with your investigation, so don't take it that way." I was angry that I sounded so defensive. "I promised Brett I wouldn't say anything to the police about our conversation, at least not until later. He didn't even trust his lawyer with the information he gave me. Besides, there was no proof there actually was a credible threat. You and I both know a hit-and-run accident is generally not the sort of thing that leads the perpetrators to make death threats. That is," I couldn't help adding, "if it was an accident."

Charlie's eyes narrowed as he frowned at me.

"Murder?"

"Murder."

He was quiet for a minute before he asked, "Do you know who took that truck—if someone else besides Brett was driving?"

"Not for certain, but I have a good guess," I admitted.

"Dammit, Robin, who?" he shouted.

I hesitated. The wisest thing to do was let him in on what I had learned. This was too big for me to handle on my own.

"Greg Connor may have something to do with this," I said quietly.

"What about him? He's a shitbum we've been dealing with since he was about ten years old. He finally seemed to get his life on track when he went to work at the lumber mill a few years ago. You think he did all this?" Charlie asked.

"I don't know. He skipped town the same day as Thompson's death, and he was a friend of Brett's. But Brett wouldn't tell me who asked to borrow his truck. He's too afraid."

Just then the young deputy found us. He looked weary as he flipped through a little notebook.

"My sergeant went to the jail to let Lindstrom know what happened. He's still not talking. He asked for his attorney—you know, Bill Watson. Watson showed up and spent about five minutes with him. Then he came out and asked that Lindstrom be released so he could come to the hospital. That's up to a judge, though." Deputy Bradfield flipped his notebook shut with a snap, report finished.

"What do you mean he won't talk?" Charlie exploded. Although a few inches taller than Charlie, the deputy suddenly looked small next to the thundering city detective. "His sister was nearly killed tonight! Did your sergeant relay that little piece of information to him?"

"Y-yes, Sir. Watson wouldn't let him say a word, though," Bradfield said.

"All right, here's what I'd like you to do. My department would greatly appreciate it if your department would step up its search for that pickup that turned Frank Thompson into a pile of broken bones last week. It's probably the same truck that hit the girl's car tonight," he said through gritted teeth. I had never seen Charlie so angry.

"Yes, Sir," the deputy said and scurried off, probably back to tell his sergeant about what jerks the city cops were.

Charlie and I headed back to the waiting room without another word. A forty-something female doctor in surgical scrubs was sitting across from Hannah, who looked up and smiled when she saw us.

"She's going to be okay. The swelling in her brain is down, and she's out of danger for now," she said through her tears.

"I'm glad to hear that," Charlie said as I hugged Hannah.

"Will there be any permanent damage?" I asked.

"Well, it's too soon to tell," the doctor said. "We'll know more after a day or two, but I don't expect any serious aftereffects. I doubt she'll remember the accident, though. Short-term memory loss is common with concussions like hers."

Hannah left with the doctor to visit Sarah in the recovery room, leaving Charlie and me to figure out what to do next.

"How certain are you that it was Greg Connor who took the truck? Got any proof?" he asked, running a hand through his hair.

"No. Everything is circumstantial. Not a thing that could even get you a search warrant," I said.

"Damn," he muttered. "We've got nothing until Lindstrom decides to talk or we find that truck."

As Charlie started to walk away, I followed and grabbed his arm. "Look, I'm sorry I didn't tell you about the threat. We agreed we'd share information. Now, tell me something. Have you gotten any strange vibes from either of Thompson's partners?" I asked, remembering Mrs. Witherspoon's tidbit of gossip.

"No, why?"

"A few sources, who shall remain nameless for the time being," I said, holding up a hand as Charlie started to protest, "told me Thompson was having some problems just before he died, possibly involving one of his partners."

"Well, the plot thickens! I'll see what I can find out. You keep me informed of what you learn, since I know it's no use to tell you to butt out," he said and stalked away before I could make a snide remark of my own.

I wouldn't be allowed in to see Sarah that night, so I went home and got about four hours of fitful sleep.

Chapter Seventeen

AKING SHORTLY BEFORE NINE on Sunday morning, I called the hospital to make sure Sarah had made it through the night. A nurse informed me the girl was resting comfortably. Satisfied, I put Belle on her chain in the back yard and took a shower. The lukewarm water felt good on my tired body but did little to wash away the sluggishness in my mind.

Wrapping myself in a threadbare terrycloth robe, I shuffled to the kitchen for a piece of toast and glass of orange juice, contemplating the events of the last twenty-four hours. Mike Callahan had indicated that Frank Thompson's death could have been murder because the accountant had surely been afraid of something before he died. If someone had hired Greg Connor to kill Thompson, it might explain the threat made to Brett Lindstrom. Whoever was behind Thompson's death didn't want anything traced back to him—or her. And if that were the case, the only suspect I could think of was the beautiful, not-exactly-grieving widow Victoria. It all seemed like something out of a soap opera.

I began to feel energized as my mind fired up and considered the possibilities. While Charlie's hands were tied by legal red tape, I could ask all the questions I wanted of whomever I wanted. Time was of the essence. Hannah would be the next target, or maybe even Brett himself, if some answers weren't found quickly.

It was past ten by the time I left my apartment, armed with an address for Arnold and Mary Connor. I hoped they would prove to be Greg's parents, since they were the only Connors listed in the phone book. But first, on a whim, I made a return trip to the Stewart Lumber Company. Successful business people, in my experience, usually work six to seven days a week.

The whim paid off. Apparently Grant Stewart was no different from the likes of Bill Gates. The Lincoln Navigator I had seen Stewart driving last week was parked in front of the main building, the only vehicle in the front lot. I pulled in next to it and jumped out. The front door of the office was locked, so I pressed the doorbell and waited. A few minutes later I heard footsteps, and the lock turned in the door.

Grant Stewart looked surprised when he saw me standing on the large square concrete step that served as a porch, but he greeted me with a warm smile.

"You were here the other day, weren't you? Robin Hamilton, right?" he said as he opened the door wider. I nodded.

"Jack Kirksen told me you were looking for Greg Connor. Please, come in." As I stepped inside, I caught a whiff of his cologne. It smelled expensive and fit well with his classic appearance. In his mid-fifties, with neatly trimmed, thick silver hair and the body of an aging running back, he wore business attire complete with black patent leather lace wing-tips.

He saw me eyeing his clothes and said, "Pretty dressy for a weekend at the office, eh? I went to church earlier and didn't bother to go home and change. Please, come up to my office. I'm just finishing some paperwork. Would you like pop or coffee, perhaps?"

"No, thank you, Mr. Stewart," I said. "I don't want to take up too much of your time,"

He led me down the hall to the staircase I had seen the week before. As we climbed the deep red, carpeted stairs, he said, "You're from the newspaper, right?"

"Yes. I'm working on a story that might involve Greg Connor," I said. "I was wondering if you could help. Your comments would be off the record at this time, of course."

"I see" was all Stewart said as he stopped at the open door to his office and stood aside to let me pass. He closed the door behind him and indicated one of two large, comfortable, black leather, Queen Anne-style chairs in front of his massive desk. I sank slowly into the one on the right, suddenly aware that we were the only two people on the premises. The room must have taken up most of the second floor, but I began to feel claustrophobic

Stewart's office was paneled in the same dark brown wood as the hallway. The deep red carpeting in the stairwell continued uninterrupted throughout the office and felt thick and plush under my sandals.

He settled into a swivel executive chair behind the massive mahogany desk that formed an L around him, with a computer on his right. A screensaver with the name Stewart Lumber Company prevented me from seeing what he had been working on. He sat with his back to the window overlooking the parking lot. Another window to the east showed a large field and then a thick forest of pine.

"So, what is your interest in Greg?" he asked, flashing a white-toothed smile. He had the look of a man who spent a lot of time on a boat. My eyes drifted up to the wall behind him, and there it was—a framed ten-by-thirteen photo of *Scarlett*. He followed my gaze and laughed.

"She's a beaut, isn't she? Forty-two feet of fiberglass therapy. My late wife named her after Scarlett O'Hara. "Gone With the Wind" was her favorite movie," he said. "Now, how can I help you?"

"I understand Connor quit unexpectedly the week before last," I said.

Stewart looked at me for a moment, expressionless.

"I don't understand why a young man like Greg would be of any interest to a reporter, off the record or not," he said.

"Greg is of some interest to me because he grew fairly close to another one of your employees, Brett Lindstrom. I'm sure you know Brett is now in jail, charged with the death of—"

"Yes, yes, I know all about that. Frank Thompson was my accountant," he said with an edge in his deep voice, then shook his head. "Brett seemed like a nice kid, just not the brightest. It's a shame the police suspect him of something so awful. But you have to know that I don't have a lot of sympathy for him if he is proven guilty. Frank and his wife have been friends of mine for years. They were a great comfort to me when my wife died."

"I understand, Sir, and I'm sorry. I didn't mean to cause you any further pain. I just want to know if you have any idea where I can find Greg," I said.

"I still don't understand what Greg has to do with Brett. Sure, they were friends, but so what? I'm sure Brett had more than one friend," Stewart said. I was getting the feeling he didn't really want to answer my question. Kirksen was apparently right about Stewart liking Greg.

"He may have information that could help in Brett's defense," I said. I wasn't about to tell Stewart I thought Greg might have been behind the wheel of the truck that struck Thompson. "Do you know where he might be?"

"Only in a general sense. I knew Greg was looking to spread his wings. He had a tough life growing up and was thrilled when he was finally able to afford his own apartment, but that wasn't enough for him. He wanted more out of life than to just survive," Stewart said, his eyes growing distant. "I saw some potential in him and took him under my wing. I tried to show him there was more to life than working like a mule all week just to blow your wages on the weekend, drinking and partying.

"He began to develop ambition. He talked about moving south where there were more opportunities. I didn't expect him to leave so suddenly, but I wasn't surprised. When Greg made up his mind to do something, he did it without hesitation," Stewart said. He flashed his light blue eyes, the color of Lake Michigan at dawn when it was clear and cold.

"Did you notice if Connor had a nasty temper?" I asked.

"Well, yes, I suppose Greg can be short-tempered sometimes. He's a young man. He has yet to learn patience. What does that have to do with Brett Lindstrom or Frank Thompson?" he asked, annoyance creeping into his voice.

"I don't know yet. Maybe nothing. I'm tracking down every lead I can, Sir," I said. I debated whether to tell him about Sarah and decided against it. Maybe he already knew. "So you don't know exactly where Greg went?" His eyes narrowed and he heaved a heavy sigh.

"No, but I'm sure he'll let me know when he gets settled. Why don't you give me your card? I'll give you a call when he contacts me—if he wants to talk to you, that is. I think Greg just wants to get on with his life, away from the shadow of his family and old associations," he said.

As I dug one of my white business cards out of my purse, a police scanner suddenly crackled to life from a bookcase on the west wall. I jumped a little. Stewart turned and looked at the scanner, then chuckled sheepishly.

"I like to keep in touch with what's happening out there. It's cheap entertainment, but not nearly as annoying as a radio station," he said.

"Yes, I guess you're right on that," I said and handed him my card.

He escorted me down the stairs and to the front door in silence. I thanked him for his time, although I hadn't learned one useful thing from the interview.

"No problem. I'm sorry I couldn't be of more help," he said. He gave me a salesman's smile that turned the iciness in his eyes to a warm sky blue color and shook my hand.

Something about the conversation in his office seemed odd compared with what Kirksen had said. Stewart had confirmed what his manager had told me about being Connor's mentor. His take on the young man's personality was entirely different, though. I wondered who was right.

In an attempt to find out, I went to the address I'd found for the Connors. They lived about six blocks west of Greg's apartment, in a gray, one-story, clapboard-sided home in sore need of a coat of paint and a new roof. It was after eleven o'clock when I made my way up the cracked sidewalk and knocked on the twisted aluminum screen door. Getting no answer after three knocks, I was about to leave when I saw the curtain to my right shift back into place. I knocked again.

"Mrs. Connor, are you there? Mr. Connor, hello," I called.

Finally the front door opened a crack, not enough to allow me a view of who opened it.

"What do you want?" a weary female voice whispered.

"Mrs. Connor? My name is Robin Hamilton. I'm with the Daily Press. I'm looking for your son, Greg," I said. I was just guessing that it was Gregg's mother behind the door. The voice sounded old and tired.

"He's not here," the woman said, starting to shut the door.

"Wait, please. Do you have any idea where I can find him? It's important," I said, placing my right hand on the door to prevent her from closing it further.

The urgency in my voice must have touched a nerve. She opened the door a little wider now to reveal a mere shadow of a woman. She had had a recent run-in with a brutally angry fist. Her right cheek was swollen, and the area around the eye was a bluish-purple, as if coal dust had been smeared there. A frayed flannel nightgown could not cover the large bruise, resembling the imprint of a large hand, on her right forearm. The woman barely whispered when she spoke. Her eyes were filled with despair.

"No, I haven't heard from him in a week," she said. "He left with-out—"

"Mary, who the hell's at the door?" a man growled from behind her.

She threw a furtive glance over her shoulder, then turned quickly back to me. "Please leave, now," she pleaded.

She shut the door in my face, and I made no attempt to stop her. Behind it I heard the man ask to whom she was talking.

"Just some religious person making the rounds," she said in a tremu-lous voice.

"Goddamn people oughtta mind their own goddamn business," he shouted, his speech slurred. "Why the hell did you answer the door with no goddamn clothes on? Don't you have any respect for yourself?"

"I didn't—"

Her protest was silenced by a smack and followed by a cry. I ran back to my Jeep and dug the cellular phone from my purse. The newspaper had issued me the phone the day I returned, but I had yet to use it. Now seemed like the perfect time. My hand shook as I dialed those three magic numbers that would bring the police. It probably wouldn't help, but it was all I could do. After giving the dispatcher the information, I drove away muttering a prayer for Greg Connor's mother.

Chapter Eighteen

I TRIED TO SHAKE THE IMAGE of Mary Connor's face from my mind as I drove to the hospital to check on Sarah and Hannah and see if there was any new information about the accident. Church services were letting out, and traffic was heavy on the city streets. It slowed me down and gave me time to calm the trembling in my hands.

Seeing Greg's mother's situation helped me understand a little piece of his personality. His focus most of his life must have been on getting away from the screaming and hitting.

Before I knew it, I was turning down the road to the hospital. Although tiny by metropolitan standards, St. Francis is a state-of-the-art facility run by a religious order out of Illinois. It opened its doors on the south side of town in the late 1800s to drunken, brawling lumberjacks and sailors. The hospital expanded several times before finally moving to a large parcel at the edge of Escanaba in the mid-eighties.

A tan brick two-story structure, the hospital nestled back in the cool of the woods. A long winding driveway led from the highway, forking to lead motorists to the emergency room and doctors' offices or the main entrance and visitor parking lot. I took the latter and parked in the visitor lot, which was nearly empty. I remembered seeing a sign last night stating that Sunday visiting hours didn't start until noon. I looked at my watch. Quarter to twelve. By the time I would reach Sarah's room, it would be time. I strolled to the covered portico, graced with a figure St. Francis deep in prayer. Large gold crosses were etched on the double doors that automatically opened with a heavy swoosh as I approached. The lobby was deserted, a note on the desk phone advising visitors to dial zero if there was no one at the desk. I did so and asked for Sarah Lindstrom's room number.

"One moment, please," an elderly voice croaked. After a short pause, she informed me that Sarah was in Room 212.

Although the elevator was just a few feet away, I searched the three hallways radiating from the front desk until I found a sign indicating the stairs. I hate elevators.

When I came out on the second floor, the dreaded hospital smell, faint downstairs, hit me like a wrecking ball in the stomach. It was a noxious mixture of ammonia, unappetizing food and sickness. It reminded me of those awful last few months of my mother's life. Hospices were just getting started then and weren't an option for her, so she ended up spending most of her final days at the old hospital. It had been twenty years since her death, but my stomach still shriveled at that smell—the smell of death.

I tried to block the smell out of my mind as I searched for Sarah's room. It was on the west side of the building and held two beds. The one nearer the door was occupied by a woman in her mid-fifties, instructing the balding gentleman seated next to her bed, her hand in his, on the proper way to water her flower garden. From the way she sat and the drainage tube on her left side I could tell she'd just had a mastectomy. I nodded to her and the gentleman and peered around a thin peach cotton curtain to the next bed.

Sarah was sleeping peacefully, a white bandage wrapped around her head, her face bruised and scraped. Her mother sat in a chair to the left of the bed and stared out the window. I placed a hand on her shoulder and she jumped.

"Oh, Robin, I was just daydreaming," she whispered and smiled, as if embarrassed.

"How is she?" I whispered back.

Sarah stirred in her sleep, moved her head to the side and mumbled but did not awaken.

"The doctor said she's out of danger now and should make a full recovery," Hannah said.

"That's good to hear. Have the police learned anything new?" I asked.

Hannah looked at her daughter for a long moment and then turned to me and said, "Let's see if we can get some lunch. She'll be asleep for a while."

She placed a soft kiss on Sarah's cheek, then followed me out of the room, the middle-aged couple still holding hands and smiling at one another through teary eyes as we walked past.

When we got into the hall, Hannah let out a ragged breath.

"I have never been so scared in my whole life, Robin. Nothing my ex-husband ever did to me was this bad," she said.

I didn't know what to say. I just waited for her to find the words to vent her feelings. What she said next, though, sent a chill through me.

"There was a message on the answering machine when I went home this morning to change clothes," she said, her voice cracking. "It was a man speaking in a muffled voice, like he was holding something over the receiver. He said, 'Your son didn't heed my warning to keep his mouth shut. Next time, I'm coming for you.' Then he hung up."

She stopped walking and turned to me, tears streaming down her face.

"What in the hell has my son gotten into, Robin? Who are these people?" she cried.

I saw a waiting room a few doors down the hall and led her there. The room was empty except for two boxy-looking stuffed couches and a table with several magazines scattered on it. A few games and puzzles were stashed in the corner for small children. Hannah cried for several minutes, then grabbed a few tissues from a box on the table and wiped her nose and face. She waved a tissue in the air.

"This is all I seem to do these days—cry. I don't know what else to do. Robin, I want to find out who's behind all this, but I can't put my family in any more danger. There's no doubt someone tried to kill Sarah last night. What if they try again? Will this all stop if Brett just takes the fall?" she asked, eyes boring into me.

Only extreme fear could pressure a mother to sacrifice one child for another. I knew the place Hannah was at right now was not one of rational thought.

"I don't have any answers, Hannah. I do know this though—the police are working hard on this case. They're doing everything they can legally do to catch the culprit. I also know that until that happens, Brett will not be safe. Even if he is innocent but decides to plead guilty and do the time, there is always the risk he will tell someone what he knows. He's a constant threat to the people who are responsible," I explained, taking hold of her hand. "I can't tell you what to do. All I can say is that if you let this intimidation work, it may never end."

"Oh God, I hadn't thought of it like that." Hannah leaned back and stared at the ceiling.

After a few minutes I asked, "Is there some place you could quietly disappear to until this is resolved? Maybe a relative or a friend out of state who would take you and Sarah in for a while?"

"Well, there's my sister in Milwaukee. I know she'd let us stay there as long as we needed. But what about Brett and my job? I can't just leave," she said.

"Brett will understand. He'd probably feel better knowing you and Sarah were in a safer place. As for your job, I'm sure you can take some vacation time. I'm only talking about a few weeks or so. Something is bound to turn up soon."

"Maybe you're right. I hate to run away from the problem, but I can't put Sarah through any more of this either."

"Did you let the police know about the message on your answering machine?" I asked.

"Yes, I called them right away. An officer took the whole machine away to analyze the memory or something." She stood up, suddenly resolute. "Come on, let's go eat. I'm hungry."

In the cafeteria on the first floor, we each ate a sandwich and a cup of vegetable soup. Hannah talked with parental pride about Sarah's plans to attend one of the Big Ten universities downstate and follow in her mother's footsteps by becoming a nurse. When we finished, she walked me to the parking lot. Stopping next to the Jeep, I clasped her right hand in both of mine and gave it a squeeze.

"Hang in there and have faith. I know this is difficult," I said. "I'll say a prayer for all of you."

"Thanks. I guess we need all the help we can get." She paused and looked down at her feet shyly, and I saw Brett in her demeanor for the first time.

"You know, I really appreciate what you're doing. I want you to keep working on this, Robin. I sense that you feel you're responsible for this thing with Sarah, I can see it in your eyes. Don't feel that way. You're getting close to the truth. Find it," she said fiercely, giving my upper arm a squeeze before turning back towards the building.

I watched her walk back, head high and shoulders straight. I admired her courage. She was right about my having touched a nerve somewhere. It was time to expose the owner of that nerve.

Chapter Nineteen

ON THE DRIVE HOME, something struck me about the message left on Hannah's answering machine. I'd have to listen to it to know how accurate her memory was, but if the person really did use the word 'heed,' saying "Your son didn't heed my warning," we were dealing with someone educated. The average person did not use the word 'heed' very often, if ever. Since what I'd heard of Greg Connor didn't lead me to believe he was much of a wordsmith, this would confirm my suspicions of a ringleader. But who?

In the past, in Chicago, when I was working on a difficult story with lots of hidden agendas, I had always confided in Mitch. We'd take long walks along the lakeshore, talking and holding hands. Mitch always seemed to shed some light on whatever I was mulling over, either with hard facts or just a fresh perspective. Sometimes he would confide in me, too, discussing some perplexing case, always careful to leave out names and other identifying information. The end result was that we had a deep understanding of each other's work and a respect for each other's intelligence, intuition and dedication. Remembering those times overwhelmed me with sadness and a renewed sense of loss.

When I got home, I hooked Belle to her leash and walked across the street to the park and down a path to the beach. The air was humid, and dark clouds threatening rain piled up in the western sky. The approaching storm had already chased away most of the swimmers and sunbathers, leaving the beach nearly empty. I found a stretch of sand away from the few people who remained and took off my shoes and sat down. Once I freed Belle, she waddled down to the edge of the water. She sniffed a small wave as it splashed her body, then waded in a bit further until she was able to paddle around. After about two minutes, she grew tired or bored or both and waddled back to me. She gave one good shake, showering me with a heavy spray of water and sand, then lay down next to me. I laughed and gave her a kiss on her damp, oily head.

We stared at the blue-gray water that seemed to stretch on forever. I felt the urge to walk straight into it until the water cradled me and carried me away from all my pain and frustration. I felt myself sinking into a deep, dark well. At the bottom was a pool of blackness that folded its arms around me in a death grip. It was sorrow over losing the only man I had loved enough to pledge my life to, sorrow at seeing friends suffer at the hands of some unknown evil, and, finally, frustration over my own inadequacies. The feelings had been gradually encroaching on my soul all week. Now they washed over me just as the waves were washing over the shore.

I couldn't bring Mitch back, but part of me still felt he wasn't really dead, just gone away for a while, possibly working some undercover assignment. When it was over, he'd call me and say, "I'm coming home." My heart still ached at the very thought of him. My grief grew rather than subsided and was now threatening to drown me.

As I fixated on the ebb and flow of the water, images of my dead fiancé tumbled through my head. Mixed with them were the images of Sarah Lindstrom lying in her hospital bed, head bandaged, her mother crying, her brother locked behind bars, and a man she probably never met lying dead in the park. I closed my eyes and tried to focus on one single thing—anything—to stop the flickering in my head, that awful television playing in the dark. I heard a seagull cry and honed in on the mournful sound. I pictured it defying the bonds of gravity and soaring above the land. I felt its freedom for just a moment, reveling in its broad view of the earth. I opened my eyes and took a deep breath, letting it out slowly. Sorrow loosened its death grip.

There was nothing I could do about my grief except to go on living.

I pictured Brett in his baggy orange jumpsuit and tried to focus again. What I needed was a break, a solid lead to tell me where Greg was and why he took Brad's truck, if indeed he was the one. I was now convinced Frank Thompson's death was no accident. Depending on whose appraisal of Greg Connor one chose to believe—Jack Kirksen's or Grant Stewart's— the young man might have been willing to commit murder if the price was right and if he thought he could get away with it. So who hired him? Thompson's wife, who may have been carrying on an affair with the chief of police right under her husband's nose? The chief himself, anxious to have his rival out of the way? Chief Joe Nelson had a lot to lose if it could be proved he were behind Thompson's death. And while he was a pompous jerk, I wasn't sure he was capable of murder, even for a woman as captivating as the vibrant Victoria Thompson.

But if not one of them, who? Who else could have wanted Thompson dead? Perhaps his partners held the key. And what about Mike Callahan? What did he know? What had made Thompson seem so fearful to him?

I looked down at Belle, who was watching me quizzically. I had been talking aloud. Unfortunately, Belle couldn't provide me with the answers to my questions, and I needed a second opinion. I stood up and brushed the sand off my backside and Belle's underbelly. I put my shoes back on when we reached the parking lot. The first drops of rain fell as we raced to the back door of the apartment. Once inside, I called Charlie Baker's home phone number.

A cheery deep masculine voice answered after the second ring. "Yello?"

"Hey, Charlie, it's Robin. You sound like you're in a pretty good mood."

"Hi there. Yeah, I guess I am. Brett Lindstrom finally cracked this morning and told us that it was Greg Connor who took his truck the night before Frank Thompson's death. You were right all along. If he's telling the truth—and I'm not convinced he is yet—it's the best lead we've had in a while," he said.

"That's sort of why I called, to talk about Thompson. Can we meet somewhere? I'd like to bounce some ideas off you," I said.

We agreed to meet at Gizzy's, a small, popular restaurant and bar just outside of town overlooking the lake, at five o'clock. First I took a long, cool shower, pinned my hair into a soft twist and applied a touch of make-up. By the time I had finished the little ritual, it was a quarter to five. I presented Belle with a bowl of meaty-looking kibble from a small plastic packet, which caused her to move from her favorite corner on the sofa and pad into the kitchen. I gave her a pat on the head as she set to eating. She responded with a grunt as I walked out the door.

Gizzy's is located about two miles south of Escanaba on the state highway. It occupies a choice piece of lakefront property and is bordered on the north and south by sprawling, half-million dollar homes. Their homeowners, both millionaires, are eager for the day when Gizzy's will close its doors, but because the bar has been there a lot longer than the homes and its owner takes delight in bucking the "snobs," the millionaires will probably have a long wait.

I arrived before Charlie and found a table for two in the corner away from the pool table and jukebox blaring classic rock. Suddenly a booming crack of thunder drowned out the music, followed by a flash of lightning. I looked out the window and saw that the storm that had been approaching slowly for hours was now on the southwestern doorstep of Escanaba. The sky to the west was an ominous shade of charcoal, broken by periodic bolts of lightning. We were in for a grand show.

I ordered a wine cooler from the waitress, Gizzy's daughter-in-law, and alternately watched the storm and surveyed the room. The place probably hadn't changed much since the mid-sixties, I mused. The hardwood floor was scuffed and faded to a dingy gray, walls filled with photographs of successful walleye tournaments from years past and shelves of various trophies. It drew a lot of middle-class golfers and fishermen and the occasional softball team looking for a place to tell stories but not necessarily get drunk.

I was halfway through my wine cooler by the time Charlie arrived at a quarter after five.

"Sorry I'm late," he said as he slid into the chair across from me. "I got called out on a B and E right after you phoned."

"Anything serious?" I asked. Breaking-and-enterings were nothing major in the big city, but in a town like Escanaba, where many people still didn't lock their doors, they could put people on edge.

"Nah, a couple came home from vacation and found the garage broken into, but whoever did it couldn't gain access to the house. They sure tried to pry the hell out of the door, though," he said, shaking his head.

"Any leads?" I asked.

"I've got a few ideas. One of our usual suspects got out of prison about two months ago after doing three years for a string of break-ins similar to this. He came right back here and has yet to do anything productive with his life," Charlie said.

The waitress came and took his order for beer and a burger and mine for a chicken sandwich. I used the opportunity to study him for a moment. His waves of sandy brown hair were short and recently trimmed, as was his thick mustache. Khaki shorts and a white t-shirt with a Detroit Tigers logo showed off his deep tan. He was wearing glasses, I noticed—odd because he usually wore contact lenses. ("I look like a geek with those damn glasses," I remembered him saying before I left for Chicago.) He doesn't look like a "geek" at all, I thought. He actually was rather handsome in a rugged sort of way. I wondered why he had never married.

"What?" he said and looked down when he caught me staring. "Is there something wrong? Is my fly open?"

I laughed. "No, my mind was wandering. How come you never married? How old are you now, 35?" I asked.

He looked stunned, then said, "Where did that come from?"

"Just curious."

"Yeah, I'm 35, and I don't know why I never married. I guess I just never found the right person. I have nothing against marriage. I don't know, I just—well, I don't know. Do we have to discuss this now? I thought you wanted to talk about Frank Thompson?"

I laughed at the way he dodged the question. We were more alike than I had realized. I had always dodged questions about my personal life, too, even before Mitch. Now I had a reason—the questions were just too painful.

I suddenly realized that Charlie was talking to me. "I'm sorry, what were you saying?"

He shook his head and smiled. "You haven't changed much since you left town. You always did have a tendency to drift off to that never-never land of yours when people are trying to talk to you. How in the hell did you get through all those lectures in college and still graduate with high honors?" he said.

"Natural intelligence, of course. I already knew everything," I said, tilting my chin and throwing back my shoulders.

"Oh, of course. Sorry! I forgot I was in the presence of a genius," he said and bowed in his seat.

After the waitress brought his bottle of beer and a glass that he promptly dismissed to the side of the table, his face grew serious. "I saw Sarah Lindstrom this morning. She can't remember anything about the crash or what led up to it, just like the doctor said."

"What about Brett? You said on the phone he confirmed that it was Greg who took his truck."

"Yeah, I guess his lawyer talked to him after we left the jail last night. Watson didn't want his client to say anything to us before he knew what the hell was going on," he said and took a swig from the brown bottle clasped in his right hand. "But I'll tell you something, Robin. I'm not convinced he's telling the whole truth."

"Why is that?" I asked.

"I can't understand why he would hold out so long before telling us that it was Connor who had his truck at the time of Thompson's death. So he was threatened? Lots of people receive threats. Hell, I've been threatened more times than I can count. I know they're generally just bullshit said in anger. That's not enough for me." He shook his head. "Anyway, we're just assuming that would be the case. We have no proof that Connor was behind the wheel. Who knows, maybe Greg passed the truck along to someone else."

He set about devouring the towering burger and mound of French fries the waitress placed before him. A flash went off in my head as another piece of the puzzle fell into place.

"You're right! That's it! That explains why he didn't say anything to begin with," I nearly shouted in my excitement.

"What do you mean?" Charlie asked through a mouthful of his sandwich.

"Maybe Brett's known all along who was behind that threatening phone call. What else would make him frightened enough to risk jail? Maybe he knows the person making the threat was capable of carrying it out. The question is, who and why, and can we get Brett to tell us?" I said.

"That's three questions. Besides, why not Greg Connor? He could be behind the threat. If he did run down Thompson, what would stop him from going after Sarah? That kid's got a violent streak he inherited from his ol' man. Hell, we had to arrest that asshole earlier this afternoon after we caught him in the process of beating the crap out of his wife again," Charlie said.

"I know," I answered quietly. I said a little thank-you to God that the creep was behind bars at least for a few days. It was ironic that the elder Connor was sharing a roof with the same young man his son had possibly framed for murder.

"But what about a motive? Why would Connor want to kill Frank Thompson? I can't imagine how they would even know each other," I said.

Charlie took a drink, then gestured with the bottle. "I'm telling you, Robin, we find Greg Connor and this whole mess is solved," he said.

"I don't know. Something's wrong with that. If he's still in the area, why hasn't anyone seen him? The description of the truck has been on the radio and television and in the paper for days. Don't you think someone would have spotted it by now? Even if he dumped it somewhere, how did he get a new set of wheels without anyone knowing? According to his family and some of the people he worked with, he's disappeared into thin air. The only one he told he was leaving was the manager at the sawmill, Jack Kirksen, and then he was just shooting off his mouth," I said. "No, there's got to be someone else involved."

"Damn! This started out as a simple hit-and-run. Now it's beginning to look like friggin' Watergate," Charlie exclaimed and sat back in his chair.

I debated telling Charlie about the scene I witnessed between Chief Joe Nelson and the Widow Thompson. After all, it really wasn't anyone's business what they did in their back yards. But in light of the ever-mounting complications in this case, I decided he should know what the lovely wife of the late accountant was up to before her dear-departed husband was cold in the ground.

"I saw something last night that may be important, something that wasn't intended for my eyes, something that involves the chief," I said.

"Nelson?" Charlie asked with a puzzled expression.

"Yes," I said and took a breath. "After watching the fireworks display in the park, Belle—that's my dog—wanted to go for a walk. I let her lead the way, and she headed south along the beach that runs behind Lake Shore—"

"That's private property," Charlie interjected.

"I know that. Just listen. We came upon a couple in one of the back yards. They seemed to be enjoying a private moment, laughing, talking. Then I saw who they were—the chief and Victoria Thompson. Next thing I knew they were wrapped around each other tighter than two turtles sharing one shell," I said.

"Nelson and Frank's wife? Are you sure?" he asked.

"Yes. They were in Thompson's back yard. Doesn't Nelson live next door on the south side?" I said.

"Humph, yeah. Well, Nelson's always had a wandering eye. It makes sense that it would eventually gaze lustfully upon his neighbor's luscious wife," Charlie said, then paused for a moment, his eyes narrowing. "Now wait a minute! I see what you're getting at. Don't go reading anything into this. They're two consenting adults who can do whatever the hell they want. It may not be moral, but it doesn't mean either one of them murdered Frank."

"I know that. I just thought you—." I was interrupted again, this time by the bleating of Charlie's cell phone. He pulled it off his waistband and looked at the display.

"It's the station," he said and pressed a button and put it up to his ear. A clap of thunder and the sudden rush of torrential rain drowned out the conversation. After a minute or two, he pressed the power button to disconnect the call and slowly folded the phone and hooked it back on his belt. He sat back heavily in his chair and looked at me with bewilderment.

"Well, that's that. Brett's pickup was just fished out of Lake Antoine by the Dickinson County Sheriff's office. Greg Connor's body was in the cab."

Chapter Twenty

THE RAIN FELL IN SHEETS and thunder crashed overhead as we dashed across the parking lot to our trucks. The roadway was almost invisible in the downpour. I followed Charlie's late seventies-model Ford stepside pickup, staying within sight of his taillights all the way to the Dickinson County Sheriff's Department in Iron Mountain, about an hour away from Escanaba. Iron Mountain, a tough town of about six thousand people, is situated a few miles from a lovely little body of water named Lake Antoine. The two-lane highway leading there was packed with holiday travelers, many of them towing campers behind mammoth sport utility vehicles, and the heavy traffic and fierce storm forced me to focus all my attention on driving—a good thing since my mind felt like it was about to twist inside my skull.

I had covered enough homicide investigations to know that anything was possible when it came to murder. Finding Greg Connor dead behind the wheel of the murder weapon, however, was the last thing I had expected. Could he have committed suicide by simply driving the truck into the lake? Something in my gut said no. It didn't fit Greg's profile. He was too much of a go-getter to kill himself. We were now investigating two murders.

The rain let up just east of the Iron Mountain city limit sign and quit altogether by the time we reached the sheriff's department. A twenty-year-old Chevy pickup was sitting on a flatbed trailer in the parking lot behind the jail when we arrived. I had no idea what condition the truck had been in before striking Frank Thompson dead, but it sure was a mess now. Strings of weeds clung to the door handles, side mirrors and undercarriage like rotting Christmas decorations. Colors

119

were indistinguishable. The left headlight assembly was smashed, as was the windshield. Encased in a layer of greenish-brown mud, the vehicle stank of decay.

Charlie introduced me to Sheriff Ted Webster, who shook my hand and eyed me curiously.

"Who found the truck?" Charlie asked the sheriff, who was dressed in khaki shorts similar to Charlie's, topped by a stained light yellow golf shirt. The sheriff's eyes appeared bloodshot underneath his baseball cap with the department's logo.

"An angler's line caught something and broke. He thought it was one mean fish until it happened a second time in the same exact area. He trolled over to the spot and leaned over the side of the boat and saw what looked like a vehicle of some sort. He used his cell phone to call for help. That was about two o'clock our time," Webster said. Dickinson County was located in the Central Time Zone. "We barely got the damn thing out of the water before the storm hit."

Webster took off his baseball cap and wiped the sweat off his balding head then put the cap back in place. "The medical examiner, Dr. Kathy Klopeck, said it's been in there at least a week," he said, gesturing towards the dripping hunk of metal on the trailer. It reeked of the sour smell of the lake or Connor's decomposing body or both.

"The body was pretty bloated," Webster said, as if reading my mind. "I can't give you a positive ID that it is Greg Connor. That's what the license in his wallet said, though. From what I could tell from the picture on the license, it's probably him. This is the truck that was involved in that hit-and-run a week or so ago in your neck of the woods, isn't it?"

"Yeah," Charlie muttered thoughtfully. He stared at the pickup and combed his mustache with his right hand.

"Don't you have someone else in jail for that, the guy who owns it? We ran the plate through LEIN, and it came back to a Brett Lindholm," Webster said.

"Actually, it's Lindstrom. Yeah, he's in jail," Charlie growled.

"Guess you'll have to re-evaluate that one, eh?" Webster said with a laugh.

Charlie shot him a dangerous look, then said, "I've got a couple evidence techs coming from my department. The state police will probably be here soon, too, I imagine. I'd appreciate a report from your guys as soon as possible. I'll be in touch with Dr. Klopeck."

A white Chevy Tahoe with the Escanaba Public Safety logo on the side pulled in front of the trailer. Two officers hopped out and walked over to where we were standing.

"Hi, Charlie, can we get to work on it?" the older, thickset one wearing a t-shirt and jeans said, pointing at the sad-looking heap.

Charlie looked at the sheriff, who nodded.

The younger officer in uniform retrieved a large briefcase from the Tahoe and opened it on the bed of the trailer behind Lindstrom's wreck of a truck. The other officer began to snap photographs with an expensive-looking digital camera.

Charlie turned to me and said, "Call me in the morning and see if there's anything I can tell you. Right now you can print what the sheriff said—just not the part about how long it was in the water. That might be a key in solving this whole mess.

"I assume you shot some photographs of the scene. I'd really appreciate it if I could get copies as soon as possible," Charlie said to Webster.

Webster bristled a bit and adjusted his baseball cap.

"That's fine, Detective, but I may have my own murder investigation on my hands. If this Connor kid was killed in my county, it's my case," he said.

"Actually, it's the state police's case, and I understand that. Afternoon, Sheriff," Charlie said, then went to help the officers examine the truck for evidence. He was right. The state police were typically responsible for homicide cases outside the city limits in rural areas because they had more resources. It was a sore spot with sheriffs, and I could see Webster was not happy to be reminded of it.

He turned away without another word.

Charlie, the two public safety officers, a couple deputies and a newly-arrived state police lab technician went about their work, scouring for any trace of evidence that might remain. It was a necessary but probably futile effort. The water would have washed away any prints and probably any other useful evidence.

An eerie sense of foreboding swelled in the pit of my stomach. If that truck and its occupant had gone into the lake a week ago, who had tried to kill Sarah, and who was still threatening the Lindstroms? I had been hoping for a break in the case, but this complication only led to more questions and more dangerous possibilities.

As I walked back to the Jeep, the rain began to fall again.

I went to work at six the next morning, an hour earlier than usual, so I could get a head start on the story about the discovery of the pickup and Connor.

After I finished the framework of the story, I drove to the public safety department at seven to see if I could add any new details. When a dispatcher led me to his office, Charlie was waiting for me. His desk was cluttered with reports and photos of both of Thompson's and Connor's death scenes. He looked up as I entered the room and grunted, "Close the door."

"Good morning to you, too," I said as I shut the door.

"There's nothing good about this, Robin. I've got one hell of a mess on my hands," he said, rubbing his haggard face.

"Why? I would think this would tidy things up. Connor takes Lindstrom's truck, goes out and gets toasted, takes the long way home through the park and hits Thompson by accident. He realizes what he's done, is overcome by guilt, and in the delirium of his drunkenness decides to end it all and get rid of any incriminating evidence in the process," I said, smiling slyly.

"And the threatening phone calls? How do you explain those, Nancy Drew?" Charlie shot back.

"His father trying to protect the family name. The man's obviously capable of violence. Maybe Greg let on to his family what he had done," I said. I knew what I was saying was pure fiction. Greg Connor's father cared no more about "the family name" than I did about rap music.

"A brilliant theory but wrong, dead wrong. Connor didn't commit suicide. He was murdered," Charlie said.

"Really," I said sarcastically.

Charlie screwed up his face at me. "Okay, so you were right. Here, take the badge. Maybe you should be in this chair," he said, pulling a spare badge out of a drawer and tossing it across the desk.

"No, thanks. No need to get pissed at me, either. I didn't kill him," I said. "How was he murdered?"

"A blunt force blow to the back of the head. There's no way he could have gotten a blow like that if he had just driven into the water," he said as he combed his thick mustache with restless fingers.

"Any word pinpointing when it happened?" I asked.

Charlie indicated a few photographs showing graphic views of the young man's bloated body lying twisted in the cab of the truck. Water does revolting things to a body in a week's time.

"The medical examiner is finishing her report on the autopsy as we speak. I'm sure she'll stick with the original estimate of at least a week, though. Damn!" He slammed his right palm on top of the photos before leaning back in his creaky, battered chair.

"This case just got a lot bigger than you thought it would, didn't it," I said.

"I don't need you Monday morning quarterbacking my work. I don't—"

"Nobody's telling you how to do your job," I said, knowing what he was going to say. "Look, if we work together on this we'll get somewhere. I can talk to people who won't give you the time of day without a subpoena. You tell me what you know, I'll tell you what I know, and we'll see how far we get. I have a feeling we have to work fast. Whoever is behind this isn't afraid to eliminate people who could expose him or her."

Charlie's blue eyes narrowed.

"You better not be holding out on me, Hamilton. You're my friend, but you're still a reporter," Charlie said, eyebrows drawn together so tightly they almost formed a straight line across his forehead. I knew he was mad whenever he called me by my last name.

"Charlie, I have a personal stake in this. I owe Lindstrom's mother some peace of mind again. Let's face it, right now the safest place for Brett is in jail, but you can't keep him there much longer. You have no proof linking him to Thompson's death or even Connor's," I said. Then before I even realized what I was saying I added, "Unless, of course. Brett was driving the truck Friday, set up Connor, killed him and got back to Escanaba before you arrested him Saturday."

Charlie's eyebrows shot up and out as his eyes widened.

"I hadn't thought of that," he said, straightening in his chair. "Yes, that's entirely possible."

"Then again, his mother says he was in bed asleep when she got home from work Friday morning at about eight-thirty. Since Thompson was killed at about six, it would have been a tight squeeze for Brett to dump Connor and the truck and get home—unless he flew," I said.

"Not funny. Maybe his mother is lying," Charlie said.

"That's possible and could even be expected of a devoted mother, but there's another problem. Given Brett's IQ, I think it would be too much of a stretch to make a jury believe he had the ability to think fast enough to cover up a murder in two and a half hours. Besides, who ran Sarah off the road?"

"Yeah, we keep coming back to that, don't we?" Charlie sighed.

"There's something else to consider. I had a conversation with a close friend of Frank Thompson on Saturday. This person refused to go to the police out of fear of retribution. However, this person told me Frank had been acting strange for the last few weeks of his life, like he was afraid of someone or something. This person didn't know who or what, and Frank wouldn't discuss it. The first place I would look is his professional life, maybe a partner or a client," I said, remembering Mrs. Witherspoon's story from her son about discord between the partners.

Charlie nodded. "Yeah, I guess you're right. You can't tell me the name of this source, eh?" he asked.

"No, not right now. I'll work on it, though," I said.

"We have to play this out carefully, Robin. It seems the more questions you ask, the more people get hurt. Not that this is your fault. I don't mean it that way. But unfortunately, the killer has been tuned in to your investigation. Start asking too many questions of Thompson's partners, and we may end up with more dead bodies," Charlie said.

"Any suggestions?" I asked.

"Just keep me informed. And be careful. I've got to get to work on Dr. Klopeck and find out what else the autopsy turned up," he said.

"So what can I print?"

"Just the facts, no fancy speculation thinly veiled behind your expert prose. And don't put anything in about the cause or time of death for Connor. Just say the autopsy is being completed this morning, which is true," Charlie said.

"What about that mysterious message left on Hannah Lindstrom's answering machine?" I asked.

"Oh, yeah, then there's that!" Charlie groaned. "We made a tape of it and took it to the jail for Brett to hear. He says it's the same voice as before. He was pretty upset by it, too."

"Can I listen to it?" I asked hopefully.

Charlie thought for a moment, then shrugged. "What the hell, it can't hurt." He pulled an ancient tape recorder from his desk drawer and put in a cassette that had been lying under the pile of photographs.

The sound was muffled, due to the poor quality of the recording and the tape player, but it was still decipherable. A male voice crackled: "Your son didn't heed my warning. If you keep pushing, you'll be next." The message ended with the ominous sound of a dial tone. Charlie popped the tape out and put the recorder back in the drawer.

"Well, what do you think, Nancy Drew?" he said.

I scowled at him. "There's something familiar about that voice. I mean, it's obviously disguised, but I know I've heard it before. It—."

There was a knock, followed by a dispatcher opening the door and poking her head inside. "The reporter from Channel 3 is here," she said and smiled sympathetically when Charlie snarled.

"Maggots, nothin' but a bunch of goddamn maggots feeding on a dead carcass. Tell her I'll be out in a minute," he said, then turned to me and rubbed his temples. "We'll talk later. Damn! You people are giving me a migraine."

I chuckled and blew him a kiss as I left his office. I found my way to the lobby and passed Jessica Caldwell, the epitome of the ambitious blonde TV reporter extraordinaire. Dressed in a tailored purple suit, the skirt ending well above the knee, she tapped the toe of a delicate pump on the tiled floor as she waited.

"Good morning, Jessica. How are you?" I said in my most cheerful voice.

"Just fine, Robin. Big story, huh?" she responded just as cheerfully, revealing two rows of perfect straight white teeth. Probably capped, I thought.

We were like two finalists in a beauty pageant, but rather than vying for a crown, I wanted the truth, and she wanted a network job. Sooner or later, I was sure we would both get what we wanted.

Chapter Twenty-one

I CALLED GRANT STEWART'S office as soon as I returned to the newspaper. The same perky receptionist answered the phone and put me on hold while she cleared the call with the boss. After a few minutes of silence, she came back on the line and put me through.

"This is Grant Stewart. How may I help you, Miss Hamilton?" he asked, his deep voice throaty, almost sensual. A good radio voice, I thought.

"Mr. Stewart, have you heard the news about Greg Connor?" I asked.

"No, why? Is something wrong?" he asked.

"Yes, I'm afraid so. I'm sorry to be the one to tell you this. Greg was found dead yesterday afternoon," I said.

"Oh, my God, I can't believe it! Are you sure? What happened?" he asked, each word coming slowly and quietly, almost a whisper.

"I don't have all the details. I'm sure the police will be in touch with you sometime today. I can tell you he was found in the cab of Brett Lindstrom's pickup at the bottom of Lake Antoine," I said.

Silence stretched so long I began to think we had been disconnected.

"Mr. Stewart?"

"Yes, I'm still here. I can't believe this. What was Greg doing in Brett's truck?" he said.

"I don't know. The police are still investigating. I do know how you felt about Greg, though. I was wondering if you wanted to say something about him for an article in today's paper?" I asked, fingers posed above my keyboard, phone cradled in the crook of my neck.

He paused for a moment, then said, "Well, sure. What can I say? Greg was a good employee. He had dreams of improving himself. Any-

126

one can tell you he wasn't satisfied with just being a worker in a sawmill. I respected his ambition and tried to help him by showing him the business side of things," he said, then quietly added, "He had a difficult childhood and some tough breaks along the way but really seemed to be trying to turn his life around. This is just unbelievable."

"Thank you, that was very helpful, Mr. Stewart. Again, I'm very sorry," I said and hung up the phone. I wondered if he had ever had children. The emotion in his voice belied more than the average concern for an employee, more like that for a son.

I wrote what I hoped were two informative, interesting articles, one about the discovery of the truck and Greg Connor's body, including Stewart's reaction, and a second one with the details about Sarah's accident, excluding the threatening message left for her mother. Reading them over one last time before filing them in the system, I saw all the unanswered questions they raised. I wasn't the only one who saw that my stories were stories had more holes in them than Swiss cheese. After deadline, Bob Hunter called me into his office.

"What's the real scoop here? I know there's a hell of a lot more to all this than what you wrote," Hunter said as he hunched over his desk with hard copies of my stories in hand.

"Honestly, Bob, there's not much to tell except that Frank Thompson's death is looking more suspicious with each passing day." I blew my bangs out of my eyes, as frustrated as my boss.

"Well that's certainly an understatement!" Hunter bellowed. "Two dead bodies and now this deal with Lindstrom's sister and you're telling me it's 'suspicious.' Come on, Robin, you're holding out on me."

"It doesn't take a rocket scientist to figure out that Thompson was probably murdered," I replied tartly. "The most logical guess is that someone hired Greg Connor to do the job and implicate Lindstrom in the process, then covered it up by eliminating Connor. The problem is, that's all just speculation, and we can't print speculation. We'd have libel suits coming at us left and right, and you know it."

"Hmm" was all Hunter said for a while. We sat in silence, lost in our own thoughts. My head was throbbing, and I suddenly felt very tired as the events of the weekend caught up with me. I felt like my blood had taken on the consistency of toothpaste. I wanted to curl up in bed in a cool, dark room and not come out for a week. I was on the verge of falling asleep right there in my chair when Hunter finally spoke again.

"I'm assuming this accident involving—what's her name—Sarah is related to all this, too. The story you wrote said the passenger told police they were run off the road by another vehicle, possibly a truck," he said.

"Yes, Bob, it's all related," I said and rubbed my eyes. I related my talk with Brett Lindstrom at the jail and his tale of mysterious threats and the strange message Hannah received after the accident. When I finished, Hunter took off his glasses and set them gently on his desk, leaned back in his chair and studied a spot on the wall a few feet above my head. I could almost hear the gears turning in his mind.

"Okay. Who is behind this and why?" he asked.

"That's the question of the day. There are at least two possibilities that jump out at me at this point. One is Thompson's wife, who I believe was carrying on an affair. Maybe she was sick of Frank but didn't want to go through the hassle and expense of a divorce. I would bet he had a pretty good-sized estate, considering he was a successful accountant in private practice with no children to drain his bank accounts.

"The other possibility is one of his partners. Maybe one or both of them wanted him out of the picture for some reason," I said.

"Do you have any reason to believe either of those theories to be true?" he asked in a tone of, obvious skepticism.

"Only what could turn out to be coincidences. Let's face it, Bob, contract killings are few and far between in towns like this. The police are just now beginning to consider Thompson's death a homicide and only because Connor was obviously murdered." I felt more tired by the minute. "I have a city council meeting in Gladstone tonight so I have to shave some hours today. I'm going home to get some sleep. I'll keep asking questions and see what I come up with. I've got a good relationship with Detective Charlie Baker, so if anything happens, I'll hear about it. We won't get scooped on this one."

"All right, but keep me informed. This is the biggest story of the year so far, maybe even the decade," Hunter said.

I left his office and trudged back to my desk. As I was putting away some files, the publisher walked up to me looking amused.

"Strange turn of events, eh, Robin?" Sam Burns said, peering at me over the edge of his spectacles, which, as usual, were sliding halfway down his nose.

"Excuse me, Sir?" I responded, my mind too exhausted to leap into another long conversation.

"Them finding that young man's body in the truck supposedly driven by that other young man sitting in jail. Fascinating," he said. He sounded like Mr. Spock examining some strange new species on a distant planet.

"Yes, Sir," was all I could muster.

Burns leaned over my desk and whispered, "I have a reliable source who says the lovely Mrs. Thompson will soon receive the tidy sum of one million dollars from her late husband's life insurance. Fascinating, isn't it?" he said again and winked, then strolled back towards his office on the other side of the building with a smug smile on his face.

A Chicago homicide detective once told me, when investigating a murder, always to follow the money or the sex angle first. One or the other usually leads to the killer. Was it a case of both with Frank Thompson's murder?

I grabbed my purse, note pad and Gladstone City Council file and left the safety and comfort of the air-conditioned newsroom. It was noon and a sticky eighty-eight degrees outside, according to the thermometer attached to the north wall of the building. The heat made my headache worse. I was feeling downright crabby. I slammed the door of my Jeep and gunned the engine. The noise didn't help my head, but the act released a bit of tension.

When I got home, the apartment was steaming. I turned on both fans in my bedroom, put Belle on her chain in the back yard and placed a large bucket of cold water in a shady spot for her. For some reason she was agitated, her ears sagging, eyes alert, muscles taut.

I went back upstairs looking forward to a long nap, but when I passed the living room, the answering machine caught my eye. It showed I had one message. I pressed the button, figuring it was my dad inviting me dinner. It wasn't.

"I've been watching you, Robin. Perhaps you think you're Lois Lane. But I can assure you, no Superman is going to be able to help you if you don't back off. Frank Thompson is none of your business." Click.

Chapter Twenty-two

OW IN THE HELL DID he get my phone number? I'm unlisted!" I shrieked at Charlie as I paced back and forth across the hardwood floor in my living room. Charlie had been my first call after I heard the menacing message on my answering machine, and he came over immediately, a rookie officer with him.

Charlie was standing next to the vile device, notebook in hand, reviewing what he had heard. According to the machine's memory, the message had been left at nine that morning. I searched my own memory but couldn't put a face with the voice. Yet I could swear I had heard it before.

"I want to know how he got my number!" I shouted again when Charlie didn't answer.

"I don't know. It's not too hard these days," he said. "It sounds like the same guy who called Hannah."

"I figured that much," I sneered. In all my years as a reporter in Chicago, covering everything from the mob to politics (the two were often interchangeable), I had never received a death threat at home. A lot of letters and phone calls at work, but never at home. I felt violated.

"This is serious. You are off this case, understand?" Charlie shouted. "This guy may be responsible for killing two people and nearly killing two others. He means business, Robin!"

"I am not going to just sit here quietly while some creep runs roughshod over my life. Nobody chases me off a story, nobody!" I shouted back. A little fear was a great motivator. I was onto something, and I wasn't about to give up now.

"Are you nuts? You're not out to win a goddamn Pulitzer here! This is police business, and I'm telling you to let me do the dirty work. If I have to, I'll arrest you for obstructing a police investigation," he threatened, shaking a long finger at me.

"You do that, and see how far it gets once the paper's lawyers get wind of it," I retorted.

"Oh, Christ, Robin! I'm just trying to keep you out of trouble!" The rookie officer, standing near the door to the apartment, shifted uncomfortably. I turned away from Charlie and promptly tripped over a throw rug. "Shit!" I screamed and kicked the rug across the floor, then continued pacing.

Charlie had a point. The problem was that if Victoria's lover, the chief of police, was behind the threats and protecting her, the cops wouldn't get too far, either. I turned and stared defiantly at Charlie. He stared back.

"I can't keep you safe, you know," he said, switching tactics. "This isn't Chicago. This department doesn't have the resources to play bodyguard to a reporter who's got her panties in a bunch about something that isn't even her problem."

I continued staring, my face growing hot. He threw up his hands and walked to one of the windows looking out over the park and the lake beyond. The rookie shifted from one foot to the other again and studied a seascape painting over the sofa.

"Do you know how to defend yourself?" Charlie finally asked.

"Yes, I've had several self-defense classes, and I've had to use what I learned once or twice," I said, sticking my chin out like a five-year-old who doesn't want any help tying her shoelaces.

Charlie turned and looked at me skeptically. "You're pretty small, Kiddo. Do you have Mace or pepper spray?" he asked.

"I have a small can of pepper spray Mitch gave me a few months before. . .before he. . . ." I couldn't get it out. Suddenly I remembered the night he had presented me with the little black spray can and taught me how to use it. A serial rapist was on the loose in Chicago and usually struck at night, when I had to work. I had resisted, afraid I would end up spraying myself in the face, but Mitch had patiently taken me through the process several times until I felt comfortable. How ironic that while he had carried a gun and pepper spray on his belt and several other weapons in his patrol car, they were of no help to him the night he was murdered.

I felt myself on the verge of tears and tried in vain to hold them back. Charlie came over and wrapped his arms around me.

"I'm sorry. I'm so sorry," he said and gently rocked me back and forth as I clung to him and sobbed. Ashamed to let someone else see what a mess I really was, I pulled away at last and plucked a tissue from a box on the coffee table. The rookie cleared his throat. "Uh, Sir, I'm going to head out if there's nothing else you need," he said.

"Yeah, sure, go on," Charlie said and waved him out the door. Turning to me, he asked, "You all right?" I nodded.

As I wiped my eyes and blew my nose, Charlie unplugged the answering machine and wrapped the cord around it.

"I don't suppose you have a gun?" he asked.

"No, and I don't want one," I said.

"Well, carry the pepper spray and your cell phone at all times," he said. "I don't know what else to tell you. Ordering you to stay put obviously won't do any good. Just be careful, please."

He gave me a peck on the top of my head and left the apartment with the answering machine tucked under his arm.

I didn't bother to remind him that a gun or a cell phone wouldn't have done Frank Thompson any good at all.

After two hours in which I paced, ate and paced some more, I finally decided to take a drastic step. Criminals often draw their power and confidence from their anonymity. If Victoria Thompson were involved in her husband's and Connor's deaths, it was time to shrink her comfort level.

I double-checked her address in the phone book before bringing Belle back inside and locking the door, and I placed a small strip of paper high along the crack before shutting it behind me. It was an old trick but still worked. I would know if someone had been in the apartment in my absence.

The Thompson house was a sprawling, one-story, modern brick ranch-style structure with large windows all around. The three-car garage formed the short part of the building's wide L. The asphalt driveway, recently resealed, was empty. All three garage doors were closed, so I couldn't tell if her car was there. My watch showed two-thirty. I knew Victoria didn't work, and it wasn't Ladies Day at the country club, so I made a bet she was home.

I got out of the Jeep, inhaled some lake-fresh air and climbed the two wide brick steps leading to a large oak door with an ornate gold knocker. I rang the doorbell and waited. Quick, light footsteps approached the door, which opened to reveal Victoria Thompson, looking as though she had just stepped off the set of an afternoon soap opera, neatly coiffed and dressed for an afternoon with the ladies at the club.

"Yes, may I help you?" she inquired in a slightly husky voice.

"Yes, Mrs. Thompson, my name is Robin Hamilton. I'm a reporter with the Daily Press. I'm sorry to bother you; I know this is a difficult time. I wonder if you could spare me a few minutes?" I silently reminded myself to hold judgment until I had all the facts.

Victoria didn't seem the least bit upset by my intrusion. To my bewilderment, the widow appeared glad to see me.

"Oh yes, I know who you are, you've been writing the stories about my... my husband's, uh, death. Please come in," she said, gesturing with a finely manicured hand towards the interior of her spacious home.

The front entry opened directly into the large sunken living room. Beyond the airy white room, looking out toward the lake, was the dining area with a cherry table large enough to feed a Little League team. Victoria led me to a cream-colored leather sectional sofa and offered me a drink. I politely declined. I felt like a fly hopelessly stuck on the black widow spider's web, waiting to be devoured. The spider sat a few feet away on the left wing of the sectional and swept her hair back with both hands before turning that cover girl smile on me.

"I want to thank you for the way you've handled all this. The media has a nasty tendency sometimes to twist things around," she said.

"I don't quite understand what you mean, Mrs. Thompson. What's there to twist?" I asked.

She sighed and fiddled with a diamond tennis bracelet on her delicate wrist, then sank back into the sofa.

"The first few articles you wrote, sort of summing up his life if you will, were written very tastefully," she said.

"Is there any reason they might not have been?" I asked, wondering where she was going with this.

She shot me a startled look.

"Uh, well, no. It's just that these things are often sensationalized when there's nothing sensational about them," she said, studying her long French nails.

"Mrs. Thompson, the articles I wrote were not done with the intent of sparing anyone any embarrassment, if that's what you're getting at."

"I—."

"Wait a minute, let me finish. They were written based on the truth as I knew it to be then. Things have changed, though, Mrs. Thompson.

I'm going to be very honest with you. I believe your husband was murdered, and whoever is behind it also murdered the young man who may have killed your husband." The widow did not look at all surprised by my candor.

"Yes, the police told me something to that effect this morning," she said. She rose from her seat and walked around the room, stopping at the wall of windows beyond the dining room table and staring at the lake for several seconds before saying matter-of-factly, "I don't understand why anyone would want to murder my husband."

"So you have no idea who may have wanted your husband dead, none at all?" I asked.

She whirled around, eyes blazing. "I don't like your tone, Ms. Hamilton," she said.

"I'm sorry if I've offended you. I get angry when people are threatening my life," I said, standing.

She looked bewildered.

"I. . .I don't understand. Why would someone threaten you? Did you even know my husband?" she asked.

"Only on a distant professional level. I doubt he could have put a name with my face. As for why me, I've been doing my own investigation into his death, aside from the police, as a favor to an old friend. I must be on the right track because I've ruffled some big bird's feathers, and it's squawking nasty messages on my answering machine," I said, my voice rising a bit. Breathe, I told myself, just breathe. My tone was more subtle when I added, "I came here to find out what you know."

Victoria came back down to the living room and sat in a matching chair across from me. Now I got up and walked around the room, casually studying the surroundings. I spied the telephone on a small occasional table in the corner near the dining room, walked a little closer and saw the last number dialing in belonged to none other than Joe Nelson.

"How do you and your neighbor over there, Chief Nelson, get along?" I asked.

Victoria shot me a startled look, then massaged the palm of her left hand for a moment as she fixed her eyes on the white brick fireplace that took up most of the south wall.

"We're. . .well. . .uh, we're friends. He's been very supportive throughout this whole ordeal," she said. Then she turned her gaze on me for a moment. A look of horror crawled across her face.

"You think I had something to do with Frank's death and that. . . that other man, what's his name? No! I didn't! You're wrong!" she shouted, frantically rubbing her hand now.

"Look, I'll admit Frank and I were not exactly happy, but I certainly didn't have him murdered," Victoria said, the last coming out as a whine.

"Then who did? Your friendly neighbor next door?" I prodded.

The widow grasped both arms of the chair and dug in her nails, like a cat extending her claws. Her dark eyebrows arched like inverted V's above her blazing eyes. She glared at me for several seconds, then relaxed.

"So you do know about that. You are good. Are you really a reporter or a private detective in disguise?" she sneered.

I laughed. Look out, Sherlock Holmes! Here comes Robin Hamilton!

"No, Ma'am, I'm not a detective. I've just been around the block a few times," I said. I thought Victoria would have been disappointed to know it was a wayward basset hound, not my nose for news, that had sniffed her out.

"Well, it wasn't Joe. He was as shocked as I was when my husband was—when he died. While we were no longer enjoying wedded bliss, he was still my husband, and I loved him," she said and curled her long legs underneath her.

I didn't respond, just sat examining her every twitch, like a scientist studying the mutation of a deadly bacterium. She began to fidget, twisting a tendril of auburn hair around a finger, then massaging her neck.

"You don't believe me. There's nothing I can do about what happened to him, and I have no desire to sit here and discuss my family's dirty laundry with a reporter. Besides, I'm already late to meet some friends for golf at the country club. I will say one thing, though, something I haven't even told the police," she said, straightening in her chair and placing both sandal-clad feet flat on the floor. "My husband made more than a few enemies in his career. I have no doubt he finally pushed one of them too far. In the last month or so he began to act nervous, agitated. He wouldn't discuss anything with me. Then he started receiving phone calls at odd hours, phone calls that would make him upset. I have no idea who was at the other end or what the calls were about. My husband kept his business life away from me.

"At one point, about two weeks before he died, he gave me this bracelet." She held up her right arm and jangled the jeweled gold chain. I recalled the trip Mitch and I had made to the jewelry store to search for wedding bands and the ten thousand dollar tennis bracelet I had ogled. This was its twin.

"He talked about selling his share of the firm and just leaving town. It was crazy. I didn't understand any of it," she said and shook her pretty head.

Her story of Frank's behavior matched what Mike Callahan had told me earlier. It still didn't tell me the who or why. I knew I wasn't going to get any more information from Victoria, though, so I stood and prepared to leave.

"Thank you for telling me that, Mrs. Thompson. I'm sorry to have taken up so much of your time," I said and extended a hand when we reached the front door. She shook it gingerly.

"I'm sorry, too, sorry that whatever my husband was involved in has now caused harm to others. I wish I could be of more help to you," she said, the brilliant smile, now tempered with concern, returning to her face.

"But you can be of help. You need to tell the police about Frank's odd behavior and those phone calls. I think it could be important to the case," I implored.

"I'll think about it," she said. "Good luck."

As I got into my Jeep, it suddenly occurred to me that Victoria rarely referred to her husband by his name, as though he hadn't been real, just a painting on a wall she admired, dusted and straightened from time to time.

Chapter Twenty-three

NCE HOME FROM MY visit with the Widow Thompson and shopping, I unloaded the groceries, then took Belle for a two-mile hike around the park at the fastest pace her stubby little legs could manage. The exercise made me ready for a nap by the time we arrived back at the apartment.

My answering machine was sitting on the floor just inside the downstairs entryway, with a note attached from Charlie saying he was able to make a clear tape of the message and that it was now erased. I went upstairs and plugged the machine in again reluctantly, then lay down on the couch. An hour later, the sound of children laughing in the park woke me from a dreamless sleep.

For dinner, I threw together a large green salad of vegetables freshly harvested by Mrs. Easton and plopped in front of the television to eat. The six o'clock news led off with the discovery of Greg Connor's body inside Lindstrom's pickup. The video consisted of old footage of the accident reconstruction team working at the scene of Thompson's death and reporter Jessica Caldwell standing in front of the public safety building. She had nothing to add to my knowledge and even flip-flopped the ages of Lindstrom and Connor. I snorted in disgust and thought to myself for the thousandth time that television reporters got all the glory but rarely bothered to get the facts straight. We see them as attractive talking heads while they see us as a pack of snobs.

After the weather report (turning unseasonably cool over the next few days with scattered rain), I clicked off the set and took my dishes to the kitchen, where I washed, dried and put them away. It was time to head to Gladstone for the city council meeting. After washing my face, combing my hair and brushing my teeth, I surveyed myself in the mirror.

I looked tired, older than my age. I felt about fifty. I sighed and flipped off the light in the bathroom.

I pulled my khaki trench coat out of the living room closet and grabbed my purse. Belle was sitting lopsided in front of the door, whining softly, which was odd because she was usually good about being left alone. I set the coat and purse down and took her for a quick walk around the block, thinking she had to relieve herself. She did, and we went back inside where she repositioned herself in front of the door and let out the same whine.

"I don't have time for this, Belle. What's wrong?" I said as I picked up my trench coat and purse again. My imploring tone had no impact on her. She continued to sit and stare up at me with mournful eyes.

I finally gave her hind end a nudge with my foot and opened the door enough to get through and shut it securely, replacing the piece of paper I had used earlier in the doorjamb. I heard a long, low howl that gradually grew in pitch as I descended the stairs

Clouds were piling up off to the west as I drove along the four-lane highway bordering the bay. The water was deep blue with small white-caps forming as the wind gusted. Yet another big summer storm was bearing down on us. I only hoped it would hold off until I was home.

Gladstone's city hall was a two-story brick building constructed in the 1920s. It housed all the city departments with the exception of the electric, water and sewer plants, and public safety department, which were located at different points along the lakeshore. Clint Masterson, one of the older commissioners, was negotiating the steps with care. A silver-haired gentleman in every sense of the word, he owned the only independent hardware store in the county and had somehow managed not only to survive but to thrive after a mammoth national chain built a store in Escanaba a decade before. Once people met him, it wasn't hard to understand why he was so successful. His jovial personality and commitment to customer service bred loyalty in the community. Whatever you needed, he had a way to get it if he didn't already have it.

Masterson turned and stopped when he heard my footsteps behind him. "Why hello, Robin. Been seein' a lot of your name in the paper with all those stories about Frank Thompson. He was my accountant, you know. Great guy. I'd known him for years but didn't put his services to use until about five years ago. I used to do my own books, but I don't dare now. All those tax laws are a bugger to understand, and they change 'em every year," Masterson said, shaking his head. "Shame, damn shame.

What's happening with our young people? I just can't understand how someone could run a person down in the street and leave him for dead, do you?"

"No, Mr. Masterson, I don't, either. I'm sorry for your loss. I've heard many good things about Mr. Thompson," I said. "Did you see much of Frank just before he died?"

"Funny you should ask that. Actually, I didn't. In fact, his partner, Al Klegle, is the one who balanced the books the last month. He said Frank was too busy with other clients. I called Frank a few times to find out what was going on, you know. He just said he was under a lot of pressure and felt he was spread too thin. It was strange. That was so unlike him, you know," he said.

"What was Frank like?" I asked.

"Oh, smart! Could add columns of five-figure numbers in his head and get the right answer every time. Charming, too, should have gone into sales. Why, I bet he could have sold a side of beef to a vegetarian," Masterson said with a chuckle.

He glanced at his watch and said, "We better get in there before they start the meeting without us. It's almost seven-thirty."

Masterson greeted the other four commissioners and the city manager before settling into his place on the raised platform. About a half-dozen citizens and a few department heads filled the thirty padded folding chairs set up for the meeting. I took a seat in the last chair on the right of the last row. The public safety director sat in the row in front of me and turned around.

"Hey, Robin, what's all this about them finding the pickup truck with another body in it?" Bob Lincoln whispered and pushed his glasses up higher on his small, straight nose. He was wearing his uniform, one of the few local chiefs who did.

"The guy in the truck was a friend of the kid in jail. This thing is getting messier by the minute," I whispered back.

"No kidding. This is the most excitement we've had around here in years," he said. I grinned. Small town cops like their peace and quiet, but even they get hungry for a nice juicy homicide once in a while. It's something to tell their grandchildren about in their old age.

The agenda was short, with only a proposed low- to middle-income apartment complex being a possibly contentious issue. Everyone agreed there was a need for affordable rental housing, but no one wanted it in their neighborhood. After more than an hour of discussion, with vocal opposition from a few citizens, the council voted to appoint council-woman Jane Meade to study the issue further.

It was past nine o'clock when I made it out to my Jeep. The clouds had blanketed the town in premature darkness, and thick raindrops were beginning to fall as I pulled onto the highway. There was almost no traffic, not unusual for a Monday night. The downpour started within a minute. Rain flowed over the windshield like a waterfall, the wipers having little effect. I crept along at forty-five miles an hour, trying to peer between slaps of the wipers and judge where the white lines on the blacktop were, praying I was between them, my fingers on the steering wheel white with tension.

I was concentrating so hard on the road ahead that I didn't see the vehicle creeping up behind me until the interior of the Jeep was flooded with white blinding light from halogen high beams riding my rear bumper. I blinked and lost sight of the road. I felt a nudge and heard a thump. My body jerked as I hit the brake pedal and tried to straighten the wheels, but they slipped mercilessly on the wet road. The Jeep lurched to the right into the dirt and started to tip. I screamed and covered my head with my arms as the truck headed toward a stand of birch trees.

When the Jeep finally stopped, I found myself still in the ditch, the Jeep still upright but just barely. Shaking, I looked up the highway but saw no sign of the monstrous vehicle or the driver who had tried to kill me. I dug my cell phone from my purse, dropped it, then frantically scrabbled around the floor of the Jeep for a minute until my right hand found it under the passenger seat.

Before moving back to Escanaba I had never had reason to dial nine-one-one. Now I was doing it for third time in two weeks. So much for small town tranquility.

Chapter Twenty-four

AFTER ABOUT FIVE MINUTES, I saw the flash of a red strobe light as a state trooper pulled up behind me. It was still pouring rain, and I saw him don a large fluorescent orange raincoat before he cautiously approached my vehicle with a long flashlight in his left hand and his right hand positioned near his gun. He flashed the light around the black interior of the Jeep after nearly blinding me with its intense glare.

"Ma'am, are you all right?" he yelled as he rapped on the driver's side window. I rolled it down, letting the cold rain drench my arm and face.

"Yes, I'm okay," I answered, shaking. "But someone just ran me off the road a few minutes ago."

I had little information to give the young trooper, but I knew the routine. He was going to ask me a bunch of questions to which I had weak answers. He might even put me through some sobriety tests.

"What happened?" he asked as rain flowed off the back of his plastic-covered cap.

"Did you see what kind of vehicle it was or who was driving?" he asked.

"No, it happened too fast. All I know is, it was big, like a large sport utility vehicle, and dark in color, maybe blue or black. I have no idea who was driving or how many people were in the vehicle." I squinted into his flashlight. "Could you shine that light in another direction, please?"

"Sorry. What's your name?" the trooper asked, moving the flashlight so the beam hit the dashboard.

"Robin Hamilton. I'm a reporter with the Daily Press. I was coming back from a city commission meeting in Gladstone when this happened," I explained. The rain was beginning to let up a little, but my seat was drenched and so was I. The trooper didn't seem to mind at all.

"I recognize the name. You've been writing the articles about that hit-and-run in the park in Escanaba, right?" he asked.

Gee, I'm famous, I thought.

"Yes, Trooper—" I tried to find a name on his rain slicker.

"Trooper Winters, Ma'am," he said, shifting from one foot to the other and hunching his shoulders.

"Trooper Winters, whoever was driving that vehicle ran me off the road intentionally. It was no accident. A similar incident occurred this past weekend, only it was two teenage girls who were almost killed," I said.

Trooper Winters looked skeptical.

"Listen, call Detective Charlie Baker with the Escanaba Public Safety Department. I know I will," I said, feeling my lower jaw starting to jut out. I pulled it back in and sighed. There was no need to pout.

"Okay, Ma'am, I'll check. May I see your license, registration and proof of insurance? It's for the police report," he said.

I fished around in the glove box for the documents, praying I had put the most recent insurance slip in the Jeep. I found it and breathed a sigh of relief. The expiration date wasn't for another three months. I pulled my license from my wallet and handed everything to the trooper, who took it all back to his patrol car where he remained for several minutes before returning the bundle to me along with a slightly soggy business card. Trooper Harlan Winters, it said. He looked too young to have a name like Harlan.

"I'll be in touch with you, Ms. Hamilton. Are you going to be able to get this thing out of the ditch, or should I radio for a tow truck?" he asked, waving a hand over the Jeep.

"Yeah, I think I can get it out. Thanks anyway," I said and started to roll up the window.

"Well, okay. Have a safe trip home," he said and tapped the door. The rain began to fall hard again. I called out a "thank you" but doubted he heard me over the din of the downpour and traffic splashing past. I started the Jeep, shifted it into four-wheel drive and, after a little maneuvering, managed to get it back on the pavement. The trooper followed me all the way to the Daily Press parking lot. As I unlocked the back door, I turned and waved to him. He flipped his headlights once in response and drove away. I was sorry to see him go.

⁓❦⁓

It took an hour to put together a story about the meeting. I read the piece over a few times for clarity and, when satisfied it made sense, filed it in the system and shut down the computer. I dragged on my trench coat, dreading going out to the dark parking lot. Pulling the little can of pepper spray out of my purse, I eased open the back door and surveyed the lot.

Although fog had rolled in off the lake, the rain had stopped and left the blacktop glistening under the two tall overhead lights. The parking lot was empty except for my Jeep and a few cars I recognized as belonging to tenants of upstairs apartments on the block. I closed the door behind me softly, feeling like I was trapped in a low-budget horror movie and that when I got into my truck, the killer would jump up from the back seat and slash my throat with a jagged-edge knife. I scampered across the lot, pepper spray clutched tightly in one hand, keys in the other. The keys clattered, the sound echoing through the deserted night. I unlocked the door and jumped in, locking the doors as soon as I was inside, then shot a frantic look at the back seat. That's when I saw it.

I screamed and started to jump out of the truck, then threw another glance over my shoulder. Slumped in the rear seat was a large, formless shape. Tentatively, I reached out and touched it. The shape felt soft at first, but as I pressed it took on a hard, boxy form. I let out a deep breath. I had never taken the cooler out after the Fourth of July. My dad's golf jacket was tossed over it. I gave it a shove and growled.

The short drive home gave me just enough time to imagine all sorts of hair-raising possibilities waiting for me at my apartment, but all I found was a garage empty save for Mrs. Easton's Buick— empty yard—empty apartment except for Belle wagging her tail so hard she was about to fall over. I knelt down and scratched behind her large, drooping ears, remembering her reluctance to let me leave earlier. I placed a hand on each side of her face and grabbed her soft ears gently. I looked into her eyes and asked, "Did you know something bad was going to happen? Hmm? You got some kind of sixth sense or something?" Belle grunted and wriggled free of my grip. She gave my nose a swipe with her long, pink tongue and waddled off to the rug in the living room and plunked down, casting an eye towards the answering machine.

A cold finger of fear caressed the back of my neck. The machine showed two messages. My heart pounding in my ears, I pressed the "play" button.

"Hi, Sweetie, it's Dad. Just wondering how your day went. I heard about that Connor kid and Sarah Lindstrom. Hannah must be beside herself. I'll talk to you later. Be careful. I love you. Bye." Beep. A mechanical voice informed me that the message was delivered Monday at 8:25 p.m. Then message two played.

"I warned you to stay away. The next time, you're dead." Click. Dial tone. "Message two delivered Monday at 9:52 p.m. End of messages."

I wondered if it would also be the end of me.

After a night of less than three hours of sleep, I finally gave up, showered, dressed and ate breakfast, even though my stomach was in a knot. The clock on the kitchen wall said five-fifteen. Normally, dawn would light up the eastern windows, but billowing, dark clouds crushed any hope of sunshine this morning. The gray sky matched my mood. I felt as if my once-comfortable apartment had been turned into an isolation chamber—no way for me to get out and no way for someone to reach me. I knew all I had to do was pick up the phone, but who would I call? I didn't want to worry my dad. Charlie would have to be told, and he would be angry, especially once he found out I had paid Victoria Thompson a visit the day before.

Thinking of her led me to wonder if the killer knew about my interview with the grieving widow. I was obviously being watched.

By five-thirty it was light enough outside to take Belle for a short walk. The air was chilly, the wind breaching my light jacket. I stuck to the sidewalk, avoiding the park. My heart thudded in my chest with each paranoid beat. At the sound of a car I would turn and search frantically for its direction, ready to run for my life. But each one passed without so much as a glance, oblivious to the tired-looking woman and her chubby little dog out for a morning stroll.

Back inside the apartment, I gave Belle food and fresh water and then sat in the easy chair by the window with a hot cup of tea. I hated feeling this twisted mix of sadness, anger and fear. I had to make a choice—continue with the investigation or let it drop and get away for a week or two. When faced with a tough decision, my father always told me to do what was best for me, but that advice felt hollow now. Dropping the investigation meant whoever was behind these murders might get away, leaving an innocent young man to go to prison. I wanted to curl up in a ball somewhere and cry until I ran out of tears, sleep until the weariness left my bone, and, finally, laugh until my sides hurt. I couldn't remember the last time I had really laughed out loud. But my mind wouldn't let my body rest until this case was solved. A sense of urgency welled up inside me, and I knew who it was I had to call.

I dialed Bob Hunter's office and left a message on his voice mail saying I was taking the one personal leave day allotted to me. I didn't explain why. Next, I called Charlie at home. He wasn't happy that I caught him just as he was coming out of the shower and even less happy when I relayed the events of the night before, including the most recent sinister message left on my answering machine.

"Why the hell didn't you call me last night?" he yelled through the receiver.

"Trooper Winters said he would call you. Besides, what difference would it have made? I have no vehicle description, other than it was a big, dark thing that rides even higher than my Jeep. The voice on the answering machine is the same one as before. The only thing I learned from all this is that someone is definitely watching me, and whoever it is doesn't like what he or she sees," I said.

"She? Victoria Thompson? Robin, in case you're not up on the gender of voices, that message I heard was undoubtedly left by a man. I've heard Victoria talk, and she doesn't sound anything like a man," Charlie said. The sarcasm in his voice grated on my frayed nerves.

"Don't get snotty. I know it's a man. But who's to say someone's not behind the scenes playing the strings?" I asked.

"It's possible, but I'm still having trouble understanding what Greg Connor has to do with all of this. My mind is not able to stretch from Brett Lindstrom to Victoria Thompson with a bridge based on solid logic," Charlie said. "You, on the other hand, seem to be good at jumping to all sorts of conclusions. So, what are you going to do now, Nancy Drew? Or do I even want to know?"

"Stop calling me that, and no, you probably don't want to know," I said, then added, "Now, let me ask you a question. Have you found anything that would point you towards the killer?"

Silence.

"Well?" I drawled.

"No, not yet, but I will," he said curtly. I had wounded his pride.

"I don't mean to insult you. I know you're doing everything you can. But there are some questions I can ask and get honest answers to that you can't. Just give me a couple of days, maybe less. I may be onto something, but I need to talk to a few more people," I said.

"Why can't you tell me and let me talk to them?" he asked. He sounded almost like a child pleading to stay up an extra hour to watch his favorite TV show.

"Because, quite frankly, I don't think they'd utter a word to you," I said.

"Why not? I'm a cop. That's usually enough to get most people to open up like a flower in the morning sun," Charlie said.

"How poetic," I snorted. "Charlie, these people are scared to death. I think they know that talking to the cops could get them killed. Even talking to me might be a liability at this point. But I think I've got at least another day to use my trump card as an ace reporter. Look, I know you don't like interference in police business—no cop does—but just trust me. I really think I'm close."

"Close to what? You get too close to the driver of that truck, and I'll be talking to you through six feet of ground," he said.

After I hung up, I found the home phone number for Douglas Jordan, the third partner at Thompson, Klegle and Jordan, CPAs. It wasn't even six-thirty yet, but Jordan answered on the second ring with a chipper "Hello."

I started to explain why I called when he stopped me.

"I've been wondering when you'd get around to talking to me. I'd love to tell you all about life at Thompson, Klegle and Jordan. Can you meet me at my office at seven?" he asked.

"Sure, that sounds fine," I said, caught off guard.

"Good. Park in the side street lot and come to the back door. I'll be waiting," he said.

Chapter Twenty-five

STILL FEELING THE EFFECTS of the sleepless night before, I walked the seven blocks to the accounting office in hopes that the exercise would enliven me. Overcast skies threatened rain at any minute, and a brisk northerly wind sent a chill through my lightweight trench coat. I stuck to the alleys, a path which drew a few suspicious glances from residents leaving for work, but I simply flashed a fake smile and called a "Good morning" to ease their fears. No, I'm not a serial killer, lurking in the backyard, waiting to abduct your children and drag them off to my lair in the woods, I felt like saying.

I looked over my shoulder a few times but found no one following me, at least no one I could see. When I arrived at Jordan's office, I walked around to the rear entrance and knocked on the back door. The only vehicle in the small lot was a jade-colored Jaguar XJ-6. As I waited for someone to answer my knock, I admired the car. Its lines were graceful, like a slender woman's hand. Such a fine automobile was a rare sight in the Upper Peninsula and considered an extravagant luxury by most locals, although I noticed they were becoming a bit more common as wealthy people from Detroit and Chicago retired up north and brought their money with them.

After about half a minute, the back door to the office flew open.

"You're punctual. I like that," said the tall slim man who stood in the doorway. I looked at my watch and saw that it was seven twenty-nine.

I stepped inside and felt the blast of air conditioning, unnecessary considering the dampness and cool temperatures outside. I shivered and followed Jordan to his office. He had apparently anticipated the cold because he was dressed in a brown turtleneck and beige cotton v-neck sweater. His brown trousers were cut to accent his trim, long-legged figure.

He led me into an office much like his partner Albert Klegle's except that this one was on the west side of the building and decorated in shades of blue rather than green. There were fewer pictures, as well, just one of him and his wife, Susan Jordan, the only female circuit court judge in the Upper Peninsula, and another photo of him with three buddies hoisting some sort of golfing trophy.

He motioned for me to take a seat in front of his desk and asked if I'd like a cup of coffee or a soft drink. When I declined, he settled into a black leather swivel rocker chair and picked up a steaming cup of coffee. He took a sip, set it down and leaned back with a chilling smile.

"I think we can skip the pleasantries, Ms. Hamilton. I know why you're here. You want to know why someone bumped off the illustrious Frank Thompson," he said.

"Doesn't sound like you miss him much, unless I'm misinterpreting the sneer in your voice," I said.

"No, Ms. Hamilton, I don't miss him," he said.

"I see," I said, rethinking my planned approach to questions. I decided to follow the same hard line I had with Victoria Thompson. "Why do you think Frank's death was anything other than an accident, Mr. Jordan?"

"Please, call me Doug, and I'll call you Robin," he said, then leaned forward and folded his long arms on the desk. His lean, tan, pinched face reminded me of a funny little animal whose name I couldn't recall but I I remembered that the name was a synonym for something negative.

"Robin, I know Frank was murdered because I know Frank. I have no doubt there are more than a few people happy to see him out of the picture."

"Well, Doug," I said, putting extra emphasis on his name (something about the man made my skin crawl), "I spoke with your other partner, Mr. Klegle, the day of Frank's death. He had a lot of nice things to say about Frank."

He snorted. "Robin, what Albert told you for your article was not exactly accurate. I think perhaps the truth hurts him too much. You see, it's true that Frank and Albert worked together at Lewis and Davis, but that's about it. Albert told you they decided to leave and start their own firm. Actually, Frank left first and hung out a shingle a few blocks down from here. It was apparent that he was a natural. Within a year he built up a loyal, rich clientele—well, as rich as you're going to get for around here.

"Albert, on the other hand, was a nice guy without a lot of personality, not very good at building up a successful list of clients, which is what makes or breaks a firm in the eyes of its partners. He was on the verge of losing his job at Lewis and Davis, so he went to Frank, and Frank felt sorry for him. After all, Albert's wife was six months pregnant with their son, and Frank's firm was growing fast. So Frank hired Albert and kept him all these years, even though Al still has a small client list and brings in the least amount of revenue of all of us." He was still smiling, somewhat nastily, almost gloating.

"How did you come to know Frank?" I asked.

"I was also employed at Lewis and Davis. I was anxious to become a partner, and Frank knew it. You see, Susan had dragged me up here a few years before when she took a job with a law firm. I left a large, well-established firm in Southfield to follow her. I took a job at Lewis and Davis, but there were too many accountants competing for one partnership, so when Frank offered me a partnership with his firm, I accepted. That was about two years after he hired Albert," Doug said.

"How did Albert become a partner? If he was about to lose his job, it's unlikely he had the money to buy into the firm right away," I said.

"No, no. He became a partner the same time I came into the firm, so it was a three-way split, although Frank was the controlling partner with forty percent." Jordan stopped smiling for the first time.

"I fail to see what any of this has to do with Frank's death," I said and shifted in my chair.

He drummed his fingers on his desk for a few seconds, then leaned back in his chair again, ready to launch into his theory of murder and mayhem.

"On the surface, it has nothing to do with it, but read between the lines and you'll see an entirely different picture of Frank emerge," he said. "Let me spell it out for you. Frank Thompson put on this wonderful St. Francis of Assisi act for the public, but it was all bullshit!"

The ferocity with which he cursed made me sit up straighter.

"Maybe Albert really believes everything he told you. He owes his career to Frank, but he'd have to be blind not to see the truth. Frank was a dishonest accountant, covering up for clients who wanted to shave more from the profit line on their tax returns than the law allowed.

"I can't say he stole from the firm, at least nothing I can trace. But I know one reason he had such loyal clients is because some of them would have gone to prison, right along with him, if the truth ever came out about their activities. Frank was a financial wizard. He would have been much more at home on Wall Street." The self-assured man behind the desk shook his head ruefully. "Anyway, going back through the firm's files a few months ago, I noticed some billing irregularities pop up with a few of his clients, beginning about ten years back." He paused to take a sip of his quickly cooling coffee.

"How did you find these irregularities? Was it your duty to audit Albert and Frank's work?" I asked.

"No, Frank had a skiing accident while on vacation in New Hampshire around New Year's last winter. He was in the hospital for two weeks. I took it upon myself to look after his clients who were getting ready to put together their tax returns." He paused again for a moment and sat watching me, as if to judge my reaction to his story. When I didn't say anything, he shrugged and continued.

"In the files, I noticed Frank had billed for work on days I knew he was gone, like out of the state on vacation or at conferences. He had access to financial account numbers and, in some cases, was even authorized to make withdrawals. When I went to match the business paperwork with his. . . well, let's just say the end result looked like Swiss cheese."

"So you're saying Frank was taking kickbacks for fudging the tax returns?" I asked.

"That's exactly what I'm saying. I'm certain those irregularities were payment for his creative accounting skills," Jordan said, leaning back in his chair with a satisfied nod.

If Frank Thompson really had been a crook, I thought, it would make it a lot easier to narrow down the list of suspects. Perhaps he had threatened to talk and someone decided to eliminate that risk permanently. It made sense—if Jordan were telling the truth.

"Did you ever confront Frank? Do you think this has anything to do with his death? Do you know who killed Frank and Greg Connor?" I asked.

He laughed. "You're smart and blunt. I like that. Of course, I confronted Frank. He said he hadn't had a chance to reconcile the statements and put everything in order. He even thanked me for pointing out the 'errors' and said I had saved him hours of work. He was smooth, that man." This time he seemed to be shaking his head in admiration.

"As for your other questions, Robin, I really don't know who killed Frank and that other young man. I don't know anything about that guy in that truck," he said and waved his hand in the air.

"Why not go to the police about Thompson's financial shenanigans?" I asked. "After all, your wife is a judge. It doesn't look good for you to be harboring a criminal, does it, even if that criminal is now dead?"

"The police? What good would that do now? Frank's dead. A revelation like this would only spoil the good reputation of the firm and bring down a few successful local businesses that employ a lot of innocent people." He ran a hand through his thinning brown hair and sighed as he let his eyes wander around the room.

I couldn't help feeling I was being played like a Stradivarius.

"May I see those files?" I asked.

Jordan got up from his chair, stuffed his hands in his pockets and walked to the window, which overlooked a small plot of pansies.

"I wish you could, but they're gone," he said after a long pause.

"Gone? All of them?"

"Yes, gone. At least the ones that might show anything illegal. A couple days after Frank's death—Sunday I think. Yes, it must have been Sunday. I came down here to start putting his files in order. I found the key for the large lateral filing cabinet in his office. Several files were missing, including the ones I had reviewed earlier. The file cabinet with information on his individual clients is intact from what I can tell. I haven't cross-checked the files remaining with his client list," he said, continuing to stare out the window.

"What do you think happened to those files? Who had access to them other than the firm's employees?" I asked.

"I don't know. I haven't called the police because I'm not sure they're stolen. I just don't know where they are," Doug said, sounding annoyed. "I suppose anyone could have gotten in here. Victoria had a back-up key to the office. Who knows?"

"I see. Does Al know the files are missing?" I asked.

"Yes, and he was just as surprised as I was. But I do know this," he said and turned to face me. He walked around his desk and leaned against the edge, his legs inches from mine. "If you find those files, I bet you'll find the killer. I believe the key is in those files."

If there really were missing files, and I wasn't sure I believed Jordan any more than I believed the world was flat, they would provide a valuable clue. I asked to see Frank's office.

Doug Jordan led me to the corner office on the other side of the building, next to Klegle's. After unlocking the door with a key from a set in his right front pocket, he pushed it open, releasing a stale odor from the room. The blinds were drawn, making the office nearly pitch black, with the dreary skies outside providing little natural light through the cracks. A clap of thunder broke the eerie silence that had settled over us. We jumped. He let out a nervous laugh.

"I sort of feel like a kid snooping in my grandmother's attic," he said and flipped a switch behind me causing overhead fluorescent lights to flicker to life.

Thompson's office was a little larger than those of the other two partners, with plush mauve carpeting, an ornately carved cherry desk and leather chair identical to Doug Jordan's. The walls held several citations from various community groups, as well as photos of Frank with several dignitaries, including a former president of the United States. The room was attractive, if a bit "over the top," considering what I knew to be Frank's rather low-key manner. I said as much to Jordan.

He pulled the photo of Frank and the President off the wall and examined it for a moment before answering.

"Victoria handled the interior decorating for the whole building. It was her idea to have all these photos and whatnot on the walls. She said it was important to show his clients he was a man of high standing in the community if he wanted to get anywhere in life," Doug said.

"Where did she want him to get?" I asked.

He put the photo back in its place and sat in Frank's chair, looking suddenly small despite his height. "I'm not sure," he finally said. "I don't think Frank knew, either. You see, he came from a very poor family, so poor that his older brother died from malnutrition as a baby. He never forgot that—or I should say, Victoria never let him forget it. It's like he was always fighting back this invisible pack of wolves at the door. No amount of work or money would ever vanquish them." His voice trailed off to nothing.

I sensed Jordan had let his guard down and finally said something that was the whole truth and nothing but the truth. I could imagine the not-so-grieving widow pushing Frank to the edge.

Turning my attention to the two black lateral filing cabinets on either side of the door, I tried the one to my left. The top drawer slid open effortlessly. It was half-empty, as were the other two drawers. I leafed through what remained, but none of the names of the businesses stood out in my mind.

"I didn't see any reason to lock it if the important files were gone," Doug said from his perch behind me. "The other cabinet, where the non-business client files are stored, that's locked. Here's the key."

He tossed me a small silver key on a faded brown leather fob he pulled from his pocket. I unlocked the cabinet and found each drawer crammed with large manila expanding file folders full of statements, notes and letters. Each folder had a label typed with the client's name. Many of the names were familiar to me as prominent local people. I closed the drawers and tossed the key back to Doug.

"Who had keys to this file?" I asked.

"Just Frank and his secretary, Cindy. She's the one who sits at the front desk. And possibly Victoria. I got this one from Cindy," he said.

"Who would gain by killing Frank Thompson? For the sake of argument, let's say he was hiding large sums of money for a client or two and suddenly developed a conscience. The smart thing would be to sell out and leave town," I said, remembering Victoria saying that was exactly what was on Frank's mind in the days before he was killed. "Running him down in the street accomplishes his silence—but at what price?"

Jordan stared at me for a minute. He stared a lot, I was noticing. It gave the false impression that he was a little slow.

"I don't know what they expected to gain. I'm not Sherlock Holmes. All I can say is, as in politics, follow the money. His largest clients were Dixon Motors, T and T Enterprises, and Drexel Engineering. Maybe it's one of them. Or that money-hungry wench he married. I really don't know," he said firmly.

"Could it be you?" I asked.

He chuckled. "No, not worth it. I have nothing to gain by Frank's being out of the picture. Yes, I now own half the firm and Albert the other. But it really just creates a headache for me because Frank brought in so much more business than Albert. Now I have to figure out how to clean up this mess, too," he said and glanced at his watch. "I'm sorry, but Albert will be here soon, and I don't want him to know I've spoken with you. It would distress him."

"Thank you for your time," I said as he walked me to the back door.

"Good luck," he called after me.

As I walked home in a drizzling rain, thunder periodically breaking the silence, I played over in my mind everything Jordan had said. No doubt he was right about following the trail of money.

Chapter Twenty-six

WHEN I ARRIVED HOME shortly after eight, Belle and I headed back out into the drizzle. She splashed from puddle to puddle while I mulled over Doug Jordan's claims. I had mixed emotions about his tale of deception. I didn't understand his motives for sharing such unflattering details about his late partner, especially if they were true. What did he have to gain? Somehow I couldn't accept his portrait of Frank, either. What little I knew about Thompson didn't fit with the mastermind crook profile. Then there was Victoria. She was having an affair with the public safety director, but did that make her a murderess? Rather than finding answers, I only had a lot more questions after my interview with Jordan.

I was brought back to the present by whining at my feet. We had stopped near a towering oak tree three blocks from home, and Belle was focused on something behind us. I turned quickly but saw nothing. There was only heavy mist and a thick fog rolling off the lake, wrapping its long, twisted fingers around the trees that lined Lake Shore Drive. Then within seconds, I saw headlights pierce the grayness and heard an engine rev. My heart stopped, but the rest of my body moved into a run. Dragging Belle behind me, I darted between two large Victorian-era homes and prayed the yards weren't fenced. The engine grew louder. I ran behind the house on my right and sneaked a peak around the corner, but the vehicle had already passed. I stood there for at least a minute, my heart pounding in my ears. Belle's thick body shook as she let out another whine. I cursed the fact that I'd left my cell phone in my purse in the apartment.

Did I dare go back home? I considered knocking on the door of the house sheltering me but instantly banished the thought. I could hear the talk now: "She pounded on the door, shouting something about someone in a vehicle chasing after her. Must have gone crazy or been high on drugs. She just moved back from Chicago, you know." I had enough problems without my new neighbors thinking I was nuts.

Instead I approached the alley, creeping along the wall of a garage, and made my way back to the apartment, keeping close to the buildings on the right and staying alert for any sounds of an approaching vehicle. The only noise was the foghorn periodically sounding off near Sand Point Lighthouse at the north edge of the park.

Back home, I grabbed an old ragged towel and dried Belle but not before she managed to drench the kitchen with a couple shakes of her floppy ears and chunky body. Once the mess was mopped, I changed clothes and fixed a cup of tea. The wind, rain and close call with God-only-knew-who had left me chilled to the bone. I wrapped an afghan around myself and settled into my recliner with the warm cup of tea in my hands and Belle at my feet, picked up the phone and dialed the police station. Charlie was away from his desk. I left a message for him to call me as soon as possible.

I didn't feel safe at home, but I didn't know where else to go. I was obviously a target. Someone was watching my every move. For all I knew my phone was tapped. The thought did nothing to calm my frazzled nerves, but I drank my tea and tried to clear my head, focusing on the oil painting hanging above the sofa. The scene, a 19th-century schooner being guided through stormy seas to safety by a lighthouse perched atop a rocky cliff, always calmed me.

I realized I needed to find someone who could confirm Jordan's story. Then it dawned on me that one of the women in the accounting department at the Daily Press had worked for Thompson, Klegle and Jordan for several years. Molly Ashbrook had mentioned the connection in passing on the day of Frank's death, but I was so busy I hadn't paid much attention. "There's quite a story there," she had said. She would have inside knowledge of Frank's behavior and clients and, most importantly, might be willing to share it. I called her office and asked if she'd meet me after work to discuss her former employer. She readily agreed to meet me at five at my desk—the safest, least visible place that came to mind.

I felt more confident after making that appointment, and it was time to check up on victim number three. Perhaps Sarah Lindstrom had remembered something. It was raining hard by the time I arrived at the hospital, but this time I had wisely brought along a cheap black umbrella. The wind fought me all the way to the front doors.

It was after ten-thirty by the time I made my way to Sarah's room. The first bed was now empty; the mastectomy patient, I hoped, was home and on her way to another twenty good years. Sarah was sitting on the edge of her bed dressed in jeans and a yellow t-shirt with a small glittery silver butterfly imprinted on the front. The white bandage around her head been replaced with a large Band-Aid over her right eye. She looked up from tying white canvas sneakers with platform soles and silver and white laces and beamed at me.

"Hi, Robin!" she said. I was surprised she knew who I was, considering we had never been introduced.

"Hi, Sarah. Looks like they're letting you out," I said, returning her smile.

"Yeah, I'm psyched to be going home. This place smells awful, and it is so-o-o-o noisy. It's, like, impossible to sleep," she said and rolled her eyes.

"How do you feel?" I asked.

"Fine. There's still some tenderness here," she said, pointing to the bandage, "but I feel okay. Everything checks out with the doctors, so I guess that means I'm back to normal. They said there's no permanent damage."

"That's great. I'll bet your mom is relieved."

"Yeah, I guess so. She's still really worried about Brett, though," Sarah said and looked down at her shoes, then up again. "Hey, I heard on the radio they found his truck with some other guy in it at the bottom of Lake Antoine. Does that mean Brett's off the hook?" she asked, full of hope.

"I'm afraid not," I said. I sat down next to her. "There are still a lot of questions the police want answered."

Without my having to say it, Sarah seemed to understand what I was alluding to—that Brett was now a suspect in two murders. The hope in her eyes changed to despair.

"Robin, I know Brett would never kill anyone. He's a very simple guy. His biggest thrill is taking Scampers, our dog, outside to play Frisbee. I have no idea what's going on, I just know Brett's not the type to get involved in murder!"

"Do you remember anything about the accident?" I asked.

She shook her head. "No, not a thing. The last thing I remember is talking with my friend Lacy about how excited we were about our senior year. The next thing I knew, I woke up here with a major headache," she said and rubbed the bandage.

"Sarah, did you know Greg Connor?" I asked.

She looked puzzled, as if trying to remember something, then said, "Oh, yeah, he's the one they found in the truck. No, I never really met him. Brett did mention him a couple of times. My friend Nikki came to visit me yesterday, and she said he was bad news."

Hannah, wearing her nursing uniform, walked in just then, and Sarah and I stood like recruits ready for inspection by the drill sergeant. Sarah was a good five inches taller than me and thin as a picket in a fence.

"Are you ready to go, Sweetheart?" Hannah asked.

"Yeah, Mom, all set," Sarah said and picked up her denim jacket and duffle bag.

"Whoa, sorry, you have to go out in a wheelchair just like everyone else," Hannah said and went back into the hall. I thought it a bit strange she had ignored me. When she came back, she was followed by another nurse pushing a wheelchair. Sarah hopped in, set her jacket and bag in her lap and waved.

"'Bye, Robin," she said with another bright smile.

"Mary, will you please take her down to the main lobby? I'll be right there. Thanks," Hannah said to the other nurse.

"I came to see how Sarah was doing and if she remembered anything from the accident," I said.

"She doesn't remember it at all, which is just as well as far as I'm concerned. Robin, I'm trying to shield her from as much of this as possible. Please don't ask her any more questions," Hannah said, and she stalked out of the room.

⟡

Belle welcomed me home with a thorough sniffing-over, then settled on her favorite rug in the middle of the living room. After throwing my damp trench coat over a chair in the kitchen, I followed her lead and sat Indian-style on the rug next to her, my back against the front of the sofa. I leaned back, closed my eyes and tried to relax. Belle nestled her head in my lap while I stroked her ears and mentally tried to fit the pieces of the jigsaw puzzle of Frank Thompson's and Greg Connor's murders together.

One by one I ran through my list of suspects. The obvious one was Victoria. She had two possible motives—money and love. With Frank gone, she got a sizable life insurance settlement and a chance to explore her relationship with Chief Joe Nelson. My personal opinion that Nelson wasn't worth the risk of life in prison without parole was immaterial.

Next on the list were the partners, Doug Jordan and Albert Klegle. Klegle didn't have the guts to pull off something like a hired hit and certainly couldn't kill anyone himself. I would have bet the few measly thousands sitting in my savings account on that. Jordan, on the other hand, struck me as a conniving man with a taste for the good life. Now that there were only two partners, he could get a larger share of the profits and split up Frank's choicest clients, saving the most lucrative for himself. In addition, my guess was that the firm had some sort of life insurance policy on the partners in case of an untimely death. Perhaps he had dreams of buying Klegle's share in the firm.

Then there was the silencer angle. If Jordan were telling the truth about Frank's "creative accounting" and Frank had decided to go straight, it was possible someone hired Greg Connor to kill Thompson, then got rid of Greg as the only solid witness. I thought about the three companies Jordan had mentioned.

Dixon Motors was a conglomerate of about a dozen of the largest automobile dealerships in the northern part of the state. Founded in the late 1940s, it was run by the Dixon family, a nice bunch of people active in the community and known for good customer service. I graduated with Mike Dixon, the youngest son, now general manager of the Chevrolet dealership in Iron Mountain. I knew the Dixons were very religious and definitely law-abiding. I couldn't see them cooking their books, let alone murdering anyone.

Drexel Engineering was a relatively new business that I knew little about. Its founder was sort of the local equivalent of Microsoft's Bill Gates, but I couldn't even recall his first name. I did know the business was growing fast and had just completed a multimillion-dollar expansion. With all the government projects the company was working on, Drexel would have too much to lose to take a chance on cheating Uncle Sam.

That left T and T Enterprises. The Ts stood for Tanner and Tanner, brothers who operated a construction firm. I remembered my dad telling me something about how they had managed to get some pretty big jobs, including the new science and technology building at the local college, despite rumors of shoddy workmanship due to cost-cutting, with the savings being pocketed by the owners. Nothing had ever been proven, and business was booming, if their signs at many of the construction sites around town were any indication of success. I made a mental note to check the Daily Press archives for any information on T and T Enterprises.

I was jolted from my musings by the ringing of the telephone. I stared at it for several seconds, fearing who might be at the other end. I looked at my watch. It was noon, too early for my dad to call. Tentatively, I crawled over to the end table and picked up the receiver, cradling it gently in my right hand.

"Hello?"

"We need to talk." It was Charlie. I let out a sigh of relief.

"When and where?" I asked, rising to my feet.

"Now, and I don't care. How about Eddie's?" he said. He sounded rushed.

"Okay, see you in a few," I said and hung up the phone. In my relief over hearing Charlie's voice, I forgot to ask what he wanted to talk about.

The rain had stopped but the sky remained gray and the air damp and chilly. I parked my Jeep about half a block away from Eddie's and spied Charlie's unmarked cruiser parked across the street as I hurried into the restaurant. Eddie's, a favorite place for retired folks to gather for breakfast in the mornings and office staff and shopkeepers to eat lunch, was a family-style joint located on Ludington Street in the heart of what businesses in the small, aging retail district liked to call "Downtown." Luckily for us, Charlie was already seated at a table in the back. Every table, booth and stool was taken, and the room was filled with the chatter of voices and clatter of dishes.

"What's up?" I asked, squeezing into the chair across from him.

He looked around as if to ensure no one was eavesdropping, leaned forward and whispered, "We've got a witness."

"To what? The truck going into the lake?" I asked, my eyes popping open and pulse quickening.

"To your incident last night," he said.

"Oh," I said. Then his words sank in like a booted foot in a mud hole.

"Wait a minute. How is that possible? It was nearly pitch black and pouring rain. How could anyone have seen anything in that mess?" I asked skeptically.

"Shh! Keep your voice down," Charlie hissed. He looked around again. No one was paying any attention to us, but I began to worry that his melodramatic behavior would draw attention.

"What's the big secret?" I whispered back.

"There are open ears everywhere. I'm not sure who can be trusted. Anyway, where you went off the road there's a bluff with a lot of houses overlooking the lake. Last night a man who lives up there was taking his dog for a walk. He came to the edge of the bluff where there's a small clearing next to the safety fence and stopped to watch the traffic for a minute. He saw you and a large vehicle without lights come up behind you. Then the driver behind turned on his lights, hit you from behind and took off when you hit the ditch. But your headlights shined on the other vehicle long enough for him to see that it was a large, black or dark blue SUV," Charlie said.

A vision of such a vehicle flashed in my mind, but it was gone before I could grab onto it. I said a quick, silent thank-you prayer, though, for all dog owners who brave the elements for the sake of their four-legged friends.

"Okay, that's a start. Unfortunately, there are probably hundreds of SUVs like that in Delta County alone," I said.

The waitress arrived and took my order for an iced tea and grilled chicken salad. Charlie ordered a pasty, a Cornish meat and potato-filled pie that was Eddie's specialty.

"A pasty?" I asked. "I thought you hated those things."

"I've been working hard, and I'm hungry," he said with a grin. "Anyway, you're right about the SUVs, but at least it's something. Now I can go to the Dickinson County cops and have them ask if anyone saw a vehicle like that around when Greg Connor took a swim."

"I've got some news, too," I said and relayed what Doug Jordan had shared with me that morning.

"That's interesting," Charlie said. "I didn't really knew Frank Thompson, but I never heard anything like that about him. It does add a twist to things, doesn't it?—If it's true, of course," he added dubiously and cocked a bushy eyebrow at me.

"That's just it. I suspect Jordan has some pretty strong motives for wanting to tarnish Thompson's reputation. I'm meeting with someone later today who may be able to help me sort things out."

"Who?" Charlie asked.

The waitress delivered our meals and big bottle of ketchup, which Charlie nearly emptied on his steaming pasty. When she was gone, I said, "Thompson's former assistant."

"Robin, be careful. The killer knows you're digging into this and may not stop at just scaring you next time," Charlie said.

"I know. I'm being watched," I said and peered around the room, half-expecting to find someone peering back at me from behind a newspaper. I saw several people I recognized, including the publisher, to whom I smiled and waved, and Grant Stewart in deep conversation with the senior Mike Callahan. "I wonder what those two are taking about," I mused aloud, then turned back to Charlie. "I'm getting close, Charlie. I can feel it. I swear, it's like I can feel the killer breathing down my neck."

"And vice versa, Robin," Charlie warned. He took a swallow from his coffee, set his cup down and took my hands in his. "You know, as a friend, I gotta tell you, you're starting to sound obsessed with this Lindstrom thing. Don't lose yourself to save this kid. He ain't worth it."

I pulled my hands back, grabbed a paper napkin and began twisting it.

"It helps me forget," I finally said, swallowing hard.

"I know. But you can never really forget until you allow yourself to remember." He stood up, threw a $10 bill on the table and left me alone with my reflections.

Chapter Twenty-seven

I WAS ANXIOUS TO BURY myself in the Daily Press archives, but first it was time for Belle's afternoon constitutional. The sky was clearing, with sunlight streaming periodically through the thinning clouds. The temperature had also jumped about ten degrees to a comfortable sixty-eight, according to the State Bank's time and temp sign in front of the building on the corner of Main and Eleventh Street.

Belle seemed eager to get out of the house when I rattled her leash. Before leaving the apartment, I shot a furtive glance at the answering machine but saw it was blank. "Thank God," I said to Belle.

Mrs. Easton tapped on the kitchen window and waved as we passed. I waved back and shouted a hello. It occurred to me that, being an observant woman, she might have seen the offending SUV in the area.

Walking our usual path along the lake, with frequent stops for Belle to smell various trees, blades of grass and assorted food wrappers (which I picked up and deposited in the nearest trash can), we made it back to the house in half an hour. Mrs. Easton was in the front yard, weeding the flowerbed that lined the left side of the porch. She turned and looked up from under her wide-brimmed straw hat when she heard us approach.

"God sent us a beautiful day after all that rain, didn't He? You've been in and out all day. Didn't you go to work, Dear?" she asked.

"No, I took a personal day to work on some things. Say, Mrs. Easton, have you noticed any suspicious vehicles in the neighborhood over the last week or so?" I asked.

She pulled off her gloves and sat back in the grass, thinking. After a long pause, she said, "I can't say as I have. What exactly do you mean? Is something wrong?"

"I'm not sure, but if you see a large black or blue sport utility vehicle, like a Chevy Blazer or Ford Explorer, driving by too often or parked within a few blocks, would you let me know? It's important," I said.

"Of course. I'll keep my eyes open. What is this all about?" she asked.

I wondered how much to say. I didn't want her to worry, but I also didn't want her to be unprepared if someone came around asking for me.

"I'm looking into the death of that accountant," I said, motioning to the spot where Thompson was hit. "I may be making some people nervous."

"Oh, do be careful, Dear. I'd hate to see anything happen to you," she said and reached up and grabbed my free hand.

"Don't worry, Mrs. Easton. I'll be fine," I said. I gave her a weak smile and took Belle upstairs.

Arriving at the Daily Press offices, I darted to the side door, through the newsroom and down the stairs to the basement without garnering much notice. The basement was dim, even after I flicked a switch that turned on the few light bulbs hanging from the ceiling.

The space was divided roughly in half, with newspapers from the past year stored in cubbyholes along two walls in a small dreary conference room on the left. Behind, a door led to a much larger room where the circulation department stored newspaper racks and delivery boxes for rural customers. There were nearly a hundred years of clippings in the long row of antique filing cabinets, and the room had a musty smell, sort of like an old library. I found it comforting, as though I were visiting an old friend with a treasure trove of tantalizing, long-forgotten secrets.

The archives were filed according to numbers beginning with one and stretching up to about three thousand. Each topic or name was assigned a number on an index card and then placed alphabetically in a card file, just like the old Dewey Decimal System card files used in libraries in the old days. I went straight for the T's and quickly found T and T Enterprises listed as 2856. I found the appropriate drawer and said a little prayer that no one had the file out for any reason. I was in luck. The file, although thin, was in place. I pulled it.

The file contained five articles, three of which concerned construction projects at the college and one regarding the hospital addition. It was the last article in the file that drew my attention, a story written when the business was formed five years ago. It was a basic piece that obviously had run on the Business page and sounded more like an advertisement than news.

What caught my eye was a name I hadn't expected to find. I went back and read through the article again, word for word, my interest growing with each sentence. It turned out that Richard and Raymond Tanner were only managers and part-owners of the firm, while owning fifty percent was none other than my favorite local sawmill entrepreneur, Grant Stewart. According to the article, Richard Tanner had worked for Stewart for several years as a salesman and Raymond had fifteen years of experience as a construction worker. Stewart was quoted as saying he saw an opportunity when the two men approached him about the deal, and now he looked forward to a "prosperous, long-term relationship."

The arrangement made sense. Stewart would supply not only the materials for construction projects but the labor as well and make a small fortune in the process. Now I wondered what else we had on Stewart. I put the Tanner file back in its drawer and looked up the lumberman's name. It was listed as 2010 and was much thicker than the Tanner file. I looked at my watch and cursed. I had to meet with Michelle in a few minutes. I took the Stewart file upstairs with me and tucked it in the back of a deep drawer in my desk.

The newsroom was empty except for the news clerk, who was shutting down her computer. She grabbed her coat and umbrella and turned to leave, then spotted me.

"What are you doing here, Robin?" she asked with a tired smile. "I thought you took the day off."

"Just doing a little research. You look beat. Rough day?" I asked.

"Rough doesn't describe it. Every reader with a gripe decided to call today, and of course, Hunter was tied up in interviews most of the day," she said, readjusting the load in her arms.

I gave her an encouraging pat on the shoulder and wished her a good evening.

A clamor of footsteps down the stairs announced Molly Ashbrook. As she blew through the front door to the newsroom, it was hard to remember she was nearly forty. She bounced around with the energy of a teenager. With a bubbly personality and wide, toothy smile, she was one of those people no one could dislike.

She plunked down on the floor by my desk what looked more like an overnight bag than a purse and sat down breathlessly.

"I was so excited to get your call! I've been wanting to talk to someone about the firm since this all happened, but I didn't know who would want to hear it all," the petite, cheery brunette said.

"I'm glad you're taking the time to talk to me, Molly. First of all, anything you tell me is off the record. This is all background information," I said.

"Oh, I understand. That's fine," she said, jumping out of her seat to remove her iridescent turquoise raincoat and drape it across a neighboring desk before sitting down again. Her stylish red skirt and matching jacket contrasted beautifully with her pale complexion.

"How you long did you work for Thompson, Klegle and Jordan?"

"Well, let me see. I got my associate's degree in accounting in. . . um, I worked there sixteen years. I started right out of college as a sort of secretary/receptionist/assistant to Frank, but I helped Al and Doug from time to time, as well," she said.

"What did you think of them all?" I asked.

She scrunched her eyes and nose for a moment, as if organizing her thoughts.

"Well, they were three very different men. Frank was very community-minded. He liked to feel useful. Some people thought he did all that charity work—you know, being co-chair of this or that fund-raiser or whatever, even pro bono work—just for appearances. That wasn't true. He really supported any organization focused on children. He loved children and always talked about wanting a houseful, but he and his wife never had any kids. Because of that, I think he poured the love and affection he would have given to his own children into charity work.

"As for Al, well, he's nice enough, but he doesn't have much personality. Actually, he seems kind of slow sometimes. I always thought it was weird that he went into accounting. He seems better suited for a job that doesn't require so much contact with the public. If it weren't for his wife and his secretary, he'd be lost," Michelle said with a laugh.

"What about Doug?"

She paused for a moment and clicked her long red nails together before answering.

"I never trusted Doug. There was never anything I could put my finger on, but he just seemed. . . I don't know, sly, I guess would be the word. Like he was planning something all the time," she said, frowning. "He kept odd hours, usually working early in the morning and then leaving for the day around noon. He liked to snoop, too. More than once I caught him rooting through Frank's files."

"Did Frank suspect him of anything?"

"Frank was a very trusting soul. He believed the best of everyone, even Doug," she said.

"To your knowledge, did Frank ever cheat on his wife?" I asked.

"Good Lord, no! He was devoted to Victoria, although I don't think she appreciated it. He always remembered her birthday and their anniversary. He was actually rather shy around women. He told me one time that if Victoria hadn't made the first move, he probably would still be single," she said.

"I see. He sounds like a very honest, sincere man," I said.

"Oh, he was, to a fault. If I made a mistake in a single entry, he caught it like that," she said, snapping her fingers.

"What about his clients? Did he ever have any confrontations with the owners of, say, Drexel Engineering, Dixon Motors, or T and T Enterprises?" I asked.

"Those weren't his clients—they were with Doug," she said. "Frank handled mostly individuals. Doug took care of the business clients. Al handled most of the nonprofits."

"Are you sure?" I asked.

"Of course. I maintained Frank's files and took care of his billing," she said, adjusting her scarf. "The only exception was Grant Stewart. He was with Frank from the beginning, and when he started Stewart Lumber, he said he wanted Frank to continue as his accountant. But after a while Grant left the finances of the business to his manager —um, oh heck, I can't think of his name."

"Jack Kirksen?" I said.

"Yes, that's it. He's the one Frank dealt with when it came to Stewart Lumber," Michelle said.

"That makes sense. What about T and T Enterprises? Why did that account go to Doug? They're in partnership with Stewart," I said.

"You know, it's funny you should ask that. I remember Grant requested Doug handle them. I don't know the reason, but Frank obliged his request," Molly said.

"Did Doug and Frank get along?"

"For the most part, I think. They weren't the best of friends. They didn't hang out together after hours or anything. It might have had something to do with Victoria. You see, she'd been having an affair with Doug when she joined the firm. After she got to know Frank, she dropped Doug like a hot coal when he wouldn't leave his wife," she said.

"Really?" I said and wondered if another piece of the puzzle had just fallen into place.

"Yeah, it was always a bit awkward at office get-togethers. Everybody knew except Doug's wife, Susan. Truthfully, I don't think he ever got over Victoria," she said.

"What about Al and Frank? Did they get along?" I asked.

"Absolutely. In fact, Al owed a lot to Frank, career-wise. He asked Al to be his partner a few years or so after he started the firm," Molly said.

"Are Al and Doug as honest as Frank?" I asked.

"I'd say Al is, but Doug—well, I suspect he bends the rules for his clients sometimes. That was another point of friction between him and Frank," Molly said.

"Can you think of anyone who would want Frank dead?" I asked.

She concentrated for a moment, then shook her head.

"I've been asking myself that same question ever since the accident began to look like it wasn't an accident. I never knew Frank to have a cross word with anyone. I really liked him," she said, her eyes filling with tears. She wiped them away and apologized. "I just get so mad when I think about it."

"There's no need to apologize. I understand. You obviously liked working for the firm. Why did you leave?" I asked as I handed her a tissue.

She blew her nose. "My husband went to work for Carlson Sweeney—you know, the other big accounting firm in town. It just seemed weird to be working for his competitor, so when the job opened up here, I took it."

"Just one more question, Molly. Did Frank ever break his leg on a skiing trip?" I asked.

"No, that was Doug. I wasn't there, but it happened last year around Christmas, I think. I heard about it from one of the secretaries there," she said, looking puzzled.

"Really? Interesting. Listen, you've been a great help. I don't want to keep you any longer," I said and stood.

"It's not a problem. I hope you find out who's behind all this," she said.

We walked to the parking lot together, where she headed for a sporty red Pontiac, while I searched the area for the ubiquitous dark monster truck. The coast was clear. I waved as Molly drove away, then stopped dead in my tracks. The image that had flashed through my mind when Charlie had told me about the witness seeing the vehicle come up behind me flashed again. This time, it stayed.

The first time I had seen Grant Stewart was when he drove up to his office in a dark blue Lincoln Navigator, a large luxury sport utility vehicle. I felt a rush of fear, adrenaline and anger all at the same time. The pieces were beginning to fit together.

I tried a scenario out in my mind. Stewart saw something vulnerable in both Greg Connor and Brett Lindstrom. He developed a rapport with Connor, a troubled young man, and Stewart offered him a large sum of money to kill Frank using the truck owned by Connor's trusting friend Brett. Then, out of fear of discovery, Stewart got rid of Connor. He probably had plans to do away with Lindstrom, too, eventually. Still, why? And what did Douglas Jordan or Victoria Thompson have to do with it?

Jordan had fed me a line of garbage about Frank to throw me off the trail. I wondered if someone, maybe Grant Stewart, was getting nervous and had put him up to telling me a story, figuring I'd eventually want to talk to him anyway. My guess was that Jordan was the thief, but who was he stealing from?

Like a beagle in search of a fox, I could smell fear. When criminals are afraid, they make mistakes. Forgetting about the Stewart file secured in my desk, I drove home energized.

Chapter Twenty-eight

I BOUNDED UP THE STAIRS to my apartment, eager to talk to someone about what I had found out from Molly and the files. Bits of information I had collected over the last week and a half swirled around in my brain like debris in a tornado. I needed to talk it all through with someone. My first thought was to call Charlie, but a dispatcher at the station told me he was gone for the day, and he didn't answer at home, either. I left a message for him to call me as soon as possible and dialed my dad's number, praying he would answer. On the third ring, I heard his cheery "hello."

"Are you busy? I need to talk to you about this Lindstrom thing," I said.

"Come on over. I'll put some burgers on the grill," he said. He sounded happy to hear from me. I took Belle for a quick toddle around the block, then lifted her into the Jeep. I only looked in the rearview mirror a half-dozen times during the short trip.

I could smell the hot charcoal briquettes as soon as I pulled into the driveway. My dad poked his head out the front screen door and called a hello. I lifted Belle back out of the Jeep, and she trotted towards him with tail wagging and ears flopping crazily. He let out a hearty laugh.

"I can't get over how funny she is," he said as he bent down to scratch her ears and rub her sides. She rewarded him with a gratified howl and waddled into the house. He held the door open for me and said, "I tried calling you at work, but they said you took the day off. Then I tried your apartment but didn't get an answer. Is everything okay?"

"I was working on the Thompson-Lindstrom case. I spent the day talking with three people who provided me with some very intriguing information. That's what I wanted to talk to you about. Why did you try to call? You don't usually call me at work unless something's wrong," As we walked from the living room and into the kitchen, I grabbed some glasses and a pitcher of iced tea from the refrigerator. He held the sliding door open for me, then closed it as I stepped onto the patio.

"No, nothing's wrong, but I got a phone call from Hannah, and I thought you should know about it," he said.

We sat down at the round table with the patio umbrella shielding us from the evening sun. The clouds were nothing but a memory. The sun blazed, still four hours from setting, but the air was only pleasantly warm, not suffocating as it had been for so many weeks.

"I saw Hannah this morning when I visited Sarah. She seemed less than thrilled to find me there," I said.

He took a sip from his glass and walked over to the grill to turn the sizzling burgers, then came back and sat down in the chair across from me.

"Hannah took Sarah and left town. She said she was too afraid of what might happen next if she stayed." He brushed something I couldn't see off his dark green golf shirt.

"Then she took my advice. I told her to get away for a few weeks, just until this was resolved. Did she say where she was going?" I asked.

"She has a sister in Milwaukee. She gave me the number and asked me to keep her informed of what's happening. She also said you were in danger, too. What's going on, Robin?" He cocked an eyebrow at me. I squirmed a little and wondered who had told Hannah about my run-in with the mad rammer.

"Yes, I suppose I'm next on the list. It seems I'm getting too close to finding out who's behind all this," I said. I didn't know how much he knew, but I didn't want to add to his worries by getting into details.

"Robin, if anything happens to you, I'm going to blame myself. I'm the one who pushed you into investigating this," he said and began picking more invisible lint off his shirt.

"Dad, look at me," I said, taking both of his hands. "Nothing is going to happen to me. I can take care of myself. Besides, even if something did, I'm the one taking the risks. I choose what I will and won't do. If I get myself into a mess, it's my fault, not yours. I'm not eight years old."

He squeezed my hand. "I know, but you're all I've got, and you've already been through so much this year. Maybe you should just let the police handle it from here on out," he said.

"I am. All I'm doing is gathering information. Don't worry," I insisted.

He didn't look convinced, but he let it pass, and we went to work in thoughtful silence devouring juicy hamburgers, green salad and watermelon. My mind automatically drifted to Hannah. I felt a twinge of envy, wishing for a moment that I too could run away from it all. But that's exactly what I had done two months before, fleeing Chicago to return to Escanaba, and look where that had got me.

To my dad, I said, "I wish I knew what Brett knows. I wouldn't be surprised if it has something to do with Grant Stewart."

His eyebrows shot up as he finished his last bite of watermelon, and he put down his fork, pushed the plate away and sat back in his chair. The metal creaked under the force of his movement.

"Why don't you tell me what you've found out so far," he said.

I rehashed my discovery about T and T Enterprises and my interviews with Doug Jordan and Molly Ashbrook while we watched Belle try in vain to chase three squirrels zipping around the yard. When I finished my story, he stared into his empty glass for a few minutes. Finally he said, "It sounds to me like this Jordan guy and Grant Stewart might be in it together."

"I know, but if that's the case, why did Jordan come to me? I never really considered him much of a suspect," I said in exasperation.

"Does he know that Michelle works at the Daily Press now?" he asked.

"He must. She's been with us for a few years and has kept in touch with the firm." I watched as Belle gave up the chase and collapsed on her side with a moan. The squirrels chattered at her from a birch tree branch overhead.

"My guess is, Jordan is trying to implicate Grant Stewart," Dad went on. "We all know there really is no honor among thieves. Do you have anything to tie Stewart to the case besides his relationship with that Connor kid and Brett?" he asked.

I hesitated. If I told him about Stewart's vehicle matching the description of the truck that nearly hit me, I'd have to explain last night. I fudged.

"I saw Stewart driving a dark blue Lincoln Navigator. It loosely matches the description of the vehicle that ran Sarah Lindstrom off the road," I said. It wasn't a lie. It just wasn't the whole truth.

"You're right. There is something missing—a motive," he said as he refilled our glasses.

"I know that," I wailed. This wasn't helping at all. Maybe I was grasping at straws. Maybe Frank Thompson's death really was an accident.

Maybe Brett Lindstrom really did hit him and was trying to cover it up. Maybe Greg Connor was helping Brett by ditching the truck and accidentally got caught when it went into the lake. Maybe I needed to find a new line of work, like horticulture, something that kept me far from people and all their problems. I felt a nasty tension headache starting behind my right eye. Then my dad said something that made me forget the pain.

"Grant Stewart has killed before, you know," he said casually, as if he had just told me my shoe was untied.

"What?!" I shrieked, sitting bolt upright.

He took a long sip from his glass and grinned.

"Oh, yes, Mr. Stewart may have already gotten away with murder. A lot of people believe he killed his wife. No one could ever prove it, obviously." He took another drink, then set his glass down and folded his hands over his slight paunch, teasing me with a long, drawn-out pause.

"Dad! Spit it out. You're driving me nuts! What are you talking about?" I nearly shouted.

"I'm surprised you didn't hear about it down in Chicago. It was a huge scandal here. It happened four or five years ago.

"Grant and his wife owned a big cabin cruiser. It was a real beauty, custom-made, worth about a hundred grand. They liked to take it out on little excursions around the bay. They usually had friends with them, but this one particular evening in late July they went out by themselves. Grant later said Claire—that was his wife—was feeling a little depressed and thought a boat ride would cheer her up. So off they went about eight-thirty, according to neighbors who saw them shove off.

"It was a beautiful evening, warm and humid. About two miles offshore they powered down and just drifted. Grant went below to get some refreshments from the little refrigerator on board. All of a sudden, he heard a splash. Thinking Claire had decided to go for a swim, he ignored it and went back to mixing drinks and making sandwiches. But after a few minutes, he realized it was too quiet. He hurried up on deck to find it empty. He searched the water, saw nothing. He shouted her name for several minutes, but there was no answer. He radioed for help. Night was starting to fall, so a Coast Guard helicopter flew up from Sturgeon Bay and searched the water with a spotlight, as did the sheriff's department with its little boat. They never saw any sign of her. Grant was devastated, went through a big funeral all weepy-eyed, vowed he'd never remarry.

"The reality is that his wife was a bit of a drinker. She had reason to drink, God knows, with the way Grant ran around on her. But Claire was also a very good swimmer, and it's unlikely she would have gone in the water by herself two miles from shore in near darkness, even with a few drinks in her. I knew her quite well from the country club. We used to talk golf and politics. She was very intelligent and had strong opinions about everything. One night she told me she came from a very wealthy family downstate.

"Stewart inherited a great deal of money when she died. In the millions, Robin. She didn't have any brothers or sisters, and her parents were dead, so Grant got it all. Now, while the police knew all this, they had absolutely no proof of foul play. They never even found her body."

I sat in stunned silence. The whole thing sounded like the plot of a television movie of the week. I finally asked, "How do you know it was murder? Why didn't you tell me before?"

He laughed. "Come on, Robin. I was a firefighter in this town for thirty-three years. I know just about every cop and paramedic within a hundred miles—and they all love to talk. As for why I didn't tell you, frankly, you never asked what was going on back here. I guess I just figured you wouldn't be interested."

He was baiting me. I could tell by the smug look on his face. He'd needled me for years about my "pursuit of excitement in the big city." I wasn't going to get drawn into that debate again.

"I don't understand. I thought Stewart Lumber was doing brisk business. Why would he need to kill his wife to get money?"

"Greed? I don't know. Grant is rumored to be a high-rolling gambler—and not just at the Native American-run casinos around here, mind you. I'm talking big games in Vegas and Atlantic City," he said.

"So what's his game with Doug Jordan?"

"I couldn't tell you. I don't know this Jordan character. But I've heard he's pretty slick, spends a lot of time schmoozing for business—which I suppose is necessary in that line of work, but I don't like it," he said with a shake of his head.

Goosebumps popped out on my arms as night fell around us. It was nearly ten o'clock, and I could feel the lack of sleep catching up with me. I didn't want to go home, though. Something was nagging at me. Besides, I didn't want to go back and find another message on my answering machine from The Voice.

"Do you mind if I stay here tonight?" I asked.

"No, not at all," he said and cocked a bushy gray eyebrow at me. "Are you all right? You look like you've been battling a five-alarm blaze for two days straight."

"I'll be fine. I just need some sleep. The sooner this case is solved, the sooner everyone will be fine," I said emphatically and got up to clear the table. While Dad cleaned the grill, I parked my Jeep in the garage—no need to advertise where I was.

Afterwards, I telephoned Mrs. Easton.

"Oh, I'm so glad you called, dear. A man was here about two hours ago looking for you when I was out in the garden. He was very nice-looking with thick silvery hair, very business-like, but much too old for you. He'd be much more my type," she said with a giggle.

"Did he tell you who he was or what he wanted?" I asked.

She sensed the steeliness in my voice and asked with alarm, "Was that the person you were talking about earlier, the one in the large, dark SUV? He asked if you lived here, and I said yes, but that you weren't home. He wished me a good evening and left. I didn't get his name, but he looked familiar. Did I say too much?"

"No, that's okay. Did you see what kind of car he was driving, Mrs. Easton?" I asked.

"You know, I think he must have walked. I didn't see any car. You sound so concerned. Is something wrong, Robin?" she asked, fear creeping into her voice.

"Yes, something is wrong. That man you saw may have murdered three people," I said. I heard her gasp at the other end of the line. "Listen, I won't be home tonight, and I'd rather you didn't stay there, either. Is it possible for you to go to your sister's? I know it's short notice, but I'd feel better if you weren't home alone."

I hated alarming her, but it occurred to me that she was a witness to Frank Thompson's murder, and I didn't want her to end up dead because of me.

"My sister is in Houghton visiting her grandchildren, but I could stay with my friend Mildred. She'd like the company. She just lost her husband this spring, you know," she said.

"That's perfect. Promise me you'll go to Mildred's," I said.

"Yes, dear. I'll call her right now," she said and hung up.

Maybe I was being paranoid. I didn't care. Too many people had been hurt already.

Despite the familiar surroundings, my dad just down the hall, and Belle at my feet, it was a long time before I fell asleep.

Chapter Twenty-nine

WHEN SLEEP FINALLY CAME, it was sound. I barely heard the alarm at five o'clock. I found the clock on the nightstand next to the bed and fumbled around for the off button. Belle grunted when the noise ceased, and I sat up in bed for a few minutes to orient myself. This had been my bedroom since I was brought home from the hospital as an infant, but I hadn't slept in it since Christmas the previous year when I brought Mitch home to meet my dad. I shook my head, rubbed my eyes and stretched. I didn't want to think about that now.

Dawn was breaking, and weak light passed through the flimsy white curtains hanging over the east windows. The room was rather bare, with just a full-size bed, nightstand and large empty dresser for furniture. The rose-colored carpeting, although worn, was soft and clean. The books, stuffed animals and assorted childhood memorabilia had long since been moved, sold, given away or lost. The white walls still gleamed but were marked by a multitude of tiny holes, telltale signs of where favorite photos once hung.

I suddenly felt as empty as the room, as if everything that had ever mattered to me—my fiancé, my mother, my shot at a Pulitzer—was gone. I was back working at a job I'd given up six years ago, constantly on edge for fear I'd start crying hysterically, and hiding out from someone I couldn't identify, in a bedroom once adorned with a Wonder Woman poster. I'd never felt more pathetic in my life. Why am I doing this, I wondered? What was there to look forward to? "Why should I even get out of bed?" I asked the ghosts of my childhood.

The only answer was another grunt from Belle, who looked up at me with droopy brown eyes, pleading to be let outside before her little bladder burst. It wasn't much inspiration, but it was enough to motivate me to throw my legs over the side of the bed and shuffle out to the patio door to let her out.

I watched my dog toddle from tree to tree for a few minutes before she picked one that met her specifications, squatted and let go. She ran back to me, thick paws drenched with dew, and I finally took notice of the sun rising amid patches of wispy clouds. The effect was one of simple yet glorious beauty. I stood on the patio for several minutes, enjoying the quiet of the morning and the colors with which God had chosen to paint the sky. I took several deep, clean breaths and decided to live at least one more day.

⚓

Leaving Belle with my dad, I drove by my apartment. The old house was still standing, silently basking in the glow of dawn over Ludington Park. I turned on the radio in time to hear a prepubescent-sounding female announcer give the weather report—a picture-perfect summer day with clear skies, temperatures in the lower seventies and moderate humidity. It was the kind of day Yoopers (the whimsical and not always flattering name given to residents of the Upper Peninsula) stored in their memories to keep them warm come January.

My stops at the city and county police stations showed it had been a quiet night except for a break-in at a local pizza joint. The culprit had made off with a safe, the third such case in two months. It was worth a short story on the front page below the fold on an otherwise uneventful news morning. After deadline, Bob Hunter called me into his office.

"What's going on with the Thompson case?" he asked gruffly.

"I think it's about to break wide open, Bob," I said.

He peered at me over the rims of his wire-framed glasses.

"Really? What's up?" he asked. The old newshound smelled a T-bone grilling on the fire.

"I'm almost certain one of Thompson's clients is involved somehow. I need another day to research some background. I took my one personal day yesterday to talk to some people, and I have a few leads I want to track down. I just need a little more time," I pleaded.

"All right, but I want this wrapped up soon. This could be the biggest story in a decade, and I don't want that sassy little TV reporter to scoop us," Hunter said, shifting restlessly in his chair, which creaked under his weight. "I'll reassign Tony Lundin the two stories I had planned for you to work on today. Do you need any help from me?" he asked. His eyes were sparkling with excitement.

"You're enjoying this, aren't you?" I asked.

He settled back in his chair and grew wistful.

"I remember a time when I chased down some incredible stories and had a lot of fun in the process. Nearly got myself killed once or twice, but that's what this profession is about, not —." He waved an arm at a wall covered with a multitude of awards from the Associated Press and Michigan Press Association.

"Thanks, Bob. I don't think you'll be disappointed," I said.

I left Hunter's office, retrieved the Grant Stewart file from the back of my desk and headed down to the basement where it was quiet. The file contained miscellaneous business stories about various entrepreneurial honors and new happenings with Stewart Lumber Company. After about five minutes of leafing through the slightly yellowed clips, I found what I was looking for.

The articles regarding Claire Stewart's untimely death began on July 15 with a sixty-point headline across the top of the front page screaming "WIFE OF LUMBER MAGNATE DIES IN BOATING ACCIDENT." The article contained a brief description of Claire. The only child of a wealthy Ann Arbor family, she had been educated at the University of Michigan and had earned a degree in art history. She had married Grant Stewart at the age of twenty-four about six months after she met him while working for the interior design firm which decorated his office. The was no mention of how she found her way to our remote town in the first place. My eyes were drawn to the full-color, two-column photo of an extremely attractive woman with shoulder-length hair colored an expensive shade of sunny blond. Most striking though were the eyes—sharp hazel flecked with gold and framed by perfectly arched dark brows. They seemed to say to those who dared to look deeply, "I know things you'll never know." I had seen those eyes before. They epitomized the word 'mysterious.' But where had I seen them? I concentrated on the photo for several minutes but eventually gave up, knowing the answer would come to me in time.

The rest of the article followed pretty much the story my father had told me. The couple had decided to go for a late evening pass around the bay. Grant Stewart claimed he went below deck to prepare drinks after anchoring about two miles offshore. He heard a splash, ignored it, then returned topside to find his wife gone. Later articles focused on the ensuing investigation but revealed no useful evidence. I tried to read between the lines of what the reporter, a woman I'd never heard of, may have really thought; however, the articles gave not even the slightest hint that Grant Stewart might have dumped his wife overboard. On September 12, the Daily Press ran a story quoting the sheriff as saying, "Claire Stewart's death is being ruled an accident. Case closed." Stewart told the reporter the finding did nothing to ease his grief.

I put the file back in the proper drawer and searched for anything on Douglas Jordan but found little. There were only a few small items mentioning him as a partner in the accounting firm or photos of him by his wife's side for some charity function. I slammed the drawer shut and sat back down to think.

What motive would either Jordan or Stewart have for killing Frank Thompson? I went over again what Jordan had told me the day before. In a lie that complicated, there might be a grain of truth. The firm's former secretary had said it was actually Jordan who had been in an accident and missed a few weeks of work, not Thompson, as Jordan had claimed. Perhaps Thompson had gone through Jordan's files and found something wrong. But that was six months ago. At what point did Thompson become a threat, and what was the scheme Jordan and Stewart had plotted? A hunch told me the answer was probably contained in Grant Stewart's files at the accounting firm, either for T and T Enterprises, the shady corporation he had set up with the request that Jordan handle the account, or his own Stewart Lumber Company. I pondered how to get my hands on that file. I needed to get into Jordan's office after hours. Suddenly I remembered the photo of Thompson that I had borrowed from Klegle the day of the murder.

I took the stairs two at a time from the basement. The photo was in the Thompson file in my desk. I made a quick check of the computerized photo archive to make sure the Daily Press had a copy on file for future use, then checked myself out on the board by the receptionist's desk and walked with a spring in my step to the firm of Thompson, Klegle and Jordan.

It was just after eleven, and Ludington Street was alive with summer traffic. Tourists walked along the wide sidewalks, stopping often to peer into the windows of antique, gift and clothing shops and discuss whether they wanted to enter. The roadway was jammed with large recreational vehicles, teenagers cruising with music blaring, and pickups pulling boats on trailers.

As I walked, I formulated a plan to get back into the accounting office that night so I could get a look at the files. I dug a piece of stale bubble gum from the bottom of my overstuffed purse and popped it in my mouth, took a deep breath and walked into Thompson, Klegle and Jordan. The same receptionist sat behind the workstation and smiled her welcoming greeting when I entered. We exchanged pleasantries about the weather, and then I asked if Mr. Klegle might be available for five minutes. She said she would check and disappeared around the corner, leaving a trail of light, fruity-scented perfume behind. In her absence I tried to remember whether the back door had a deadbolt lock in place. That would make my plan a lot more difficult. I had a little knowledge of lock-picking but wasn't too confident in my skills. My scheming was interrupted by the receptionist's return. She directed me back to Klegle's office.

He hadn't looked good the day I'd met him nearly two weeks before, but he looked even more haggard now. The dark, baggy circles under his eyes contrasted sickeningly with the grayish cast of his thin skin. His desk, so neat and tidy when I had last seen him, was now cluttered with myriad papers. He looked up from one particularly messy pile when I entered. The look in his eyes made me stop in my tracks. They held a frantic sheen, like a wounded animal fearing for its life. I felt almost guilty about what I was planning.

"I'm sorry. It looks like you're busy. I just stopped by to drop off this photo I borrowed." I held up the small manila envelope with the two-by-three photo inside.

Klegle stared at me for a moment. He seemed, his mind adjusting slowly to the intrusion of another person. Finally he spoke, although I could barely hear his whispered reply.

"That's fine. Just set it over there," he said, gesturing towards a small table in the corner supporting an antique-looking lamp. I did as he asked, then stood in front of his desk.

"Mr. Klegle, are you all right? You don't look well," I said, genuinely concerned.

He made a sound that was probably supposed to be a laugh. It sounded more like he was gagging.

"Ms. Hamilton, Frank's death has created a gigantic pit of misery, and it is swallowing me up a day at a time," he said, and he turned back to his piles of paper, leafing through one on his desk, reminding me suddenly of Ebenezer Scrooge bent over his books in his frigid little London office before he had learned the true meaning of Christmas.

"Mr. Klegle—."

"Please, just go," he said, dismissing me with an impatient wave of his hand.

I turned and poked my head out of his office to make sure the hall was empty, strolled briskly to the back door. There was no deadbolt. I opened the door, a solid, steel-insulated slab painted tan, took the wad of gum out of my mouth and filled the hole in the door jam for the latch mechanism. I looked over my shoulder, half-expecting Klegle or one of the junior partners to ask me what I was doing, but the hall was still empty.

I stepped out into the warm sunshine, took a deep breath of lake-fresh air and let the door close softly behind me. I pushed against it and it slid open easily. I let it close again and walked casually back to the Daily Press, all the while praying my little trick wouldn't be discovered. It was an odd thing to pray for, but I hoped the Good Lord would accept the need for a little deception to bring the truth to light and justice to fruition.

Chapter Thirty

I ACCOMPLISHED LITTLE THE REST of the afternoon. My body felt like a mass of electrical connections all short-circuiting at once. I kept wondering if anyone would guess what I was planning. It was a good thing I had chosen to live the life of a generally law-abiding citizen because I would have made a lousy criminal. If I didn't have a nervous breakdown before committing a crime, when the cops took one look at me they would know I was guilty of something.

I didn't understand how I had gotten so deeply involved in this case. Something about it appealed to the tiny little humanitarian in me, I guess. I had met Frank Thompson only a few times, but something in my gut told me he was not the type of man to defraud clients. The man had a generous spirit that enabled him to reach out to others not blessed with his talent, drive and charisma, and he had used his business sense to provide a hand up to children who otherwise might have gone without. He had been tragically cut down at a time when he was beginning to have a sizable positive impact on the community.

Then there was poor Brett Lindstrom. I couldn't help but believe the simple young man had little or nothing directly to do with Thompson's or Connor's murders. He was a fall guy, maybe an easy target because of his need for acceptance, his loyalty and naiveté. I hoped in the end he would be able to build some sort of life for himself and be happy. I knew he would always be at risk from the con artists of the world, but before they had another crack at him, I had to tie all the ends of the frayed rope that made up this case and get Lindstrom a "Get Out of Jail Free" card.

At four o'clock, before leaving the newspaper, I considered calling Charlie. Not to tell him of my plan—a felony that could put me in prison for an uncomfortably long time—but to see if he had learned anything that might make my escapade unnecessary. In the end I decided against it. I had a feeling Charlie would need a lot of convincing before he believed Grant Stewart was a murderer. He also had no leads to justify a search warrant on the accounting firm. All he had was the second-hand tale told to him by a reporter who would never take the stand as a witness to reveal a confidential source. I had promised Doug Jordan his words would never see print, not in the Daily Press or on an affidavit for a search warrant.

I went home to check on Mrs. Easton. She was in the back yard tending to her vegetable patch, kneeling between a row of tomato plants and a row of cucumbers when I drove up and parked on the small slab of cement in front of the garage. One of her many big floppy straw hats, this one a violent shade of turquoise, shielded her pale face from the blazing rays of the afternoon son.

She waved and called, "Hello, dear. I hope it's safe to be here now. I couldn't let my veggie garden go to seed, you know." She smiled in such a charming, playful way that it seemed she must be over the shock of seeing Thompson killed. The former schoolteacher was actually enjoying the intrigue now.

I walked over to where she was pulling weeds and squatted at the garden edge, trying to keep my short cotton dress from revealing my unmentionables. The garden was a loving tribute to Mother Nature, where leafy carrots, cucumbers, tomatoes and many other healthy delectables flourished. The recent rains had been a boon for the vegetables, as well as for Mrs. Easton's prize-winning roses, which were in full bloom around the perimeter of the yard. The whites, pinks, reds and yellows created a tranquil, fragrant atmosphere humming with happy bees.

"Yeah, I think it's safe," I said, smiling. She studied my face for a minute.

"What's wrong, Robin? Something is really bothering you. I mean even more than usual." Her voiced was laced with motherly concern.

"More than usual?" I asked. Was I always so uptight?

"You're always so serious. It's like there's a great heaviness on your heart. I know about Mitch, but I believe this has been with you a long, long time. Most people still have some childish sense of fun in them, but only if they had fun as a child. I think your mother's death had more of an impact than you acknowledge, Robin," she said quietly. Her eyes squinted at me from under the wide brim of her hat.

"Maybe you're right" was all I said in reply. Everyone wanted me to feel things, but I had neither the time nor the deSire to get into a heart-to-heart with myself or anyone else about death. I had avoided all such conversations for twenty years, not venturing into that place inside where I had long ago locked away my pain. Damned if it didn't keep resurfacing at the most inopportune times, though.

I stood and said, "I've got a job to do tonight, and I need to eat and get some sleep. I'll talk to you later, Mrs. Easton."

As I walked up the steps to the back door, she called, "No matter how busy you are or how fast you run, your past always catches up to you. Believe me, I'm speaking from experience," she said.

At the moment, my past seemed like a speeding car, trying to run me over.

It was eleven o'clock and pitch black outside when I set off on foot to the accounting firm, dressed in black knit pants, black turtleneck, black sneakers, my hair tucked under a black Oakland Raiders baseball cap. I looked like a cat burglar. I had also managed to get about five hours of sleep and felt ready for anything. Leaving Belle at my dad's earlier, I called to tell him not to worry and that I would pick her up tomorrow after work.

"Robin, I don't mind taking care of Belle, you know. She's a great dog. But I'm awfully worried about you. What's going on?" he had asked.

"Dad, please, just trust me. I know what I'm doing," I had said—a lie if ever there was one. I was flying by the seat of my pants. I had never broken into a building before. I wasn't even sure I knew what I was looking for. And in the event I did find something useful, what was I going to do with it? Make copies? Steal it? Either way was not going to be of any help to Charlie because the evidence would be inadmissible without a valid search warrant based on probable cause. And what if I were caught? How would I explain my stunt in such a way as to keep me out of jail? I had no idea.

I made one small concession to reason and called Charlie's house just before leaving my apartment. There was no answer, which was fine with me. I left a short message saying where I was going and why, but not how I was getting inside. At least if I disappeared, he would know where to start looking.

As I drew close to Frank Thompson's former office, my stomach shriveled into a tight ball in my abdomen. I clenched and unclenched my fists and took deep breaths through my nose and let them out through my mouth. The exercise worked to keep my nerves in check. I thought about all those whodunits I had read throughout the years, with strong female characters able to battle the forces of evil and barely break a sweat. V.I. Warshawski, Kinsey Millhone and Dr. Kay Scarpetta made it sound so easy. I felt more like Laura Ingalls lost in the big city, trying to keep from crying for her Ma and Pa.

I slunk through the alleys, praying I wouldn't disturb any dogs. A cold front was making the night almost chilly, a small blessing because it meant everyone would be inside rather than enjoying nightcaps on the patio.

The last few blocks before the office were heavily patrolled by the police because of the low-rent housing that drew transient and not always law-abiding tenants, so I slowed my pace and stayed close to the buildings. I kept a cautious eye out for the telltale sweep of a moving spotlight from a patrol car. I wasn't sure how I would explain to a cop my manner of dress or being out so late all alone in an alley.

I was nearly through the Second Street alley between First Avenue South and Ludington Street when I saw it. I froze in my tracks and held my breath. Parked at the corner, across the street from the accounting office, was a large, dark sport utility vehicle. Its chrome grill gleamed in the light of a street lamp towering over it. It looked like a shark, jaws wide open, poised for attack. I could just make out the emblem on the hood. It was a Lincoln Navigator. Grant Stewart was somewhere nearby.

When I could move again, I looked around for a place to hide that would still allow me to see the office and Stewart's truck. I spotted a line of four steel garbage cans to my right and ducked behind them. By peering between the cans I had a clear view of the office and the truck, which appeared to be empty. Faint light showed through the front windows of the office, as if someone had only turned on the lights in the rear of the building, but I saw no lights on the east side where Thompson and Klegle's offices were located. Who-all was in there? I briefly considered trying to get a peek in the windows but shot down that idea as way too risky. I looked around for other vehicles, but the street was deserted save for Stewart's menacing machine. I couldn't see the office parking lot from my vantage point.

What was Stewart doing there, anyway? Destroying evidence? Plotting with Doug Jordan? I wondered how long I'd have to wait behind those cans. A whiff of their contents made my stomach roll, and my legs were getting stiff. Suddenly the lights went out across the street. I waited breathlessly for Stewart to walk around from the rear. To my surprise, the front door opened, and he stepped out, looking first to his right then left before taking a key and locking the door behind him.

I was watching Stewart so intently I failed to notice I had company. My nose sensed its presence before my eyes saw it. As Stewart jogged across Main Street to his truck, I looked down and saw a big black feline with a white mask and feet crouched an arm's length to my left. I squeezed my watering eyes shut and tried to hold my breath. It was the one and only thing to which I was allergic. The fat furball's dander carried on the night breeze, dancing across my scrunched face. I stretched out my hand to shoo the cat away. It stared at me with large yellow eyes. Don't let me sneeze, oh please, God, don't let me sneeze, I screamed silently. I pinched my nose and breathed through my mouth, a fruitless effort.

As Stewart grabbed the door handle of the Navigator, the loudest sneeze I had ever heard exploded from my every pore. To me, it sounded like a cannon going off, the echo bouncing off the garbage cans and the walls of the buildings up and down Ludington Street.

Stewart stopped and looked in my direction. I pinched my nose again and tried to crouch as low as I could get to the ground. My eyes and nose were both watering like faucets now, and my legs were cramping so bad I wasn't sure I'd be able to get up and run if I had to. Stewart stepped away from his truck and began walking slowly towards me. I suddenly remembered that he had at least ten inches on me in height and was in remarkably good shape for a man in his mid-fifties. I immediately regretted my foolish decision to go snooping. I wasn't ready for this!

He came closer and closer, his eyes scanning the yard behind where I hid, the street and then settling on the rusty old steel cans that provided me little protection. His right hand went to the pocket of his light gray jacket and pulled out a small pistol.

My clenched stomach felt like it was in my throat as he crossed Second Street. A patrol car turned the corner off Ludington and pulled up alongside him, but not before he stashed the gun back in his pocket. The officer lowered his power window and shined his flashlight at Stewart.

"Good evening, Mr. Stewart. Anything wrong, Sir?" the young officer asked with a smile that did not reach his eyes.

"Good evening. I'm not sure if there's anything wrong or not. I was down here visiting a friend. When I went to leave I heard a strange noise and wondered if there was an intruder around," he said.

"Okay, I'll look around. Why don't you just go on home, Sir?" the officer said, still smiling, although his tone of voice said his request was not to be denied.

Stewart looked back in my direction and hesitated. Finally, he said, "Well, all right, but I think there's someone over there." He pointed to the garbage cans. I swallowed hard. The cat still stood beside me. I gave it a shove with my foot, silently asking for forgiveness for being unkind to an animal. It let out a shrill angry yowl then took off across the street. The officer laughed.

"Ah, it's just a cat. See, nothing to worry about," he said.

Stewart looked back at the cans and frowned. Without a word he strolled back to his truck, got in and started the engine. He took off east down Ludington, then turned onto Lake Shore Drive with a squeal of tires. The officer shook his head and drove off into the night. I heaved a sigh of relief, stood, stretched my legs, then sprinted across the street to the accounting office and around to the back door. I turned the handle and pushed. The door opened effortlessly.

Chapter Thirty-one

THE BUILDING WAS CLOAKED in blackness and silent as a tomb. I fished the penlight from my pocket. It gave off a tiny beam of light, enough for me to find my way around yet not enough to draw the attention of anyone passing on the street.

Deciding to start with Frank Thompson's office, since it was closest, I made a left down the short hall and stopped at his door. It was closed, but the handle turned easily under my grip. The blinds were drawn, so no light passed through from the street. The office was just as empty as it had been two days ago when Douglas Jordan had brought me in here.

I opened the top drawer of the filing cabinet to my left. It was still empty, as were the other three drawers. The file cabinet on the right, however, was surprisingly open, and I flipped quickly through those files. There was nothing that indicated Grant Stewart was even a client of Thompson's. I found a few files for nonprofit organizations, mainly information about audits, something I knew was required for grant funding.

On a hunch, I looked behind each cabinet but found only a few dust bunnies. Next I turned my attention to his desk, but it was empty except for a few pens, paper clips and a pad of notepaper with the firm's name emblazoned on the top in royal blue letters. I started to put the pad back in the top right-hand drawer where I'd found it when I noticed the imprint of some writing. I held it at an angle but other than "T&T" printed at the top, I couldn't quite make out what it said. It looked like a column of numbers. I ripped the top sheet off and carefully rolled it up like a scroll, secured it with a rubber band and tucked it into my right pocket.

The office had been cleaned of its contents. Even the walls were bare, the photos showing Frank Thompson with various VIPs and his awards now gone, perhaps turned over to Victoria. Whoever had cleaned the office had left only the files of clients that could be handled by anyone in the firm. I wondered what had been in that other file cabinet. Jordan had said business files, but Molly Ashbrook had said Thompson normally only handled individuals and nonprofits these days. Then it occurred to me that perhaps Thompson, as senior partner, was keeping close tabs on the other players in the firm. In addition to Klegle and Jordan, there were two junior accountants. Maybe the missing files were personnel related.

I made a quick search of Klegle's office but found nothing of consequence. His desk was now clean, the mess of papers I had seen earlier stashed away somewhere. His lateral filing cabinet was open, so I leafed quickly through its contents. His files suggested he mainly worked with small retail operations in the area and nonprofits, as Molly had indicated. His desk was locked, though, and I didn't think I had time to fuss with the lock. I gave up, closed the door behind me and crossed the hall to the offices of the two junior partners. Neither office held anything of interest to me.

I made my way back around to the other side of the building to Jordan's office. The door was locked. I cursed aloud and decided to risk a few extra minutes and try my hand at picking the lock on the flimsy wooden door. I took a few bobby pins from my hair and maneuvered them within the keyhole for several minutes. I was beginning to get frustrated when I heard a tiny click in the doorknob. I held the pins in place and turned the handle carefully. It opened without a sound. I pulled the pins from the keyhole and put them back in my hair.

As in Klegle's and Thompson's offices, the blinds were drawn; however, there was one major difference—this office was a mess. Someone, probably Grant Stewart, had gone through the files, tossing them willy-nilly on the floor next to the two filing cabinets on each side of the door. The desk had been searched as well, the contents strewn about the floor underneath it. Papers were scattered around as though someone had been desperately searching for something vitally important. I searched through the drawers, anyway. The files still there were a jumbled mess, shoved back in twisted piles. I moved them around but found nothing of interest.

As I had in Thompson's office, I pulled against the cabinet and moved it a few inches from the wall and played the pinpoint of light behind. There on the floor was what appeared to be a letter. It was folded to fit into a number ten envelope.

I stretched an arm as far as I could, pinched with thumb and forefinger, grabbed it and pulled it out. When I unfolded it I nearly shouted "Eureka!" The letterhead was emblazoned with the Escanaba First

National Bank building and logo. A full page in length, it was signed by none other than Mike Callahan, Sr., president, and was addressed to Frank Thompson. It was dated June first of this year and read:

> *Dear Frank:*
>
> *The purpose of this letter is to inform you of abnormal activity in one of the business accounts held by Stewart Lumber Company. Being the accountant for the business I thought you should know what is happening. It was brought to my attention that several large withdrawals have been made from the checking account in recent months bringing the balance from $2,304,245.17 on January 1 of this year to $156,890 today. This account normally carries a balance of somewhere around $2 million and, as you know, is used to cover such things as payroll expenses.*
>
> *While it is true the business is current on both loans it has through this institution, I am concerned about such a drastic change in the checking account. Could you please give me a call and let me know if I have any reason to be concerned? Thank you for you time and consideration in this matter.*
>
>

Sincerely,
Michael A. Callahan Sr.
President
>

This was probably the letter that had started it all. Both Callahan and the dean at the college had said Thompson had been acting strange for the last month or so of his life. He must have done some investigating and come up with answers that made somebody nervous. Grant Stewart? But why would Stewart siphon money from his own business, especially if he had plenty of his own, thanks to the inheritance from his wife? Then I remembered that Molly Ashbrook had said he was not the one in charge of the books for Stewart Lumber, that the man who kept the books was Jack Kirksen.

I visualized the foreman, and felt a jolt, suddenly remembering where I had seen Claire Stewart's eyes before. I estimated Kirksen to be in his early to mid-thirties. Claire would have been the same age as Stewart, about fifty-five, which would put her age when Jack was born somewhere in her early twenties. Was he given up for adoption or hidden away somewhere? A girl from a wealthy family with a good name would certainly not have been able to keep a child born out of wedlock. Kirksen's birth probably also explained Claire's move to the Upper Peninsula. Who was the father, I wondered?

I folded the letter several times to fit inside my bra, since I had no other safe place to put it, then looked at my watch. It was nearly twelve-thirty. I had been in the building for more than an hour already. It was time to leave and get this letter to Charlie.

As I turned to leave, my little beam of light settled on the big leather chair Jordan had occupied so arrogantly the day before. A note written in large black marker on a sheet of yellow legal paper was stuck to the back with an ornate silver letter opener. The note read, "YOU WON'T GET AWAY WITH THIS!" The violent manner in which the note was scrawled and stabbed into the chair sent a shiver through me. What was Jordan trying to get away with? And why did Stewart have a key to the accounting firm and to Jordan's office?

I needed to talk to Charlie. He wouldn't like my methods of infor-mation-gathering, but he wouldn't be too proud to use what I'd found in any way he could. I locked and closed Jordan's office door, then hurried to the rear exit and poked my head outside. The parking lot was deserted. I dug the gum out of the lock and let the door close with a soft thud behind me. Now I just had to get home without being spotted by a cop. Rounding the corner of the building, I looked down the street and saw it was deserted.

By the time I saw movement behind me out of the corner of my eye, it was too late. I turned to find Jack Kirksen towering over me, the fury in his golden eyes burning into my skin. Before I could do anything but gasp in horror, he grabbed my right arm, whirled me around and clamped a hand over my mouth while his other arm pressed against my throat.

"Utter so much as one little peep, and I'll snap your neck," he whis-pered hotly into my ear. He needn't have worried. I was too busy trying to convince my heart to start beating again. I couldn't breathe between his hand over my mouth and nose and his arm squeezing my throat.

To emphasize his point, he jerked his arm hard against my wind-pipe. The pain was excruciating. Then he removed his hand from my mouth and withdrew something from his pocket. My mind raced. A gun? A knife? I heard a ripping sound and felt him jerk his head to one side. Before I knew it he was taping my mouth with what appeared to be packing tape from one of those handy dispensers favored by the Postal Service. Once my mouth was secured, he twisted my right arm behind my back, then let go of my throat and quickly grabbed my left wrist. This was ridiculous, my mind screamed. I was going to end up at the bottom of Lake Michigan if I didn't do something quick. As he tried to tape my wrists together, I landed a good strong mule kick on one of his shins. He let out a grunt and yanked my arms up and back. Tears came to my eyes. I had never felt so much physical agony in my life.

He dragged me to the front of the building, keeping us between the office and the line of small evergreen shrubs that decorated the perimeter. When we reached the front, he poked his head around and looked both ways. Satisfied that no one was around, he hooked one long arm through mine and began dragging me across the lawn. I prayed for a cop to come along. Where are they when you need them?

We stopped, and I looked up to find him opening the tailgate of a large black Chevrolet Suburban. It was Kirksen all along! Grant Stewart was innocent, at least of these last two murders. I was amazed at how strong Kirksen was as he picked me up and tossed me into the back. As soon as I hit the floor I started kicking, hoping to hit him square in the face, but he was too quick. He pounced on my legs and quickly taped my ankles. Then he slammed the tailgate shut and got behind the wheel.

In my most defiant voice, I said, "Where are you taking me?" Unfortunately, it came out as "Mm mmf mmfmmf mm?"

"Shut up!" he whispered fiercely. Still, he seemed to understand what I was asking because he said, "We're going for a little ride."

The drive took less than ten minutes, an eternity when waiting for the Cavalry to rescue you and a blink of an eye when faced with impending death. The taste of the tape's glue was nauseating, and the Suburban's carpet burned against my cheek every time we hit a bump. I tried to formulate an escape plan but couldn't focus on anything except the pain in my arms. For the second time that night, I mentally kicked myself for taking matters into my own hands. I should have listened to Charlie and let him handle this mess.

As the streetlights ended and the highway began, I noticed my heart was beating again. Pounding in my ears, actually. I had to find a way out of this! I couldn't think! On the edge of panic again, I heard a voice in my head, Mitch's voice. "Stay calm. An opportunity will present itself if you just stay calm." I took a deep breath through my nose as the truck came to a stop. I craned my neck to peek out the window. The sign on the side of the building announced that we had arrived at the Stewart Lumber Company.

Chapter Thirty-two

KIRKSEN GOT OUT OF THE TRUCK but didn't immediately come to get me. Instead, I heard the jangling of keys and the sound of the front door to the building being opened. I struggled up and saw that he had parked along the side of the building and was disappearing into the dark main office. Within seconds a distant light appeared from the hall. He reappeared through the front door, face resolute.

I didn't see a weapon of any sort and grew hopeful. Kirksen glanced back at the highway, deserted at this late hour, jogged to the tailgate and opened it. He hoisted me over his shoulder in one efficient move without uttering a sound. I cursed my lack of bulk. I tried kicking again, but he was holding me too tight. I relaxed and let my muscles go limp.

"That's right, Ms. Hamilton, save your strength," he snickered quietly, as if he were afraid of being overhead. I quickly scanned the lumberyard. The place was as deserted as the fairgrounds in January.

Without turning on any lights in the front office, he carried me to the hallway. There he shut the door leading from the office to the hall before proceeding to the end and up the stairs toward Grant Stewart's office. The door to the owner's office was locked, too, but Kirksen quickly produced a key and reached to his left and flicked on the lights. His strength and lithe movement awed me. Then he dumped me in a heap in the middle of the floor on the plush red carpeting and settled himself in Stewart's chair with his elbows perched on the desk. He stared blankly at me for a moment, then smiled a bone-chilling smile. He's insane, I thought suddenly. Something somewhere along the way had snapped in the mind and soul of Jack Kirksen, something that had already driven him to murder twice.

I scowled at him. He laughed.

"It's a shame to have to kill you," he said and stopped smiling. He ran a hand through his thick, wavy hair and sat back in the chair. "You know, you really are a cute girl. You should have gone into a tamer profession, Ms. Hamilton. I warned you to stay out of this mess. This is none of your business. It's a personal matter to be settled between Grant Stewart and me." He spit out Grant's name as though it were a worm in an apple, folded his hands across his flat stomach and watched as I wriggled around on the floor into a sitting position. He snickered again, remarkably calm.

"Struggle all you want, lady. You won't be leaving here alive," he said, still smiling. I ached to kick him right in his pearly whites. After a few seconds of watching me seethe, he said, "I suppose I do owe you the honor of letting you in on the whole story before you die. It's what people in your profession call 'quite a scoop.'

"Why did Frank have to die? It's simple. He suffered from the same fatal disease as you—extreme nosiness." Kirksen paused and looked at the ceiling for several seconds, as if distracted by some errant thought. When he looked back at me he shook his head.

"I knew you wouldn't leave things well enough alone the moment I met you. You have an obvious determination to pursue truth and justice. Did they teach you that bullshit in journalism school?" he sneered.

Then his voice softened. "You see, Claire Stewart was my mother. She fell in love with my father in college. Unfortunately, my father was a poor student studying philosophy on scholarship, so her lofty family wouldn't allow her to marry him, let alone have his child. Luckily for me, abortion was illegal in those days, so she carried me to term and gave me up for adoption.

"Yes, isn't it neat how with an extended vacation to some distant aunt, the reputation of the Vanderkellen family was saved? I ended up with a couple of alcoholics who put on a good act for the adoption agency but had no business raising a child. When I turned eighteen, I started looking for my parents. I found my dad first because he was also looking for me. He told me the story, and I tracked her down. By then she was nearly two decades into her marriage to Grant Stewart and didn't want to jeopardize her relationship with him. So she kept me a secret. She did help me get through college, along with my father who, ironically enough, is a very successful trial lawyer in Chicago."

Kirksen got up and strolled past me to the window, his hands stuffed in the pockets of his clean, faded jeans. "After getting my business degree,

I came back here and landed a job with Stewart Lumber. The old man never knew who I really was, and I had no problem keeping my mouth shut. I had it made. I got to see my mother once in a while, and I had a good job. But then I noticed Stewart treated my mother like shit—running around on her, keeping her on a leash when it came to money. He controlled her like a puppy. And then he killed her," Kirksen said softly and fell silent, his back still to me.

When he turned around, the maniacal smile was back. Circumstances of his life had twisted him, and now I was going to die, as Frank Thompson and Greg Connor had, for revenge against an act none of us had anything to do with.

"Stewart played right into my hands. It was all so easy. First I convinced him to put me in charge of the books. That's when I discovered his little game with that lousy construction firm he set up. I could have blackmailed him on that alone, but blackmail was too good for him. I wanted him to pay for his sins. I waited until the time was right and slowly bled the cash from Stewart Lumber. I was ready to make a break for it with a cool two million in hand when Thompson got in my way. He figured something was up and then guessed about my mother. Obviously, he had to go. What better way than to pin it all on Grant Stewart? The plan all along was to put the blame on him. Brett Lindstrom was just—well, let's call him an interim fall guy, if you will," Kirksen said and bowed his head.

I marveled at the brilliance of his plan. It had almost worked. If I hadn't come across the letter from Callahan to Thompson, the police would probably have fingered Stewart. Then I remembered I was the only one alive who knew about the letter except Callahan, and Kirksen was not going to let me live much longer.

He came and knelt down by me, his face inches from mine. I wanted to kick him with both feet still taped together but saw the futility of trying anything now.

"You're a very brave woman. I see anger but very little fear in your eyes. If I were you, I'd be afraid, very afraid," he said, then stood up again and grabbed my wrists. I let out a muffled cry as the pain ripped through my shoulders. He dragged me to the chair behind the desk and threw me in it. Placing his left knee in my lap to hold me in place, he took the roll of packing tape out of his right jacket pocket, then taped my ankles to the base of the chair.

He stood up and surveyed me calmly.

"There, you won't be going anywhere now. Might as well get comfortable. This is where you're going to die." He said it as though he were a bellhop showing a guest to a hotel room.

"This building will soon be nothing but a smoldering pile of metal and ashes. If you're lucky, the smoke will kill you before the fire reaches you," he said and strolled to the door. He opened it, turned and saluted. "Good-bye, Robin Hamilton." The slamming of the door echoed through the empty building.

I listened as his footsteps quietly thudded down the thickly carpeted stairs. Then silence. I sat motionless for at least a minute, trying to gather my senses and figure a way out of my predicament. I had to free myself from the chair. I tried wiggling my wrists, twisting and pulling frantically. Kirksen had wrapped them with a lot of tape but because my wrists were so small, in his speed he hadn't wrapped them tightly enough. Thanks to the sweat pouring from my hands, the tape began to lose its adhesiveness. After another minute or so of struggling, I wrenched my right hand free—red, raw and sore, but free.

My ankles were a different story. The tape was so tightly wound it wasn't long before my feet went numb. I tried to bend over to reach the base of the chair and toppled over, chair and all, yelping in pain as my head hit the edge of the desk and then the floor. I twisted out from under the chair and began to search the big desk for a pair of scissors, a letter opener or anything remotely sharp. In the center drawer I hit pay dirt. It was mostly empty except for a few pens, a yellow legal pad and the most beautiful stainless steel scissors I had ever seen in my life. I snipped the remaining tape off my left wrist and sliced through the great wad of tape at my ankles.

I stood and took a few tentative steps before feeling the blood circulate to my feet again, followed by that uncomfortable prickly feeling that comes from being in one position too long. I shook it off and darted for the door. I knew it would be locked from the outside, and it was. Worse yet, it was also hot to the touch. A loud pop came from the direction of the garage. I caught a faint whiff of smoke and figured the sound I heard was a propane tank exploding on one of the forklifts.

Blood from the cut on my forehead trickled down my face along with perspiration. Jack Kirksen may not have been able to sense fear in me, but I was terrified now. My worst fear from the time I was a child was burning to death in a fire. I suppose it came from my father being a firefighter and being surrounded by talk of fires all the time I was growing up. Now that fear was about to become reality. I was going to roast like a Thanksgiving turkey if I didn't find a way out fast. I estimated that I had a minute or less to escape before the smoke overtook me.

The lumber mill was about a half-mile from the nearest house, and, with little traffic on the two-lane highway going past it at this time of night, it could be a long time before anyone spotted the fire. It would take even longer for the fire department to assemble and arrive, depending on whether the mill was in Escanaba's jurisdiction or that of a volunteer unit. I couldn't remember.

I tried to focus on Mitch's voice and his words I'd heard—or imagined—earlier. "Stay calm." My eyes darted around the room, which was quickly filling with smoke pouring in from underneath the door. The only way out was through the windows.

I got down on my knees and crawled to the window closest to the desk, slid it sideways and peered down through the screen. It was at least a twenty-foot drop to hard concrete. I darted to the window on the east wall. This one overlooked several more pieces of heavy equipment parked close to the building and nothing soft on which to land. I'd have to take my chances at the first window. The room was now so full of black smoke I had to feel my way back to it. I yelled in triumph as my fingers found the frame.

Pulling myself up blindly, I could hear the flames roaring outside the door as I kicked out the screen, trying to control my coughing. I stuck my head outside and took in a lungful of fresh night air as black smoke billowed out around me. I climbed onto the windowsill, perched in a ball, grateful now to be built like a bird. I wanted to turn around so I could hang by my hands and then let myself down as easy as possible, but there wasn't time. Fire burst through the door, feeding on the oxygen flowing through the open window.

The force of the backdraft blew me out the window, and I was overcome by a strangely pleasant sensation of floating for what seemed like hours, though it was in reality only a second or two before I landed on the ground about ten feet from the building. In the distance, I heard the faint wail of sirens before the world went black.

Chapter Thirty-three

AWOKE TO THE ACRID SMELL of smoke, a sharp pain in my left ankle and a thundering ache in my head. I opened my eyes to a world of flashing red, white and blue lights, men yelling and the sound of hundreds of gallons of water hitting flames all at once. Thinking that being able to feel my legs was a good sign I wasn't paralyzed, I tried to move.

"Whoa! Stay still! An ambulance should be here any second," said a familiar voice nearby. I turned my head to the right and saw Lee Grenville, the young security guard from the paper mill, clad in Nomex fire gear, kneeling at my side. He flashed me a grin.

"Man, I knew you were trouble from the moment I first laid eyes on you, but I didn't think I'd see you leap out the second story window of a burning building! Who do you think you are, James Bond?" he kidded gently.

" I don't need a comedian now, I need a cop. Can you get Detective Charlie Baker from the Escanaba Public Safety Department here ASAP? I really need to talk to him," I said and struggled to sit.

"Hey, hey, I told you to lie still," Grenville said, pushing me back down with a gloved hand on each of my shoulders. "Just relax, I'll try to reach Baker. The state cops are already here." He stood and walked a few steps, then motioned to the ambulance that had just pulled in the driveway.

The next half-hour was a blur, as emergency medical technicians prepared me for the trip to the hospital, being careful not jar my spine just in case I had broken a vertebra. I saw no sign of Charlie—or any other cop for that matter. I was finding it hard to concentrate with all the chaos around me and the wooziness in my head. The EMTs asked me questions about my name, the date, who the president was, but nothing important, like what the hell just happened here. Any time I tried to say anything else, I was told to "be still." I felt like a bored five-year-old squirming through a long Sunday sermon. I knew I had to talk to Charlie, but I couldn't remember why. Once I was hoisted into the ambulance, I told the female EMT riding in the back with me, a husky, curly-haired redhead with bright blue eyes, that I needed to talk to the police.

"I'm sure they'll want to talk to you, too," she said with a smile and patted my hand. Then the colors in front of my eyes swirled and faded, and I was gone again.

I awoke next in a hospital bed in a darkened room, the only light coming through the half-open door leading to the hallway, through which I heard the distant sound of nurses chatting. I felt I wasn't alone in the room and looked to my left where a figure was sitting in the chair next to my bed. In a flash I remembered how I'd gotten there in the first place. Jack Kirksen had come back to finish the job!

"Robin, are you awake?" a soothing male voice asked.

"Dad? Yeah, I'm awake," I mumbled with relief. My lungs and throat felt like I'd swallowed a few yards of barbed wire.

He stood and walked over to the side of my bed and caressed my face.

"Tell me something, did you pull this kind of crap when you were working in Chicago?" he growled.

I let out a pathetic laugh and said, "No, nothing like this. Have the cops been here? I really need to talk to them."

"Yes, that Charlie Baker has been in here three times already checking up on you," he said.

"Did he say anything? I mean, about what happened?" I asked, struggling to sit up. "What time is it, anyway?"

He hit a button on the controls nestled between the mattress and guardrail, and the bed slowly shifted me into a sitting position.

"It's almost five-thirty in the morning. And, yes, Charlie said they had made an arrest, but he didn't go into details." He took my hand in his and asked quietly, "Robin, what happened?"

I filled him in on what I had done, breaking and entering and all. When I finished he shook his head.

"This is my fault. I pushed you into getting involved in this mess, but I had no idea how dangerous it would get. I guess I should have known," he said and squeezed my hand.

"Your hand is so tiny, not much bigger than when you were a little girl and used to walk with me to the grocery store and put your hand in mine whenever we crossed the street."

His voice thickened, and he turned his head away from me, but not before I saw the tears welling in his eyes.

"Dad, I'm okay. This isn't your fault. I made the choice to follow this through to the end, or at least what I hope is the end," I said, feeling a stab of guilt for upsetting him. To change the subject, I asked him about Belle.

"You know, that damn dog knew something was wrong. She was pacing around the house all evening like a caged lion. Then she started howling sometime around one. It scared the hell out of me, so I called your apartment. When I didn't get an answer I knew you were in trouble, so I called the cops. They were no help. Then the phone rang at about two o'clock, and it was that Baker guy, saying you were in the hospital, but that you would be all right," he said.

"Of course she's all right. She landed on her head, didn't she? Nothin' in there to hurt," a sarcastic voice called from the doorway. Charlie flicked on the light, causing me to blink furiously.

"Thanks, ol' buddy. Just what I need—a blinding light in the eye. Are you going to break out the rubber hose and beat something out of me now?" I snapped.

My dad let go of my hand and laughed. "Listen, I'm going to leave you two alone for a while and see if I can round up a cup of coffee. You want some, Sergeant?" he asked Charlie.

"Yeah, coffee sounds great. Black with two sugars. Thanks, Hank," Charlie said and sat down in the chair. After my dad had left, closing the door behind him, Charlie turned to me and shook his head.

"Jesus Christ, Robin, are you trying to give your old man a heart attack? He doesn't need this shit, and neither do I," he scolded.

"Spare me the lecture, okay? Jack Kirksen was behind the whole thing. My dad said you arrested someone—was it him?" Squirming to get comfortable, I became aware of the heavy cast on my left foot and the bandage wrapped around my head.

"We got him. A state trooper out on patrol saw his Suburban peel out of the driveway of the lumberyard and then saw the flames coming from the office. He radioed for the fire department, then took off after Kirksen. It was a harrowing chase until he crashed into a stand of nasty old pine trees at about a hundred miles an hour. He's dead," Charlie said and rubbed the back of his neck. "It's a good thing I got your message on my answering machine about Doug Jordan, though, so we arrested him about three hours ago, just as he was packing. So far he hasn't said a damn thing. That leaves me in a tough spot because I don't have the first clue what the hell he or Kirksen had to do with any of this. I'm hoping you can shed some light on the mess, Nancy Drew."

I sank into the cotton sheets and stared blankly at a spot high on the wall. I felt a strange twinge of sadness at Kirksen's death. Grant Stewart, if he had indeed killed Jack's mother, had a hand in her son's death too. What a waste of human life.

"Yeah, I know a little. It was revenge. Claire Stewart was Jack Kirksen's mother. She'd given him up for adoption a few years before she met and married Grant," I said and proceeded to fill him in on what I had found in the accounting office and what Kirksen had told me.

"Wow! He might have gotten away with it, too, if not for you," Charlie said.

"Did Brett know it was Kirksen behind the calls and Thompson's death?" I asked, my own voice sounding far away to my ears.

"No, I don't think so. He says Kirksen and Connor didn't seem to get along all that well, so he didn't connect the two of them," Charlie said. "But Connor must have made some deal with Kirksen—for money most likely—and conned Brett into letting him use his truck to do the job. Of course, Brett had no idea what the hell was going on. Connor just told he needed it to haul some stuff."

"What I don't understand is what Douglas Jordan has to do with any of this. Why did Stewart leave that note on his chair? And what was he doing in there in the first place? Did he suspect Jordan was the one who had taken the money? This isn't over yet, Charlie," I said.

Charlie stood and walked around my bed to the window. I could see the rosy reflection of the early morning sun on the feathery clouds.

"We've been investigating T & T Enterprises for about a year now. Kirksen didn't tell you that he provided us with information about shoddy building practices that saved the company a truckload of money. The money was then funneled into a private account by Stewart. Jordan was the accountant for T & T. My guess is he had some part in the scam. Maybe he wanted more money and was threatening Stewart, or maybe he was working with Kirksen. I don't know. But when I leave here I'm heading back to the office. Grant Stewart's been sitting in one of our holding rooms since five o'clock. I want him good and ready to talk when

I get there. Let him stew in his juices for a while," Charlie said, still look-ing out the window.

He finally turned around with a somber expression on his face and heaved a sigh.

"Robin, I underestimated you. I knew you were a good reporter, but I didn't know how far you'd go to get a story. We usually don't have your kind of newshound here—or these kinds of crimes, either. Hell, even when we do have a murder, it's usually some drunken domestic battle that gets out of hand." He sighed again and shoved his hands in the pockets of his jeans. "I guess what I'm trying to say is, you didn't need to do this alone. You could have relied on me a little more. I feel awful that you're lying there as it is, but if something worse had happened to you—well, I don't know if I could have faced your father. This really shook him."

"I thought I told you to spare me the lecture," I said hoarsely.

"Okay, I know you're going to do what you want, anyway. But next time, will give me a heads-up when you set out to get yourself killed?" he said.

"Yeah, okay, it's a deal. Just don't get in my way when you think I'm wrong," I said and smiled.

Before he could think of a comeback, there was a knock at the door and my dad came in with two large Styrofoam cups of steaming coffee.

"Did you talk any sense into her?" he asked as he handed Charlie a cup.

"Hah, why bother with the impossible! I gotta get back to work. Thanks for the coffee," he said to my dad and clapped him on the shoul-der. When he reached the door, he turned back to me and said, "I'll let you know what the lumber baron and the accountant have to say."

"Hey, Charlie?" I called.

He returned to the doorway and cocked an eyebrow at me.

"Do you think Grant Stewart killed his wife?" I whispered, my strength fading.

"Do I think Stewart killed his wife? Is that what you asked me?" he responded, stepping back into the room.

"Yes."

After a long pause, he looked at his shoes, then at me, then back at his shoes. "You know, the funny thing is, I just don't know. There's been rumors of that since she disappeared. I know he cheated on her, but I always sensed that, in his own weird way, he loved her. I just can't see him doing that. He's never dated anyone since. Does that mean anything?" he asked, peering into my soul.

I thought about the prospect of ever loving someone besides Mitch. I couldn't even picture it.

"Yeah, that means something," I said and settled back into the bed. My dad squeezed my hand as Charlie walked out the door.

"You okay?"

"Yeah. Will you look up Bob Hunter's home number and hand me the phone?"

I wanted to go to sleep, but I needed to earn my paycheck first.

"Hey, Bob, have I got a story for you," I said when his craggy voice came on the line. When I hung up half an hour later after dictating the whole mess, my head was fuzzy and my ankle was throbbing. I pressed the button to bring the head of the bed down, mumbled something about needing an aspirin and fell into a deep restful sleep.

━✦━

I let out a yelp as the doctor poked and prodded the goose egg on the back of my head.

"Sorry about that. Hmm, everything looks to be healing nicely. Your brain got rattled a little when you hit that concrete, but there's no permanent damage. Must have a hard head," he said with a grin.

"Ain't that the truth?" my dad added and smirked.

I curled my lip in a snarl and glared at them. It had been three days since my fall, and I was anxious to be away from the sterilized stench of St. Francis Hospital. Jack Kirksen was dead, Grant Stewart and Doug Jordan were being arraigned in district court right about then, Brett Lindstrom was on his way to Milwaukee to see his family, Victoria Thompson was a million dollars richer, and I was going home.

After being wheeled down to my dad's pickup and hoisting myself inside, I drew in some fragrant summer air filled with the fresh scent of Lake Michigan. I felt like the one just released from jail.

My dad got into his truck and started it up. Partial to revamping old Chevys, he had painted this one, a mid-sixties model, metallic candy apple red, and it sported a monster of an engine, with dual chrome pipes coming up the sides behind the cab.

"When are going to trade this heap in on a Cadillac?" I teased.

"When you stop adding to the silver in my hair," he shot back.

"Touché!"

"Where to, home?" he asked.

"Sounds good to me. I need to check my messages and sift through the junk mail," I said, wondering how I was going to climb up and down the stairs several times a day. Even though my dad was going to take care of Belle until I was in a walking cast, I still had to go to work. I was pondering this when my dad asked me about the arraignments.

"So what did they end up charging Jordan and Stewart with? Not murder, I take it?" Dad asked.

"No, no. Stewart got busted for defrauding the state on the contract for the construction of the new office building on the highway, and Jordan was nailed for being an accessory. From what Charlie said, they could still get Jordan for blackmail. He was holding what he knew over Stewart's head and bleeding him for money." I scratched the bump on the back of my head. It was still sore, but the cut from where I hit the concrete was healing and itching like crazy. I felt like I had fleas.

"Did Jordan have anything to do with Kirksen's shenanigans?" he asked, making the turn onto Lake Shore Drive.

"No. In fact, when he came across that letter I turned over to the police—which by the way, had fallen out of the folder when he swiped the Stewart Lumber Company files from the firm right after having Thompson killed—Jordan thought Stewart was the one who had drained the account. They had been in cahoots a long time, and Stewart purposefully wanted him to handle the accounts of T & T Enterprises because he knew Jordan was dirty. Thompson was a choirboy. You were right about there being no honor among thieves. Charlie said they were both tattling on each other like second-graders," I said. "That night I stayed at your house, Grant Stewart stopped by my apartment to warn me that he thought Jordan was behind both murders and might come after me. He never had a clue about Jack Kirksen."

I laughed to myself. What was that line from Shakespeare? "Oh, what a tangled web we weave when first we practice to deceive?" I wondered how this all was playing with Victoria Thompson and Joe Nelson now that she was a legitimately rich widow.

As we pulled into the alley, the sound of barking reached my ears even before I caught a glimpse of Belle bouncing wildly at the end of her chain in the back yard. Mrs. Easton came out the back door and waved. My dad motioned that he would help me out of the truck, but I waved him away with a crutch. I needed to figure this out myself. With some difficulty and a few stops along the way, I made it upstairs to my apartment. My dad had thought to open the windows, so it didn't smell too bad, nor was it too hot. I collapsed on the couch and let Belle slobber over me while my dad and Mrs. Easton made off to the kitchen to put something together for lunch.

I sorted through the mail—mostly junk—and listened to the two messages on the answering machine. One was from Bob Hunter.

"Hey, kiddo, hope you're feeling better. Great story. Now that's the mark of a true reporter, meeting the deadline from her hospital bed. See you soon!"

As a reward for my hard work, he had sent over a bottle of champagne. Now I could get drunk and break the other ankle.

The second message was from Hannah and had been left that morning.

"Robin, I can't thank you enough for what you've done. I'm so sorry you got hurt, though. Brett got here early this morning. He's a little thinner and pretty ratty-looking, but he's free. We're going to stay here another week until things settle down a little, then I want to take you out to dinner. Take care and say hi to your dad for me. Bye."

The joy in her voice made me feel better, but I couldn't help wondering what kind of impact all this would have on Brett. Only time would tell, I thought.

As for me, my mind kept drifting to the voice I had heard in the back of Kirksen's Suburban. I wanted it be real, for Mitch to be there always, whenever I needed him—even in death. Again, only time would tell.

About the Author

Award winning journalist, Nancy Barr grew up in Michigan's Upper Peninsula. She graduated *cum laude* from Lake Superior State University in Sault Ste. Marie.

Her journalism career spans two decades beginning at the *Daily Press* in Escanaba, Michigan, reporting on police, court, school and local government news.

In 1998, 1999 and 2005, she received the Good News Award sponsored by area churches and has also been honored by The Associated Press and Michigan Press Association.

A lifelong connoisseur of mysteries, her favorite memories as a young child are of weekly trips to the neighborhood library with her mother to spend hours poring over Nancy Drew mysteries

More about Nancy Barr at www.nancybarronline.com.

BAR LEISURE